DARKLY

BOUND

BETRAYAL

VAL KNOWLES

CRANTHORPE
MILLNER
PUBLISHERS

First published by Cranthorpe Millner Publishers (2023)

ISBN 978-1-80378-108-2 (Paperback)

www.cranthorpemillner.com

Cranthorpe Millner Publishers

I would like to thank my family and friends for all their love and encouragement.

PROLOGUE

Somerset
Saturday 30th May, 2020
3 p.m.

Dry, with long periods of sunshine had been the weather forecast that morning and it certainly hadn't been wrong. It was yet another hot, sunny afternoon. Bees were circling around their favourite flowers, buzzing happily as the pollen collected on their little furry bodies. Butterflies wafted their fragile wings; their lovely colours enhancing their chosen flowers as they too took their share of the pollen. Dragonflies hovered; their gossamer wings almost transparent until the light caught them and their shimmering colours became fluorescent and even more beautiful.

Everything should have been perfect for Talya's eighteenth birthday. In fact, it should have been idyllic, except that it wasn't, and it couldn't be. The new coronavirus (COVID-19) had taken its evil hold on the world and no one was safe, although the UK was just about to take its first steps to emerge from a national lockdown.

But Talya was never one to be suppressed. Like a whirlwind she burst into the garden, startling Anna and Nick who were lazily relaxing in the sun.

"I've just taught Grandmamma how to do Zoom but she couldn't get the hang of the audio button so we had to talk on our 'phones as well. It was just so funny; she kept talking when I was trying to talk. They send their love, and they want us to pop over for a drink in their garden one day next week, now that we can meet up again."

Nick smiled at her fondly. He wasn't in agreement with the scientists who were supporting easing of lockdown measures too quickly. His support lay with those scientists who urged caution, and were trying to persuade the government to ease lockdown measures slowly.

"Well, we'll see. They're both in the vulnerable group but they don't have to shield, so meeting outside in their garden for a short time might be OK."

Anna smiled to herself as the image of Talya and her mother-in-law trying to out-talk each other flashed through her mind. Talya seemed to have inherited more than her fair share of her paternal grandmother's volatile genes. More than once Anna had breathed a secret sigh of relief that Mikey had inherited his father's more pragmatic approach to life.

"Hey, Dad, quick, you're on!" shouted Mikey from the living room. His parents exchanged an amused smile at the excitement in their son's voice. They'd forgotten just how proud he was of his father's work, and now that he was home from his final year at Oxford University during the COVID-19 lockdown, his enthusiasm and pride in his father's prominent role in the fight against the virus seemed to fill the house. Reluctantly, Nick and Anna dragged themselves up from their comfortable loungers.

They all trooped into the living room just as the prime minister was finishing his briefing, gesticulating enthusiastically, his pale hair flapping around his face as he did so.

"I'll now pass you over to Professor Nick Karev, a prominent viral immunologist whose research work on T-cells, which are among the immune system's most powerful weapons, has shown a link that bodes well for the development of long-term protective immunity. Karev and his team are investigating findings in the important role that T-cells play in the battle against SARS-CoV-2, the virus that causes COVID-19. They are looking at significant data that seems to link levels of vitamin D with the activation of T-cell response."

Nick's face filled the screen as he started to explain his research in a simplistic format, and to answer questions. After a few minutes, Nick reached forward and turned off the TV.

"Enough, this is boring stuff. It's a lovely day, let's get outside again and start celebrating Talya's birthday. Now, who wants a Pimms?"

After the usual fight over the most comfortable lounger, Talya and Mikey raised their glasses with their parents. Talya took a sip of her drink, pulled her long, dark hair away from her face and smiled sweetly at them.

"Grandmamma also reminded me that you'd promised to tell me and Mikey all about it when I reached eighteen." She paused expectantly as Anna and Nick exchanged a long look.

Anna's heart sank as she gazed across at Nick. Of course she remembered that promise and she and Nick had discussed it between themselves more times than she could remember, but Anna had still dreaded this moment.

"About what, darling?" she asked, playing for time.

Talya shrugged impatiently, her voice rising. "Oh, Mummy, don't play dumb, you know exactly what I mean. We're not stupid, or kids anymore. The past – yours and Daddy's past – that dark, secret, mysterious family history that you won't talk about. Look, we know that I'm named after Grandmamma and my middle name is after your mother, even though I never knew her. You've told us that Mikey's middle name is after Daddy's father, although we never knew him either, but why break an obvious pattern? Why isn't he also named after your father?" She leant forward, almost shouting now. "Why was he named Michael? Who was Michael? We don't have anyone in our family called Michael. We don't *know* anyone called Michael. So why would you give your first child that name rather than the name of your own father? And why is it all such a secret? Why so many secrets? What really happened to your father, Mummy? How did he die? You never want to talk about him. You said he had an accident at work, but what kind of accident? And what happened to Daddy's father? Grandmamma will only say that he died young, but she won't talk about him until we know his story. Daddy says he never even met him. We don't know anything about either of them. And why can't we visit their graves, like we do your mother's? It's not fair. Why do we have to live with so many secrets…?" Her voice tailed off and she brushed a tear from her eye.

Mikey kept silent, watching his parents with something like sympathy in his dark eyes as Nick leant across and briefly squeezed Anna's hand.

Nick took a deep breath and settled back in his lounger, drink in hand, frowning slightly in concentration.

"Talya, Mikey, your grandmamma is right. I'm sorry, we've tried to shield you but for too long. It's time to tell you the truth and unlock the secrets of the past."

He smiled reassuringly at Anna as he started to slowly and carefully relate the well-rehearsed and much edited version of the story of their dark and tragically entwined past, from which neither of them would ever be able to fully escape.

But even before he started to speak, at Talya's mention of Michael, Anna's thoughts had drifted back to that evening in May, 1996.

CHAPTER 1

Somerset
Friday 17ᵗʰ May, 1996
8 p.m.

The doorbell rang and she got up and walked slowly to the door. Her father was standing on the doorstep. The moon was dim and her father's unsmiling features were in semi-shadow as she moved forward to greet him. Then, as he stepped backwards away from her and faded into the darkness, her reaching hands found only the smooth contours of a wooden coffin and a scream echoed around her head. The doorbell rang again, jolting her from her restless dreaming state.

Anna sat up abruptly, her head as heavy as her heart, confused as to where she was. What time was it? What had startled her? The doorbell rang yet again, followed by a heavy banging on the door. With an effort equivalent to the most hungover of mornings, she dragged herself off the sofa and ran her fingers through her hair, glancing briefly in the mirror over the fireplace as she did so. Grimacing at the sight of her hair almost standing on end, she stumbled to the door. The dream had evaporated but the emptiness had not yet had time to engulf her. Distraction is the antidote to grief, and she'd experienced more than her fair share of grief these last couple of days, what with her father's death and Michael going missing.

She pulled open her front door, which always stuck in damp weather. How often had she intended to get someone to fix it? It was him again; a large shape silhouetted against the teeming rain.

"Miss Hamilton, I am so sorry to disturb you again but I'm afraid I do have a few more questions to ask, and some more information to share with you."

Anna stood, undecided for a moment. *Do I say, no? Can I even say, no*; *s*he, who until recently, had only ever spoken to a policeman once before, as a child, as a dare? "Ask him the time, Anna, I dare you." She could hear Sarah's voice in her head now, as if that dare had been yesterday rather than nearly twenty years ago. She looked up at Detective Inspector Paul Ravell in his smart dark jacket, wet hair dripping over his eyes, but still upright and stern.

Would he be amused if she asked him the time? Did he have a sense of humour beneath that stiff exterior? Did he laugh or cry? Could he ever make passionate love? she wondered. Could he let himself go? He wasn't bad-looking after all: tall and fair, a bit broad perhaps. Not her type – she preferred men with dark hair – but a lot of women would find him attractive...

"May I come in, please? I'm actually getting very wet standing here," he pointed out.

She glanced briefly at her watch, shocked to see it was only eight p.m. The early darkness and heavy rain, coupled with her uneasy afternoon sleep, had fooled her into believing it a much later time. She looked back at him as he stood dripping on her doorstep. Behind him, the sky looked black and threatening.

"Oh, I'm so sorry. Yes, please do come in," she said, stepping back to allow him to enter, closing the door behind him and shutting out the unfriendly night.

Where had all this rain come from? It had started as the most beautiful of May mornings, the hottest day of the year so far (so the weatherman had said at lunchtime); fresh at first with dew, but later, hot and heavy with the scent of the flowers as they emerged to enjoy their freedom, the smell of the lilac blossom as it regained its territory from enforced sleep. Anna hadn't enjoyed this day though; how could she? She'd fallen into her fitful doze about five p.m., exhausted from her constant grief and worry, and now she felt cheated. *I've woken up from my sleep but I don't feel refreshed. Where has my day gone? Where has daylight gone? Surely it can't be dark yet?*

Anna waited as the inspector carefully wiped his wet shoes on her mat, and then she led him through the hall and into the sitting room (badly named, Michael had always said; more of a lying down room than a sitting room, with its deep white sofas, soft cushions and crazy,

9

colourful rugs).

Ravell instinctively ducked under the low doorway as he entered the room. *Michael always did the same*, she thought with a pang. She mentally shook herself, trying to get Michael out of her head and concentrate on what this police officer might want to ask her.

"I am sorry to bother you," he began, looking slightly ridiculous in his sodden jacket that had dripped its wetness across the floor and into her sitting room.

She smiled – for the first time since her father's death.

"Please, do take off your jacket, you're soaking wet. I can find you something else to wear. Your jacket will be ruined if you leave it on." But he looked so stiff and formal. Would he even take his jacket off in front of her?

Ravell glanced around him, admiring her cosy room, tastefully, if rather untidily, arranged. He looked at her in the soft light, cursing the reason he was here, wondering why he had ever chosen this as a career. He wondered briefly how Caitlin would have reacted to the situation he was about to create were she the one who was standing across the room from him as a stranger, small, alone, and looking, he realised with a start, slightly annoyed. He jumped back to the present. "Thank you."

He took off his jacket, embarrassed as the rain water dripped large pools onto her rugs. He wanted to shake his head like a dog as his hair was falling down over his eyes, but he had to content himself with running his fingers through it, just to be able to see again.

"No, it's so warm," he said. "I'm fine thanks, I don't need anything else."

So it is, she thought to herself, as she took his sodden jacket from him and carried it through to the kitchen to hang over the back of a chair. *Let it drip there, out of the way*. She glanced out through her kitchen window. It was dark outside, but it felt so humid that there must be a storm brewing.

She returned to her sitting room where he had his back turned to her and was looking at the framed photographs on her desk. How often she had studied them herself these last two days, looking for some clue, some indication that might explain the events that had recently befallen them.

There was one of her mother, her father and herself, taken some years ago in some forgotten French restaurant on some unmemorable holiday. Was it the Dordogne, or had it been Brittany? Did it really matter? And then there were the ones taken in the garden: the one of her mother, her father, Michael and herself taken just weeks before her mother died. Why had she not noticed before how thin her mother was getting? Then one of her and Michael, arms around each other's waists, leaning into each other, wide smiles on their faces, and another of Michael and their father smiling but standing stiffly apart. Why had she not noticed that distancing before?

But her favourite was the one of Michael and herself,

taken, she remembered, on a fairly recent trip to Polzeath, Cornwall. It had been a couple of relaxing days in a small hotel, where she and Michael had enjoyed the sun and the surf and her father had sat with his nose in a book the whole time. Michael was still wearing his wetsuit in the photograph. If only she could have foreseen the short time they had left to be together as a family.

He turned quickly as he heard her come back into the room, his look inscrutable. She sat down on one of the sofas and indicated for him to do the same on the opposite one. He looked doubtfully at the deep sofa and tentatively lowered himself down onto it, sinking rather more deeply into its welcoming interior than he'd obviously expected. He recovered almost immediately and looked across at her, his expression sombre. She found herself lowering her eyes, catching his mood.

He spoke slowly, almost with painful accuracy.

"I really am sorry to have to disturb you again. I do realise that I have questioned you already and that this is a very painful time for you, but I do need to speak to you again about your father and your brother. It is rather important."

Anna looked down at her tightly clasped hands, her nails digging into her palms, and quickly pulled them apart. *Try to look relaxed*, she told herself. *I don't want to talk about this again, absolutely I don't. I can't remember what I said before and you might catch me out.* Her thoughts were in turmoil, her mind desperately seeking control as she wanted to say to him, "You tell me. I don't have any answers, all I have is questions, and they are beyond your understanding. There is so much I need to know and I can't ask you; you wouldn't know where to start."

He waited patiently, seeming to sense her confusion, her loss of control.

With a huge effort, she took a deep breath, smiled (calmly she hoped) and replied, "Yes, of course, but would you like a drink first?" He looked surprised, not expecting that response, her sudden composure knocking him off balance, making him reply without thinking.

"Like what?"

"I've got gin, whisky, wine, tea or coffee."

Paul was very tempted to ask for a neat whisky, realising he'd lost his brief advantage and she was back in control of herself now, but this was work.

"Well, I am on duty so just a glass of water please."

Anna got up, went slowly to the kitchen, returning seconds later with a large glass of water liberally filled with ice cubes.

When she handed him the drink, he hadn't quite recovered his equilibrium and spoke more harshly than he'd intended.

"There are certain aspects that don't add up in the murder of your father."

Her world spun and her composure deserted her. The word 'murder' echoed around her head, bringing with it its horrible connotations. Murder: my father murdered, brutally killed, done to death, blood spilt, words unspoken, love destroyed. With an effort she controlled her thoughts.

"I'm sorry, but I don't understand. I thought the police – sorry, you – thought it was a pointless act of violence." Why not say a mugging? The word 'murder' was so dirty. Anna couldn't associate it with her neat and introverted father.

"I'm sorry if I have distressed you. I understand this is still such a shock, that you are still grieving for your father, but other information has come to light and there are certain things that I must tell you."

All these apologies, she thought sadly. *We don't mean them really; we're lying, trapped in some moral code of civilised behaviour, of polite spoken language. But I can't be moral, for even now I'm about to be less than honest with you – you, the police – and I haven't even asked you the time! Stupid thought*, she reprimanded herself, *this is no time to be frivolous*, but her thoughts refused to be silent, for in silence the memories might intrude. She looked down at her hands, still clasped tightly, and made a positive effort to relax them.

For a moment he thought he'd gone too far. At first, she'd gone pale but then she'd seemed to recover and she'd stared at him in a strange way, as if she were assessing him, although her look had become distant. It made him feel uneasy, although he couldn't say why.

He interrupted her thoughts.

"Well, more recent forensic evidence has shown that someone else was hurt in the incident that resulted in your father's death. We bel—"

Her turn to interrupt now, brittle, catch him out, make him suffer too.

"Now it's an incident? What happened to murder?" she asked coldly.

He looked across at her. She was leaning towards him, her face intense now, eyes wide, a small oval face framed by blonde hair, which, in a different life, in different circumstances, he would have liked to have got to know better. He closed his eyes for a moment as Caitlin's face appeared before him. With an effort he continued.

"I'm sorry, we have reason to believe that the person who killed your father in the laboratory on Wednesday evening was himself shot and wounded by your father, presumably as he tried to defend himself. The gun had been fired twice. We found two cartridges, and one bullet hit one of the pillars in the laboratory and fragmented. One of the fragments must have hit the other person – we've found traces of blood that don't match that of your father's."

It wasn't what she'd been expecting and it didn't lead to the cover-up she'd been prepared for. This could be worse, far worse, and she wasn't prepared for it. She sat stunned, feeling the oppressive atmosphere around her, imagining the dark thunder clouds gathering outside, willing them to go away, willing him to go away, to let her collect her thoughts and leave her alone. Paul mistook her confusion.

"I think I must have shocked you? I know that at first we told you that we thought someone must have forced their way into the laboratory when your father was working late, and either surprised him there or been surprised by him. There didn't seem to be a motive. We assumed at first it might be petty burglary, the computers for example, an opportunist crime gone wrong, a thief caught out and killing in panic. We weren't very happy with that idea – Mayhims is not the easiest place to break into – but Mr Sutherland, the managing director, initially seemed to think that your father may have been somewhat lax in resetting the security system when he went in, thus allowing another person to gain entry reasonably easily. He also told us that the security cameras have been malfunctioning recently."

"Yes, but surely if it was an opportunist crime, that would indicate they weren't expecting my father to be there, so they wouldn't have known that it would be easy to break in?" she objected.

"Exactly, we had thought of that ourselves. Mayhims is well-known locally for its security system, although we did wonder if someone might have been watching the laboratory, knowing your father's habit of working late. But it would still be a brave or foolish petty thief who tried it, and a rather unusual killer who then 'phoned the police to tell us where to find the bod... I mean, your father." He paused to loosen his tie. The atmosphere had become very heavy again, the rumblings drawing closer.

Outside, a loud crack of thunder broke the silence and they both instinctively looked to the window where a flash of lightning flew briefly across their field of vision to leave darkness and the heavy drumming of rain. Anna rose slowly and moved behind him to the window to pull across the heavy curtains, shutting out the unfriendly elements.

Time, give me time. Let me think. It's not what I'm thinking... It can't be... He couldn't have, she thought, trying to control the panic that threatened to overcome her.

As she settled back into her place on the sofa, he continued.

"The blood we found would appear to match your brother, Michael's, blood group, which, as you probably know is type AB, rather uncommon. It doesn't of course prove that Michael was the person who killed your father, or even that it was necessarily his blood, but you must understand that we have to find him to ask him where he was that night."

Michael, no. Not Michael.

Yet, that dreadful night, Michael 'phoning so late, sounding so distraught. "Anna, something terrible has happened. Father is dead, and they want me now. I have to hide, I can't see you yet. Don't tell anyone, not anyone that I've 'phoned you. I promise I'll explain but I can't come to you yet. If I do, you'll be in danger too."

She'd tried to interrupt him then, to question him, the shock of what he was saying not really sinking in, only the desperation in his voice, but he'd continued hurriedly. "I have to go. When it's safe, I'll come to you, but tell no one, remember, not even the police, that I've contacted you." And with that he'd ended the call, not even a goodbye.

She looked blankly at Ravell and then stood up to get herself a drink. Not a spirits drinker normally, apart from the odd glass of brandy enjoyed after a good meal, she nevertheless poured herself a generous portion of neat whisky and then, as an afterthought, dropped in a couple of ice cubes. The whisky was Glenfiddich single malt, a present from Michael, only because, as she'd said to him at the time, it was his favourite and he couldn't bear to be always offered red wine.

"Well, for God's sake, Anna," he'd laughed, ruffling her hair. "If you never keep any decent drink in the house, you can't be too surprised if your guests bring their own."

Even through her heavy curtains she could hear the storm building up outside, the loud rumbles of thunder getting closer, a heavy oppressive atmosphere building up to match the increasing tension within the room.

Blood type…

Michael always (well, for as long as she'd known him) had no fear for himself. How well she remembered that day; him pulling the neighbour's child back from the path of the oncoming car and ending up in hospital himself. The child was fine, a few bruises only, shaken not stirred, she'd said at the time. Not so Michael who'd spent eight long weeks in plaster, recovering from the compound fracture he'd received, and even longer to walk comfortably again. *I suppose that was when they'd tested him for his blood group*, she thought, although she couldn't remember. Perhaps he'd had to have a transfusion; certainly there was a lot of blood. Maybe they were just being careful, maybe it was just procedure. It didn't matter. Michael was group AB; that she did know. Her thoughts drifted back now, unchecked. Eight o'clock it was, one Saturday evening, six years ago.

"You have a half-brother and he is coming to live with us next week." It was her mother who had spoken, but her father who had looked across at her, engaging her eyes, forcing her to look directly at him for the first time that she could ever remember. He'd never been one for direct eye contact so why now? To assess her reaction? So might he after suddenly producing an illegitimate sibling for her, out of the blue, with no explanation given, a result of some early philandering presumably?

Had her mother known before? Was it before she'd met her father? At that moment, Anna hadn't even bothered to ask, the shock was too great.

Certainly, when she met Michael, he hadn't looked

much older than her own twenty-one years. Strange that they'd never really discussed age. Michael had always seemed to possess a certain detached maturity that belied his looks. She'd found out later that he was actually four years older than herself. He'd lived with his mother whilst being supported by her father. His mother, who was Spanish, had lived somewhere in the Midlands (Nottingham, she thought it was), and had suddenly died. Michael wasn't enjoying the job that he'd just started and was eager to come to Bath to join in the research work with her father. Initially it had been agreed that he'd actually live with them until he decided if he wanted to stay in Bath permanently.

There had been about her parents a kind of restrained affection. They had never been particularly outwardly demonstrative towards each other, her father's doing, Anna had always believed; a bit of a cold fish, she might have called him if asked to describe him to a stranger. Yet she grieved for him now. He had been her father, and she had tried to love him as much as he would allow her. An inhibited man, he was always preoccupied, but not unkind, not unlikeable, just seemingly incapable of any open demonstrations of love. But she had loved him as a child, as children need to love.

And then to suddenly produce a lovechild, and a grown-up lovechild at that. Had he loved the mother of this child? It belied comprehension and certainly at first, in the shock of it all, she hadn't even tried to understand. She had been going through a difficult time herself with no support from her parents at that time, not even from her mother, who had always shown affection to her in the past. Straight out of university with a seemingly useless second-class degree in business studies, and straight out of her two-year relationship with Craig, there was a sense of time wasted, futility, and no enthusiasm for the future. She'd screamed at her parents that night six years ago, and stormed out to stay with Sarah, not to return for two weeks, by which time Michael had arrived in their home and into their lives...

Ravell interrupted her thoughts. "Have you seen Michael since we last spoke?"

"No, I told you, I haven't seen him since the day before my father was kill... died." How difficult to comprehend a violent death for her reclusive father, so quiet and self-contained. Perhaps she'd never really known him.

"And he hasn't tried to contact you by 'phone?"

What was this? Was he trying to imply that Michael was some kind of criminal, hiding away and furtively trying to contact her? But yes, of course, that was exactly what he had done. That 'phone call. In her shock at the time, she hadn't absorbed the reality that Michael couldn't have known that their father was dead unless he'd been there himself. And he *was* in hiding. He was being so secretive, asking her not to tell the police that he'd 'phoned her, and he hadn't been back in touch since. "They're after me," he'd said (or something like that). "I have to hide." Who was after him? It could only have been the police. Michael – impossible to think that he had anything to hide. Michael, her newly-found brother, a companion she hadn't thought possible to hope for, who'd brought life and laughter into their sterile, dysfunctional family. Michael, with his dark eyes and crooked smile, wide cheekbones in a lean face; a legacy no doubt from his Spanish mother, certainly not from her father who had endowed his daughter with his pale, golden English good looks.

"No, I haven't heard from him at all," she lied.

But doubt must somehow have crept into her voice. She'd never been a good liar, and Paul looked at her sharply. *She's lying,* he thought. *I may be able to break her.* Yet, how could he think like this? He, who in his childhood had wept at the sight of a moth, batting helplessly at the light, unable to free itself from its eventual kamikaze end. How had he ever come to choose this way of life? But he knew why, really: it was because he was untainted then, out to search for justice in some naïve way, seeking a career in the police force as if it were some righteous path to put right the wrongs of the world.

"Can you tell me if he has any friends in the area where he could be staying?" he insisted.

"I've told you already of all the friends that I know of. Have you not checked with them?" She was trying not to sound as fearful as she felt.

"Yes, we've spoken to the people you mentioned and, like you, they haven't seen or heard from him since the day before the incident. A few have tried to 'phone him in the last couple of days but his 'phone doesn't seem to be switched on, which in itself seemed strange to them. Now, when I spoke with you before, you told me what you knew of his background: that he'd been to university in Newcastle, and that he'd lived and been educated prior to that in Nottingham. Did he have any connections from his earlier life that you know of? What about friends from his university days, old school friends, childhood friends or relatives of his mother's?"

"I have absolutely no idea," she sighed. "He never mentioned anyone, and no one ever visited, at least not whilst we were all living together. And I never asked; it just didn't seem right to pry. My parents were very private people, they weren't very demonstrative and... Well, as a family we didn't... We weren't very close. But Michael changed all that for me, and I didn't want to spoil it by questioning him about things he might not have wanted to discuss."

But it was strange – Michael without a past. Once she'd decided to swallow her pride and return home from Sarah's, she'd found Michael established in her home. Tall and lean, with his long black hair, he might be the antithesis to her blonde, blue-eyed family, but he had a warmth and humour that had taken only days to break down her hostile resolution and barriers. Despite her mother's illness, long known to her parents but kept from her (like a child, she'd thought in disgust), Michael had managed to bring light into their lives with a quick wit, an affectionate smile and a peculiar accent! How strange she'd found that at first; he spoke perfect English but his pronunciation failed him occasionally, with stresses on the wrong syllables that, try as he might (and she was sure he tried), he couldn't quite disguise. The Spanish mother, she'd thought, and when she'd teased him, he'd just laughed.

"I have a mixed birth, Anna. I have a strange combination of genes that we may never understand. Don't let's worry about that. Now, tell me about this new boyfriend, George, isn't it? Is he right for you or do I have a brotherly chat with him and tell him just exactly how you look first thing in the morning? It'll be sure to put him off, you know."

Equally strange was the way her boyfriends never really managed to get through to her in the same way after Michael had arrived in her life. The day that she received confirmation of her long-awaited promotion at Blastints, the culmination of her years of study and the proof that she was recognised, respected and had a bright future ahead of her, it was with Michael that she wanted to celebrate, certainly not with George who hadn't been allowed past the fumble stage, let alone to see her first thing in the morning.

And as time went on, when Anna and Michael no longer lived with their father, they'd still been constant companions. Incestuous, her friends had called it.

"Come on, Anna, don't be so greedy. Let's have a share of your hunky brother. You can't have him all to yourself, you know," Sarah had laughed, the others nodding their agreement.

Had he had many girlfriends? She didn't really know. Certainly, if he had, she'd never met them and he didn't talk of them. Close as they were, they didn't live in each other's pockets. Although, when she thought about it, he did sometimes disappear for several days at a time with no forwarding address, no explanations offered and no questions encouraged.

Paul tried again, breaking into her thoughts. "I understand that you moved away from your family home some time ago, as did your brother. When was this?"

"Well, a few years ago now I bought my cottage here just after my mother died, and Michael bought his flat in Bath before that."

"And do you know where Michael got the money to buy his flat?"

Anna was getting annoyed. "I really can't see how that is relevant, Inspector, and I really don't know. I bought my cottage with my inheritance from my mother. I assume that Michael must have had some savings with which to buy his flat."

"Thank you. So before that, when you lived in the same home, did he ever seem to be secretive? Receive or make furtive 'phone calls? Receive letters that he didn't want you or your family to see?"

This persistent policeman! What could he possibly understand of their strange family life? An increasingly sick mother, an increasingly work-obsessed father, and then her and Michael, striking up a close friendship against the odds, against the strange familial forces that beset them. She'd often wondered how he'd settled in so well and had been stronger than she had; she who'd lived with this introverted couple from birth and should at least have been able to distance herself, but hadn't; she it was who fell to pieces when her mother had finally succumbed to her pain and died, and her father had retreated into a silent world of work. It was Michael who had held her together, had handled all the practical aspects, the funeral, the…

"Are you sure that none of his friends from Newcastle University ever came to visit him?" he persisted.

"No, I've already said, none that I knew of." *What was he getting at? Where were these questions leading?*

"You must have thought it strange that this should be the case. I know, from what you've told me, that before he first came to live with you six years ago, you hadn't even known of his existence. Didn't you think that it was strange that your parents had never mentioned him before?"

She looked at him impatiently. Had he not listened when she'd tried to explain her family's dynamics? How could she possibly explain to this stolid man, whose mental boundaries probably extended no further than a wife and children at home, with work as a welcome interlude between the comfortable pressures of a normal life, that some families were very different? Of course she'd thought it strange, but then her whole childhood and growing up had been strange, as was her father with his well-paid but highly secret research work.

'We mustn't talk about Daddy's work' had been her mother's favourite phrase and, from early childhood, she had complied; to the point that when in adolescence she'd become curious and wanted to question him, she hadn't, because her mother's words still echoed in her head. All she really knew was that he left in the morning to go to Mayhims and, as often as not, returned home in the evening. When he didn't, she was told he'd had to travel abroad, and, conditioned from early childhood, she had never questioned it. Admittedly, she had met Graham Sutherland, who was the managing director of Mayhims, several times. Sometimes he would come round to dinner at their house and on occasions they had been invited to cocktail parties at his house, but work was never discussed. Rather sumptuous parties, she recollected, held at his very impressive house in Bath. Graham Sutherland was something of a contradiction: a small, slight, almost effeminate figure of a man, but with a personality that was both effusive and commanding.

She had once tried to question Michael about their work, but he'd shrugged it off.

"Anna, it's so boring, you wouldn't really be that interested. It's just that father is so secretive by nature.

Microbiology – no excitement and no glamour, I'm afraid. All we do is work in that stuffy laboratory, looking into microscopes and developing cultures, all in the name of medical research. Then, equally boring, we have to analyse it and do tedious computer data processing, trying to make sense of our findings, and usually failing. Come on, now. Look, it's a lovely evening. Let's see if anyone's up for a quick pint," he'd finished with a smile.

She knew he wasn't being honest with her for she'd overheard, but not understood, some conversations between him and their father about their research work, the only level on which they seemed able to communicate comfortably, their voices not quite able to contain the excitement of some new finding.

Paul wasn't getting anywhere with her. She was drifting away from him, lost in memories that he could see she wasn't prepared to share. Like Caitlin, she was removed from him, leaving him feeling alienated and isolated, the early childhood fears flooding back: the children on the block teasing him, bullying him, rejecting him because his values didn't quite match theirs although his financial circumstances did. His mother, always tired, trying to make ends meet, no time for him with a lively younger child to cope with.

Reduced circumstances had made her old and bitter before her time, remote and tearful, never quite accepting the poverty that she felt had been forced upon her.

He continued more gently. "I'm sorry, I didn't mean to be personal. I just meant could you just try to remember anything more that might have been said about your half-brother's early life than you have already? However small. I'm not trying to pry, but when we realised that Michael was missing, we did some background checks on him."

He paused for a moment. *How could he put this to her?*

"We couldn't find any record of him ever attending a school in the Nottingham area. There was no trace of his mother, no evidence that he was ever at Newcastle University, and the company that he was supposed to have taken a job with after leaving university simply doesn't exist. We've spoken with the managing director of Mayhims, Graham Sutherland, who said that he didn't bother to ask to see Michael's qualifications when he was first employed. As Mr Sutherland pointed out, your father's word was good enough for him..."

Anna started to interrupt, but Paul put his hand up to stop her. He wasn't enjoying this at all; it was cruel to sit here shattering, one by one, her illusions about her brother. He was beginning to guess at what a lonely life she probably had before Michael erupted into her life, how she must have welcomed him and bestowed upon him all the pent-up love that had been denied its outlet before. But he had to carry on; he was here to get some answers from her. He must get a grip on himself and stop feeling sorry for her.

"All we could find was a record of his birth on October 28th 1965, naming your father, who was still studying at Oxford University then, as his father, and one Donna Francesca Gonzales, occupation 'waitress', as his mother. But from that point onwards, his life appears to be a blank. It's as if he disappeared and then re-appeared from nowhere about twenty-five years later to stay with your family. We can find no trace either of his mother, Donna Gonzales. There are no records of her after that date that we can find. All we know about her is that she was working as a waitress and living in a bedsit in Oxford at that time. We've checked the address, which is how we know that it was a bedsit in 1965. The owner died ten years ago and no one locally knows what happened to Donna, although we have found one local who remembers a Spanish girl living there about that time."

Actually, what the elderly lady had said was, "Oh yes, I remember her. Spanish girl, long dark hair, pretty little thing, friendly enough but a bit tarty if you ask me, skirts up to her armpits. Worked in that café just down the road so didn't see much of her. No idea what happened to her."

Paul didn't think he needed to share all that detail with Anna. He continued.

"So, it's just as if Donna vanished into thin air, presumably taking Michael with her. What we would like to know is where your father fitted into all of this. There seems no doubt that he was Michael's father. Mr

30

Sutherland has confirmed that it was your father who brought Michael into your life and into employment at Mayhims. For some reason, your father colluded with Michael's fictional account of his past. When we find out that reason, we may well find a motive for his death. Please, try to think back to any clues that might help us."

Anna gazed bleakly at him as he spoke. He seemed like quite a nice man really and not that much older than herself, when she thought about it. Why did he have do this to her? The pain had been bad enough before. Why come along now and try to fill her head full of doubts about Michael? Why could he not just go away and leave her alone? What did it matter that they couldn't find a trace of Michael's mother, or of his past life? The police weren't infallible and a lot could happen in thirty years. Yet there were a lot of unanswered questions. Why was there no trace of Michael's education? They surely couldn't get that wrong. He must have lied, he *had* lied. He'd told her himself that he'd been to school in Nottingham, had done his first degree and then his MSc at Newcastle. He'd even told her how much he'd hated that first job that he'd taken, which was why he'd been so keen to move to Bath and work with her father after his mother had died.

"Anna," he'd laughed when she'd questioned his move to Bath. "I hated that job but I enjoy it around here. You try living in an inner city jungle with traffic fumes for breakfast, road rage for lunch and stress for dinner, and tell me that sleepy Somerset doesn't have something good to offer."

Why had he lied? And then if he had lied, so too had their father. And where was he now? Why had Michael disappeared and not got back in touch with her?

Paul sat quietly, waiting for her reply. Anna tried to formulate her thoughts. How could she answer him? She had no answers herself. How could she ever begin to explain to him the doubts and uncertainties that had beset her in the two days since she was told of their father's violent death? And then Michael's strange 'phone call. Why should she even try to explain to him? Wait for Michael, let him explain. Surely he could put her fears to rest. He would have a logical explanation for his missing past. He would turn up, strong, and comfort her, and they would share together the grief of their father's death. But where was he? Unprovoked thoughts intruded: did Michael and their father ever really get along, apart from their common interest in their research work? Did Michael perhaps have some sort of hold over their father? Why had he suddenly appeared in their lives, and where had he actually come from? Now it seemed that his qualifications were as fictional as the background that he'd apparently created for himself. But he must have been as good as those qualifications; he'd been welcomed at Mayhims, he'd worked there. Graham Sutherland had always been full of praise for Michael.

"You'd better watch your back, Alexander, old boy," he was fond of saying. "We might not be needing you much longer if Michael carries on this way. He'll have outstripped you soon, this prodigal son of yours."

Paul interrupted her thoughts again. "Did he get on with your father? Were they close?"

"Yes," she'd replied defensively. "Of course he did, of course they were." But she knew in her heart that wasn't true. Her father just didn't seem to have the emotional capacity to allow another person to get close to him. And Michael, who seemed to have more than enough emotional capacity for closeness, hadn't tried very hard with their father, apparently happy to keep their relationship at a superficial, work-based level.

And now her thoughts refused to be silent. Even with herself, close as they'd become, there'd been several occasions recently when they'd been alone and she'd noticed a strange expression on Michael's face, a slight narrowing of his eyes, an appraising, almost intense look. He'd looked as if he wanted to say something important to her, but then the look had disappeared, replaced instantly with his usual expression and he'd made some light comment.

"And he never spoke about his past, not even his mother? And you never asked him?"

Anna's thoughts were in turmoil. *I never asked him, you blundering fool, because we weren't that kind of a family, because he arrived and brought light into my life and I didn't want to spoil it.* But then, Michael had never offered any information, except in small doses, maybe to satisfy the questions before they were asked. But why? To prevent suspicion? What was happening here? What was this policeman doing to her? Six years she'd known Michael, and in that time she'd grown to love and trust him as a friend and companion. How dare he turn up on her doorstep to tell her that Michael's life had been one big lie, to make her doubt him! And yet, where *had* he come from? What had he really wanted from them? And where was he now?

Paul watched as the seeds of doubt formed shadows around her face. He shrunk inside as he saw her confusion, her trust under question and the pain as suspicions started to form. He saw the look echoed again in his mother's face, that look of painful disbelief when they told her that James had crashed and died at only fourteen. "Joyriding, they call it. So sorry, but common in this area, Mrs Ravell. He panicked and lost control when we gave chase. You mustn't blame yourself." Was that why, at sixteen, he'd formed the resolve to go out into the world and try to put it to rights, to stop the decay that led children like his brother James to their untimely deaths?

"I really am sorry to cause you so much distress, but you have to understand that we have a situation: your father, an eminent and respected microbiologist, has been murdered. The only person who can help us with our enquiries is your brother, and now he's gone missing. You are the closest remaining link to your brother, so I have to keep pushing you to try to remember anything that might help us solve the mystery that seems to surround Michael. He has a perfectly legitimate record of birth thirty years ago, but his whole life since then seems to have been a complete fabrication until six years ago, when he came to live with your family."

Illegitimate, she thought dully, *you mean a perfectly illegitimate record of birth.* Outside, the rain continued to hammer down relentlessly, drumming its way through her deficient gutters, almost drowning the sound of the distant thunder as it slowly rolled back towards them.

Paul leant forward to lift his glass and take a gulp of his water, just as Anna began to speak.

"I don't know the answer to your questions. I really can't help you. Yes, I agree that it does seem strange that Michael seems to have appeared out of nowhere, but I didn't know that then. He was accepted and explained by both my parents so I didn't question it. How could I have known then that none of it was true? Why should I have doubted them?"

He sat back and looked at her impassively as she spoke, as her impassioned words tailed off. He remained silent, sensing that she was near to breaking point.

Anna couldn't take any more; this final silence was too much. She continued speaking, desperate for him to go, to leave her alone, to try to collect her scattered thoughts and to make some sense of all that he'd told her.

"OK, he did contact me, but only once. He 'phoned

me late on the night our father was killed. It was after that policeman had informed me of my father's death. He just said that he couldn't come to see me yet and would get back in touch, but... But I haven't heard from him since and I don't know where he is any more than you do. Now, will you please just leave me alone? I'm tired, I can't tell you anything more. I trusted him. Please, just go." She buried her face in her hands.

Her last words were spoken so quietly that he had to lean forward to catch them. But he couldn't let it go now; he had to say it, hating himself as he saw how defeated and crushed she was.

"Do you think Michael could have murdered your father?"

CHAPTER 2

Somerset
Friday 17th May, 1996
9 p.m.

He wasn't going to go away and leave her alone. Anna looked at him in despair. Had Michael murdered their father? What had she known of him after all? She sat silently, gazing bleakly at Paul, her mind a blank except for the seeds of doubt that now were starting to grow their first poisonous roots. She gave a start, nausea rising up from within her, as the 'phone rang stridently, shattering the silence.

My God, what state am I in? she thought as she recovered herself and got up to answer the 'phone.

"Miss Hamilton?" queried a polite female voice on the line.

"Yes, speaking. Who is this please?"

"Miss Hamilton, I'm 'phoning from the police station in Bath. I am so sorry to trouble you at this hour, but would Detective Inspector Ravell still be with you?"

At this hour? What time was it then? She glanced at

her watch: nine p.m. She handed the 'phone wordlessly to Paul who had also risen as the 'phone rang.

"Oh, hello, Josie. Sorry, no, it's in my car, forgot it again," a rueful look. "I thought I'd told Aiden I was coming back out here. Oh, I see, well, yes, I'm still here."

He covered the mouthpiece and smiled across at Anna, previous tensions forgotten. "I've left my mobile 'phone in the car again."

He turned his attention back to the caller. "Yes, OK, go on." A pause. *Josie, whoever she was, clearly had quite a lot to say*, Anna thought. His expression changed from interest to frowning concentration. He glanced across at Anna, who had sat back down and was just finishing her whisky, his smile gone, replaced by what? A look of pity?

"And they really are quite sure of this?"

Another pause. He nodded as the metallic voice jabbered in his ear, and then he frowned, saying curtly, "Is that really necessary? But who has authorised this, and why can't it wait until tomorrow? Oh, I see, well tell him I'll be leaving here in the next five minutes or so. I'll come straight over with my report. Yes, thank you, Josie, you too, 'bye." He wasn't very pleased; Anna could see that from his expression.

Paul sat down again opposite Anna. He still hadn't quite got used to her deep-filled sofa and soft cushions, and it took him a minute to readjust his bulk in order to be able to sit up straight to speak to her.

"Miss Hamilton, that was WPC Grimley from the station. There have been some new developments of which I need to inform you. I'm afraid they do cast rather more doubt upon your brother. However, I've just been given a message from my superior, Detective Chief Inspector Harris. Apparently New Scotland Yard have expressed an interest in this case, so it's possible that they might also need to interview you. I'm sorry."

"New Scotland Yard," she repeated slowly. "But that must mean it's even worse than we thought. What are these new developments?"

It isn't getting any easier, thought Paul. She looked so frail, so defenceless. She seemed to have shrunk in the time he'd been with her. Unwanted memories forced their way back: his mother, who'd never got over Jamie's death, who hadn't been interested when he'd announced his acceptance into the force, who hadn't really cared when he and Caitlin had announced their engagement. She'd looked defeated and shrunken as Anna did now. The only time she'd shown any enthusiasm, the only time the light had returned to her eyes, was when they told her about the baby they were expecting... His thoughts threatened to overwhelm him. He just couldn't think about this now. He dragged himself back to the present, before Caitlin had time to re-enter his memories.

"Miss Hamilton," he began, "let's just go over what we know so far. Your father's body was found in his laboratory on Wednesday evening after a 'phone call from the laboratory alerting the police, presumably made by the person who killed your father. He'd been shot at close range, but there was no trace of the gun that was used, so presumably that's still in the possession of the person who killed him. Another bullet had been fired from the gun, presumably by your father, and we have reason to believe that a fragment of the bullet ricocheted off a pillar and hit the other person. We've checked and confirmed the alibis of all the other employees at Mayhims, including the senior directorate. Everything and everybody was in order with the exception of your brother who hasn't been seen since Tuesday, the day before the murder. He hasn't answered any calls to his 'phone, he hasn't been near his flat, your cottage or your father's house since the night your father died. His friends haven't heard from him, and, until you told me otherwise tonight, we believed that you hadn't heard from him either—"

Anna interrupted. "But you have to believe me, that was just one short 'phone call, just for a few seconds, and I have no idea where he was then, or where he is now! I wish I did!"

Paul continued gently. "Yes, I do believe you. Please, let me continue. His car has been left parked outside his flat since the incident. His very disappearance was enough to make us suspicious and eager to find him to question him. Then, when we checked his background details and discovered that his past was a complete fabrication, we became rather more than just curious.

The discovery that the blood found in the laboratory matched his blood type just makes his involvement more likely…"

"But it doesn't prove anything! Even if Michael was in the laboratory that night, and even if it was his blood that you found, it doesn't mean that he was the one who killed our father! Maybe Michael was trying to defend him and was hurt in the process by an unknown intruder." Even she knew that she was grasping at straws, fighting the doubts within herself.

"I'd like to be able to think that, really I would, but if that's the case, why hasn't he come forward?"

"Perhaps he's too frightened." His voice on the 'phone: *"Anna, they want me now."*

She could tell from his expression that he thought she was desperately defending Michael in her mind, refusing to face the facts.

"But why should he be frightened, and of what, unless he is guilty? I have explained to you, we can't find any reason why anyone would want to hurt your father. He appears to have been a highly intelligent, well-respected scientist with no apparent enemies."

"Then why Scotland Yard?"

Silence.

You've got me there, he thought. *Why Scotland Yard indeed?*

"Miss Hamilton, I've only just learnt that myself. I can't answer you, but I can tell you that the recent evidence about which I've just been informed further incriminates your brother. As you may know, the laboratory has been closed out of respect for your father. It's just been discovered today that someone has tampered with the computer data on the project that your father and Michael were working on; tampered with it to the point that no one can now access any of the data successfully. Scrambled I think is the best way to describe it. According to the person who has reported this, it could take months to rebuild the project, if at all, unless we can find your brother who is the only person apart from your father with sufficient knowledge."

"But why should this incriminate Michael? Anyone could have tampered with the data."

"No, I'm sorry, it takes as much knowledge to successfully scramble the data as it does to rebuild it. And anyway, the only prints found on the keyboard were those of your brother and the person who tried to access the data late this afternoon."

"Then it could have been that person."

"Sorry, he returned to work from holiday only today, and before you ask, yes, he can prove he was out of the country when your father was killed. He was also the only other person apart from your father, Michael and Mr Sutherland to know the password that enabled access to parts of the project."

"But how can you know they were Michael's fingerprints? Why should you have a record of his prints? He hasn't got a criminal record..." Her voice tailed off. *Oh no, was part of this new information some kind of proof that Michael had a criminal record, that they'd found evidence that he'd spent some of his missing years in prison? Maybe he was violent, maybe he'd fooled them all…*

Detective Inspector Ravell didn't seem to have noticed the fear in her voice. He looked slightly embarrassed, she realised in surprise, as he spoke into the silence.

"Well, er, as you know, you gave us a key to your father's house after we found him, and whilst we were there searching for information, we found a key to your brother's flat."

"You let yourselves into my brother's flat, without even asking my permission!" she exclaimed in a horrified voice.

His tone was defensive as he replied, "Well, yes, but we did arrange a search warrant as your brother is a person of interest who can help with our investigation into a murder enquiry. A person of interest who is currently missing. We waited until this afternoon, hoping he might turn up of his own accord. When he still hadn't turned up, we thought we should check to see if we could find some clue of his whereabouts in his flat. I'm sorry, we did try to 'phone you earlier, but you were out."

"Yes," she answered coldly, "that's correct, I was out. I was trying to sort out several matters relating to my father's funeral."

"I'm sorry, but we had to look, and I have to ask you

if you know where his passport might be? We couldn't find it and we have to rule out that he has left the country."

Anna was getting angry. "Just what did you expect to find while you were searching through his personal possessions, Inspector? A neatly signed confession next to a pile of blood-stained clothes? Such a shame if you found nothing. How very disappointed you must have been," she finished sarcastically.

She has a right to be angry, he thought. He'd probably feel the same himself if their positions were reversed.

"Please, Miss Hamilton, it was necessary," he answered in a conciliatory tone. "It wasn't just evidence that might point to guilt that we were looking for; it could have been that something had happened to your brother, and there might have been something there that could have shed some light on his disappearance and help us to find him. After all, we didn't know then that he'd been in touch with you."

She was not to be so easily mollified. "Yes, I do happen to know where his passport is. If you'd asked me before, I could have saved you the trouble of prying into his personal possessions. His passport had been damaged in the wash from when he'd left it in his jeans pocket by mistake. He sent it off to be replaced about a week ago. We were planning a trip to Brittany in June…" The anger left her voice and she looked at him sadly. "I don't suppose we'll go now, though. Did you find anything?"

"Well, we did find an old telephone bill and have now managed to get records of all his more recent calls. Most of them can be accounted for, but he made quite a few lengthy international calls to Moscow on the day your father died. We haven't yet been able to trace the exact destination of all the calls, but at least two were to Sheremetyevo Airport. But it was more what we didn't find that made us suspicious. Everything was left as if he'd intended to return, but the strange thing was that he seemed to have very few personal mementos. Most people keep all sorts of odd bits of correspondence – papers, letters, photos – you know, but the only thing that we found was his birth certificate, a few bills for household utilities, and—" He stopped, suddenly realising how strange the next words might sound. "And some photos of you, and a few birthday cards from you."

Anna stared at him, tears starting to well up in her eyes. She couldn't deal with this any longer. It would never have occurred to her to look through Michael's personal belongings, but she had noticed that he tended to destroy any post that he received almost as soon as he'd received it. Was that strange behaviour? Did it mean that he had something to hide? She really didn't know. She hadn't thought so until tonight, but now, as she brushed the hot tears away, now it seemed that whatever Michael had done, he had cared – *did care* – deeply for her. Oh, God, what was happening? What had he done? Where was he?

Ravell was speaking again. "We took prints from the flat. We had some very good prints from the keyboard and the mouse at the laboratory, and, incidentally from the telephone there as well, and when we compared them to the prints from his flat, they matched perfectly."

He stopped, looking at her expectantly. Seeing her tear-filled eyes, he wanted to reach out and comfort her rather than cause this pain.

"Is there any doubt that the information on the computer was destroyed on the night of my father's death?" she asked, so quietly he could hardly hear.

"I'm afraid not. I was told this afternoon by one of the technicians that your father had been seen working on the project earlier that day and it's highly unlikely that he would have scrambled the data himself. Why would he? It was research that, if successful, would earn him a name in the scientific circles that he moved in, those circles that he himself had so much respect for—"

Anna interrupted him. "There you are, it doesn't make sense. If my father had been working on the computer earlier, his prints would have been on the keyboard and mouse as well as Michael's. You see, your forensics must be wrong!"

"No, unfortunately that wouldn't have been the case. Because of the sterile nature of the laboratory work, every employee at Mayhims has to follow a strict cleansing routine to avoid any risk of cross-contamination. All equipment has to be thoroughly sanitised after use, and that includes keyboards, computer mice and even the telephone. The very fact that we even found Michael's prints indicates that he wasn't behaving in a normal manner. He, of all people, would have known, and followed, the protocol. And the employee who discovered that the data had been scrambled, the one whose prints we also found, deliberately didn't clean the keyboard or mouse as he realised that something was very wrong and he didn't want to destroy any evidence. Michael is the only person who could have scrambled that data. I'm sorry, I wish I could tell you otherwise, but I am convinced that Michael is heavily implicated in the death of your father, and that in all likelihood it was he who killed him. What I don't know is why. At the moment, we're keeping this out of the press but there will soon be a nationwide search for Michael. I can assure you, we will find him soon, and when we find him, we will find the answer."

Anna gazed bleakly at the man opposite her. She made no attempt now to stem the tears that were running freely down her cheeks, as the soft light of the sitting room was brightened briefly by a sudden flash of lightning, a rumble of thunder following almost immediately. Neither of them noticed.

Anna spoke haltingly, as if the words were being dragged out of her. "Then maybe I have never really known him. I have been deceived. Michael must have murdered our father."

CHAPTER 3

Somerset
Friday 17th May, 1996
9 p.m.

Everything hurt: his eyes, his head and his shoulder, and he was shivering constantly. He had become so used to discomfort these last... how long? Was it really only two days? He wasn't even sure what day it was anymore. His body was telling him to stop, *I can't take any more*, while his stomach grumbled with the punishment of no food and only rainwater to drink. He'd had no real sleep either; hedgerows offering him the only hospitality he had dared to take. The rain fell relentlessly and his jacket was soaked through. Above him, the darkness couldn't quite hide the rolling clouds as the thunder rumbled, punctuated briefly by the flashes of lightning that illuminated the surrounding hedgerows.

He thought of Anna and how her face would be filled with concern for him. How she would welcome him, wrapping her arms around him to warm and comfort him. He needed her; he couldn't exist alone anymore. Together they would be strong and find a way through this, and maybe it would be all right. If things worked out as planned, then it might just be all right. Sunday – that was the day – that was the day when it might be safe, and then he could explain. Maybe she would be able to understand.

Or maybe she wouldn't. Maybe no one would understand. No, he mustn't think that, he couldn't allow himself to think, for when he did, the darkness, the terrible blackness, descended.

He could no longer worry about the danger he might draw her into. His needs overcame his fear for her. His strength had faded, his masculinity diminished into a haze of exhaustion and pain, a longing for warmth and security; anything rather than another night out here amongst the hostile elements. He stumbled to his feet and, like a wounded animal, his one thought now was to survive.

He knew he wasn't far from her cottage. He had deliberately used his knowledge of the surrounding countryside to choose his hiding places. *Just in case*, he'd thought, *just in case I need to go to her for help*, yet not really thinking he would, overestimating himself as ever, refusing to accept reality, refusing to face the facts. How else would he have survived his life? How else could anyone have survived his life? Michael felt for the gun in his pocket. It was still there, his friend, if he needed it. He stumbled through the fields, his pace slowed by the thickets of undergrowth that wrapped themselves around his feet, placed there by a malevolent foe whose being he had never doubted.

He knew he was getting closer; the anonymous hedgerows were beginning to take on a familiarity now. (Or was he just so overcome with tiredness that even the most unfamiliar could take on shades of friendliness and recognition?) The rain, having ceased for a while, had returned, drenching him with a ferociousness akin to a physical beating. His head felt light and his body heavy. He just wanted to lie down, to rest, to forget and to absolve himself from the guilt and responsibility that now haunted his every moment.

He tripped, almost falling, as the uneven grassy terrain gave way to a hard surface beneath his feet. Putting out his hands to prevent himself from falling, he fell sideways against a low stone wall and almost cried out as pain shot through his left shoulder, coursing all the way down his left side. He could feel the sweat break out over his whole body as the pain threatened to overcome him.

He dragged himself up with his right hand, and now his outstretched hand found some bushes to grasp. He must be on the lane that led to Anna's cottage. There was no friendly moon in the dark, cloud-laden sky, no welcoming streetlights guiding his way. Instinct – that's all he had left – instinct, that had failed him so dismally before, when friends became enemies, and enemies remained enemies. No time for introspection. He had to put one foot in front of the other, progress had to be made. *Think only of Anna: her smile, her warmth and her unquestioning acceptance.* Anna would believe in him; she would never doubt him.

They were watching. From the deserted cottage across the road they had been watching and waiting for two nights and two days now, taking it in turns to wander out into the fields at the back to stretch their legs and refill their lungs after breathing in the damp, mildewed air of the old cottage. Mobile 'phones with the volume turned as low as possible constantly rang, numbers quietly tapped out, checking.

"He still hasn't turned up here."

And the guarded call from the watcher outside Michael's flat. "He hasn't come back here either. The storm's getting bad again. It's not very comfortable here."

And the firm reply, "John, instructions are to stay in place."

They'd watched Anna's comings and goings. They'd even taken it upon themselves to quietly and competently search her cottage from top to bottom in one of her absences, letting themselves in through her back window before her white Nissan Micra had even turned the bend of the shady lane. They'd seen Paul arrive tonight, causing a little flurry of activity and a quick frenzied check: didn't match the description. No, it wasn't Michael who'd arrived. It was probably the filth. Pretty obvious really from the way he walked. You could always spot one.

And back to observing again. Curse this bloody storm, so hard to concentrate.

Michael couldn't see very clearly now. The band of pain across his head was affecting everything, including his eyesight. Now that the storm had returned, the rain lashed down in torrents, the trees swaying as the wind swirled the black clouds backwards and forwards, thunder rumbling, cracking now, and lightning hissing too close, too often. He realised he must be close now. Dimly he could make out the soft glow that must be Anna's cottage, identified suddenly in the illumination of a flash of lightning. Thank God she lived in such a deserted place. He knew the cottage opposite was empty as she'd complained often enough about how miserable it was to have no near neighbours. He moved by instinct now. *Just keep moving, avoid the front gate. Even out here you never knew who might be watching. Be careful, the side opening was here, crouch low, but not too low or you might never get up again.*

He couldn't have seen Paul's car parked along the lane as the bend in the road wouldn't have allowed it, even had his eyes been able to take it in. He couldn't have seen the six eyes watching from the house opposite, as they widened at first in disbelief and then in delight at the sight of his dark shadow brought into sharp relief by the flash of lightning.

"Fuck, he's just turned up! Quick, where's my 'phone?" Impatient fingers tapped out a number. "Hi, it's me. He's just got here. What? Is he hurt? Don't know yet, it's too dark to see. What do you want us to do? OK, will do. Can you get John over here quickly, then? Remember there's a cop in there as well. Yes, OK, we'll do that."

Michael didn't care about anything now; all he wanted was to reach Anna, to hear her voice and to feel her warmth and compassion. Using his good arm, he groped his way round the side of her cottage to her back door, the branches of the trees swaying across to whip his face, dragging at his hair. He reached the door, which was unlocked, as he'd known it would be, and silently pushed it open, entering her kitchen. The room was in almost total darkness although dim light showed beneath the door that led to her sitting room. Helped briefly by another flash of lightning, he walked unsteadily across the floor, avoiding the obstacles he remembered by instinct. What happy times they'd shared in this room! He didn't notice the dark jacket hanging over the wooden chair and, even if he had, would probably not have understood its significance. One dark jacket looks pretty much the same as any other.

At the sitting room door, he paused. At first, he thought the voices came from the television set, but as he listened he could hear Anna's voice, and another, deeper voice he didn't recognise, but he couldn't make out the words. He leant against the door to listen, too heavily, for it swung open, inwards, giving against his weight, and he stumbled into the room, blinded momentarily by the light, soft as it was, to hear Anna's words:

"I have been deceived. Michael must have murdered our father."

He almost fell, but recovered himself immediately, his physical pain forgotten now, a new deeper pain emerging at those words. At that moment of betrayal, all his instincts jerked back into life, all thoughts of comfort from Anna gone now. His eyes, accustoming themselves to the light, took in the sight of Anna and a man, both of whom had leapt to their feet at his sudden arrival, turning to face him, and who were now standing as if frozen, staring at him as if he were a ghost.

Paul's reactions were too slow; Anna's words had bitten through to the heart of him. What right did he have to destroy her faith and trust in her brother? And yet it was his job to tell her the facts and the facts pointed to only one thing: Michael's guilt.

The kitchen door suddenly opening behind him had caught him completely by surprise – a man almost falling into the room, dishevelled and drenched, dark hair plastered over his face, white and desperate. He didn't need Anna's sudden cry to identify him: this could only be Michael.

Anna cried out Michael's name and made as if to move forward towards him but stopped suddenly in her tracks, frightened by the look on his face. This was not the Michael she knew, this gaunt stranger, dark eyes filled with pain and a new hostility.

"Hello, Anna," he said curtly. "Please do introduce me to your friend."

Michael was trying to hold on to his composure, but now the initial shock of his sudden precipitation into the room had subsided, the pain at hearing Anna's words cut to his heart. He leant back heavily against the tall bookcase that stood by the door, needing its support, desperately trying to think clearly, to work out who this man might be and what he was doing here with Anna.

The police? He looked like a policeman; he had the right bearing. Michael realised that he must get away again. This wasn't right, Anna couldn't help him. He shouldn't have come here.

"Michael, this is Detective Inspector Ravell. He has been asking me some questions about you, and he would like to talk to you."

Anna was trying to speak calmly, fighting down the hysteria that was rising inside her. She wanted to shout at him, 'Where have you been? What is happening, Michael? What have you done?' but she couldn't because he looked so tired, so desperate.

"Don't come any closer," Michael warned as Paul started to move slowly towards him. "I'm going to leave now and you're not going to stop me." He tried to pull himself upright, away from the bookcase. The room was spinning slightly and his shivering had started again. His hand felt for the gun in his pocket. The gun was still there. He took it out and pointed it rather unsteadily at

Paul.

Paul stopped dead in his tracks, a few feet in front of Michael.

"Don't be a fool," he said harshly. "Don't make things worse for yourself. I only want to talk to you, to ask you some questions about the death of Professor Hamilton."

"But I… I really don't want to talk to you."

Michael smiled crookedly, their faces floating before him, Anna's tear-filled eyes full of concern, and Paul's stern and unsmiling. He blinked hard, trying to focus as the room swayed in front of him, the colours and the shapes merging to form a misty blur and then the floor swung up to meet him, and he pitched forwards to fall headlong at Paul's feet.

Even if they'd been listening, they couldn't have heard the muffled footsteps outside above the noise of the storm, or the quiet click as the 'phone line was cut, the silent, strategic positioning, the soft breathing and the muted whispering.

CHAPTER 4

Oxford
1960

They had met at Oxford University in 1960, Alexander and Natalya, brilliant students both. Natalya had flashing dark Russian eyes, wide Slavic cheekbones and an unmanageable mane of dark auburn hair. Bright and witty, she was an unlikely friend for Alexander with his British reserve, his stiff manner, his precise and upright bearing.

She'd obtained permission to study abroad, perhaps on account of her English mother, who with dual nationality had long been resident in Russia, but with an Oxford degree herself. Or perhaps it was on account of her father, Boris Miloslavsky, a communist from the top of his shaven head to the end of his polished boots, a dedicated man who had risen high within the Party to become an official who could command respect and fear in friend and foe alike. The Soviet authorities had granted it and that was enough. There was no danger she'd be tempted to stay, the authorities were sure of that. She came from a loyal family back in Moscow and she would be sure to return to them – her father would not allow otherwise.

But never had Natalya enjoyed so much freedom as she did in those early heady days at Oxford. To experience the Western culture, to breathe the democratic air around her and to be able to speak freely! What bliss, what liberation, and she loved every minute of it.

Not that her life at home hadn't been comfortable. Not for her the financial restraints of most of her fellow Soviets. She and her parents had lived a life of comparative luxury; the contradictions in the communist ideology never more plainly pronounced had her father chosen to examine them. But of course he hadn't. Why indulge in introspection when there was no need? It was doubtful that he would ever have cause to read George Orwell's *Animal Farm*. Perhaps his English-born wife had, but then they had no cause to disagree with the commandment: 'All animals are equal, but some animals are more equal than others'.

The Michaelmas term had started in October 1960, that same October when Khrushchev had lost his temper with Macmillan and pounded on the desk with his shoe at the meeting of the United Nations General Assembly in the United States. This topic was raised at the first meeting of the Student Union Debating Society only a few weeks into the term. Alexander and Natalya were both present.

"How do you, as a Soviet citizen, feel about the anti-Soviet line taken by so many countries these days? For example, at the United Nations General Assembly in America earlier this month, it wasn't just Macmillan who was anti-Soviet, you know, it was the US. And even Lorenzo Sumulong, the Philippine Diplomat, had a go at Khrushchev."

The question was asked of Natalya by Alexander. She'd looked at him in surprise, this strange, blond-haired English boy; such intensity he had. She'd noticed him often although they had never spoken to each other before. They shared the same course and, despite herself, she'd found herself attracted to him. He was good-looking (in a pale sort of way), quiet usually, until he found a subject that interested him, and then there was no stopping him. That subject usually centred on their shared course: biochemistry.

Biochemistry, a subject of interest only to the dedicated, encouraged its students to have other interests, for it had been noted by the academics that too much intensity was often found amongst these budding scientists. Too much time spent peering through microscopes, of watching cultures grow, of trying to solve complicated equations, could send the introverted into total seclusion, the extroverts into babbling madness.

But she'd been taken aback at his question, not wanting to be drawn into a political discussion on such a short acquaintance.

"Alexander... it is Alexander, isn't it? I'm sure there are many criticisms that can be made of my country's politics, but I really prefer not to discuss it. I am, you must understand, a most loyal Soviet citizen, but here at Oxford, I keep my opinions to myself and abide by your Western capitalist culture," she said, adding with a smile, "Comrade."

Undeterred by her reply, he hadn't really known if she was laughing at him or not, but he had nevertheless asked her out for a drink that evening, and as much to his surprise as to her own, she'd accepted. Their relationship had blossomed, to the amazement of those around them. An unlikely couple, they developed a close friendship, based as much on their contrasting personalities as upon any affinity. But survive their friendship did.

At first, the sheer pleasure of her company was enough for him, but as time wore on, he found a deeper feeling emerging and he found himself wanting to spend more and more time with her. Natalya was happy to spend time with him but appeared completely unaware of his growing love for her. Alexander was her closest friend and it was with him that she wanted to share her deepest confidences, but that was as far as their friendship went on her part.

Eventually, he resigned himself to the role of confidante. Natalya often wanted to discuss the details of her love affairs, and who better to confide in than her friend, Alexander? Her total ingenuity removed her from the role of promiscuity. For her, the new-found freedom, the removal of external restraint, had given her the ability to explore herself and her sexuality with a lack of inhibition envied by many, not least by Alexander.

But Alexander was no voyeur; his friendship with Natalya was pure, a friendship based upon love, a love he had never felt before and was sure he would never feel again. A virgin himself when he had started at Oxford, as virginal as he knew Natalya had also been at that time, he was nevertheless determined he would not leave a virgin. As his feelings for Natalya deepened, he decided that he must prepare himself for the time when she would surely wake up to what he believed were her true feelings for him; the day when she would finally realise that she was ready for him, for he would always be ready for her.

Thus Alexander embarked upon sexual relationships, based not upon love, not even upon much affection, just a calculated intent to lose his virginity before it became a problem. Having lost his virginity within days of the formation of his plan, he set about learning the art of sex, an art, he discovered to his surprise, for which he had quite a flair. To seduce with no risk of losing his own emotions was quite an asset and Alexander rapidly became quite skilled. He discovered that he was attractive to those girls he had previously only been able to admire from afar. His only regret was that it wasn't with Natalya that he was sharing these new delights.

The course was challenging. It was a time of student emancipation, but also of dedication. The time had not yet come when apathy set in amongst students. Alexander and Natalya spent as many evenings in the laboratory as they did in the student bars, gazing intently into test tubes and petri dishes, willing their cultures to grow, to defy almost the laws of science, sometimes even to think they had.

They were both lucky to have secured student accommodation that remained available all year round, although Alexander's bedsit was basic to say the least.

Natalya survived the first year without having to return home, but when Trinity term came to its leafy end, she was called back to spend the summer with her parents, parting tearfully from Alexander, her closest friend, but not yet her lover, and with gay abandon from Guy, who happened to be her current lover.

"But, Alexander," she had exclaimed with her quaint English accent. "Alexander, I shall tell my parents all about you. They will love you too. You will come and stay with me the next time I go to Moscow. Promise me, or I shall cry all the way home."

And, laughing, (no one could make him laugh as Natalya could) he had promised to visit her country and yes, even her home at the next opportunity. Then waving goodbye with his usual reserve, he had left her at the station, returning to his dismal bedsit to feel the pangs of an emotion he had never before felt: loneliness. Loneliness: a deep emotion for the uneducated.

There are those in life who experience this feeling from an early age, and perhaps become immune, or at least hardened to its emptiness, and they learn coping mechanisms. But for Alexander, perhaps because he had never even experienced real love before, had never had to understand the concept of loneliness.

He didn't like this raw emotion, this new feeling of emptiness that he was experiencing, an aching sense of deprivation. Without Natalya, life seemed to have lost its meaning, which was incomprehensible for one who'd always been so self-contained, who'd never before really needed another person, but then suddenly found his life empty. Typically, he tried to bury himself in work, but he found that having now experienced this strong emotion, it wasn't something that would easily go away.

Not just loneliness but other emotions stirred within him: romantic love. He now knew that feeling, and he would happily have let it flourish and grow until Natalya's return but for the other feelings that crept in with it, those uninvited dark companions. Jealousy: what was she doing now? Who was she with? Desire: previously unacknowledged, but now demanding fulfilment. Confusion: why did he feel this way? But worst of all was the anger: how could she have abandoned him?

The weeks passed slowly, as weeks do when we long for them to move quickly. Time, exercising its inexorable law of confounding the human will, always finds a way of speeding towards that which we dread, and then slowing down almost to a standstill when we most desire its quick passage. Poor Alexander; he would have made a pact with the devil himself if he'd been at Oxford that summer had he thought that by doing so he could make Natalya return sooner.

But the languid summer eventually idled away its hot balmy days to its sultry end, and the crisp fresh mornings heralded the start of the Michaelmas term, bringing with it the flamboyant return of Natalya, full of joy to see her friend again, brimming with light and life and banishing Alexander's gloom and despondency with a shake of her head.

Life in the early 60s was fun. Student power was growing. They thought they were discovering it all for themselves; their parents really had no conception of what life should be about. Emancipation, copulation: any '-ation' you could imagine was there for them, for the taking. Flower power and free love were just around the corner of the future, pop groups were just starting to sing about it, but the students already lived it. And at Oxford it was never stronger; match this brave new world with the elitism of the brilliant, and the cocktail exploded.

And Natalya and Alexander shared this life, soaking it up with as much pleasure and enjoyment as the baked summer earth will greedily absorb the autumn rain. Natalya, after her closeted life behind what she laughingly referred to as, 'My Iron Curtain', had never experienced such freedom; small wonder that she embraced it with all the passion that her race had to offer. Alexander, the inhibited, took longer; he never could really let himself go as Natalya could. He would watch her enviously at the parties as she captivated everyone she met, male and female alike, her wild abandon and carefree manner impossible to withstand. But their life wasn't all parties; their companionship extended to all aspects of their student life, for they were serious students these two, dedicated to their chosen scientific discipline, vying with each other for top marks in the exams, both tipped for firsts when they completed their degrees, both expected to climb to the heights of their future careers. Alexander really felt he could ask for little more from life, except, of course, Natalya's full love. But in time, he was sure, in time she would become his completely. He could wait, they had all the time in the world. Such are the illusions of youth.

True to her word, an invitation was issued from her parents for him to accompany her back to Moscow over the forthcoming Christmas vacation. Alexander agreed readily, adding excitement and a rising sense of anticipation to his newly discovered catalogue of emotions. His disappointment was almost unbearable when he read the contents of the letter from his father that arrived just a few days before they were due to leave.

"Your mother is very ill, you must return home immediately," his father had written in the painstakingly careful print of a man unused to a pen. Alexander read and re-read the letter in disbelief. How could she be so selfish as to fall ill just as he was about to realise his cherished dream? He toyed briefly with the idea of ignoring the letter, tempted to throw it straight into the bin and disclaim all knowledge, but guilt forbade him.

He'd seen his parents only once since he had started at university, and that was only because they'd arrived unexpectedly to visit him one weekend, seemingly unaware of his distinct lack of enthusiasm at their long journey. Thinking back now, he remembered how irritated he'd become with his mother who had seemed constantly tired and lacking in any animation. At the time, he'd merely thought that she paled into insignificance compared to Natalya's vitality, but in hindsight he supposed perhaps she hadn't been well then.

Natalya's disappointment had been almost as great as his when he gave her the news, but she'd had no doubts about his course of action – of course he must go home. He could visit her family anytime; his mother was of the greatest importance. So, after a few days of resentful procrastination, Alexander reluctantly boarded the train that would take him away from Natalya and the visit to Moscow, and settled himself in the musty carriage trying, unsuccessfully, to suppress the feelings of bitterness at being deprived of her company.

He'd always felt he had nothing in common with his parents, living as they did in their provincial world in the suburbs of Birmingham, neither of them ever able to understand how they had managed to produce their clever changeling son, or how they could possibly have created him from their working-class loins. There had never been easy communication between these prosaic parents and their only child. They had tried to love him, but they had become frightened as his precocious brain had begun to develop. By the age of eight, his mental faculties had developed to the point where he could have run circles around his placid mother and his stolid, unimaginative father if he had tried, although it wouldn't have occurred to him to make the effort. Alexander's only interest as a child had been to peer into the jam jars and saucers he had stored in his room with all his various liquid concoctions and assorted selections of insects. Not for him the various toys and games that other children collected around them; for Alexander, everything had to have a purpose and, as soon as he could pronounce the word, a scientific purpose. As other children begged and pleaded for roller skates, toy cars or footballs, Alexander's hopes would be fixed on microscopes and science kits.

An insular child, he had nevertheless inspired great hopes in his teachers, whose predictions of great academic success had been fully realised when he left his local school with an impressive collection of top grade A level results, the first child from his unremarkable school to aspire and to be accepted into the higher echelons of Oxford's discerning academic society. His mother had shed a few silent tears as she and his father waved goodbye from the station, watching Alexander embark upon the journey towards his new future.

By some implicit understanding, they both knew that this was final in some way. Alexander wouldn't be one of those students who would be homeward bound at every opportunity; treasured weekends when he could get away, long holidays spent happily relaxing back at home. Not for his mother that longed-for 'phone call that other mothers accepted as their right, telling them that their student son was coming home again. Quick, clean out his room, fill up the fridge; not for either of them the gradual adjustment as boys grow to be men. Alexander hadn't ever really been a child, at least not for as long as they could remember.

Alexander got off the bus and trudged wearily through the drizzling rain along the street and up the short path to the brightly painted door of the neat terraced house that had been his childhood home. The crisp net curtains twitched in the front window and the door was flung open before he even had time to fumble for his key.

His uncle Terry erupted from the house. "Alex, thank goodness you're here at last. Come on, straight to the hospital. I've got the car round the side, I'll take you."

His protestations of tiredness fell upon deaf ears. He was ushered into the car and driven speedily to the hospital by his uncle who, after several attempts at polite conversation, lapsed into a morose silence. He'd never understood or even much liked this clever nephew of his, always with his nose in a book or peering down a microscope, too grand to even go to the local pub and play darts like his own sons.

Alexander was happy to be silent, looking out of the car window at the rows of grim-faced terraced houses gloomily regarding each other across the grey, rain-swept streets. *How different to the sedate elegance of Oxford*, he thought with nostalgia. They arrived shortly at the Victorian-built hospital whose severe facade was enough to strike fear into the strongest heart.

It was too late. His mother had tried her best to wait for him, to hold at bay the tumor that engulfed her frail body, but his delay in Oxford had proved to be the final breaking point. As quietly as she'd lived, she'd given a small sigh, and with that her life had ended whilst Alexander was on his way to the hospital in his uncle's car.

Alexander looked with detached interest upon his mother's body, his clinical mind observing her frailty, her frozen mask of death, but sadly his newfound emotions couldn't find a place in themselves for the death of his mother. His only feeling was one of regret, regret that he might just as well have gone to Moscow with Natalya. It wasn't that he didn't want to grieve for his mother; it was merely that it didn't occur to him to do so.

After the post-death necessities had been dealt with,

father and son spent a couple of silent, embarrassed days together and then by mutual consent parted with brisk efficiency, both secretly glad to see the back of the other, his father now able to indulge in his private grieving, and Alexander to await with impatience the return of Natalya.

And return she did, even more full of vitality than before, always so happy to be back. Perhaps it was the difference in culture that so invigorated her. Whatever it was, he loved her more than ever. He could only look at her and marvel. How could it be that she so affected him? Silently, he suffered within himself as she gaily returned to her lover's arms, but still wanted to spend time with Alexander, discussing her life, her hopes and her dreams.

And then that cold evening, just two weeks into the new term in late January 1962, Natalya had burst dramatically into his room. He would never forget that night. She'd heard on the news that Rudolf Nureyev and Margot Fonteyn were to dance together in London. Nureyev was her hero, not much older than herself, but she'd never been allowed to see him dance. Her father had disapproved of him, and then when he had defected the previous year, she'd given up hope of ever watching him dance.

Natalya, whose blossoming ballet promise had been cut short by her own academic prowess; Natalya, who'd never really been given the choice. Her father had looked at her sternly as she'd excitedly outlined her ambitions to him, ballet shoes dangling from her hands.

"You are a young woman now, Natalya, no longer a child. There are truths you must understand. It is true that our people are all equal," he had said, this proud unyielding man, blindly believing in his communist doctrine. "But, Natalya, you have academic promise and your future lies in the scientific discipline, not in the arts. However, I will allow you this: you may take an English education – Oxford. It is your right – you have an English mother – and it will broaden and strengthen your mind. And then you will come back, and you will help to continue the fight to undo the wrongs that our country has endured in the past, and we will move forward to become the greatest of all nations."

And obediently Natalya had complied, putting aside her ambitions of the Kirov Ballet, putting aside her dreams of dancing alongside Rudolf Nureyev, and accepting that, like a butterfly, her time was mapped out, her wings clipped like a captive bird, her horizons limited, like the good Soviet citizen that she was.

But that night in Oxford her emotions, volatile as ever, had led her to Alexander's room where he was working, frowning over his calculations, puzzling over the figures that refused to add up.

Natalya had burst into his room like a whirlwind, her dark hair in its usual state of disarray, her face full of excitement. Passionate Natalya had thrown herself onto Alexander, almost knocking him off his chair, sending his papers flying.

"Alexander, I cannot believe it: Rudolf Nureyev and Margot Fonteyn are to dance together! Can we go? It's being organised by the Royal Ballet, at Covent Garden in London. It's next month. Will you book tickets for us? Oh please, say yes! It would be all my dreams come true to see them dance together!"

And when he had smilingly nodded, she'd burst into tears, burying her head in his shoulder. At first he'd been too surprised to react, still trying to steady himself and the chair as they both bore the brunt of Natalya's sudden impact. And then, as he tenderly wiped the tears from her face, and he felt the warmth of her body, desire grew within him. He tilted her face to his, bringing his mouth close to hers, touching her lips gently at first, and then as his desire mounted, more fiercely. After a moment of surprise, she'd responded, the fire building up between them.

He lowered them both gently onto the floor, amongst the scattered papers, his calculations destined for that night to remain unsolved. Alexander lay awake all through that cold winter night, holding Natalya's sleeping body tightly, listening to her light breathing, feeling her animal warmth. He knew that he could never ask for more; he would never ask for more.

"I will never let you go," he whispered to her. "Nothing will ever come between us now."

Friends and tutors alike looked on in amazement as the love affair between this unlikely couple blossomed; the closest of friends who had now become lovers. No need to tell their parents – what they didn't know, they couldn't worry about.

As for Alexander's father, maybe he would have wanted to meet Natalya had he known that his son was even capable of entering into a loving relationship, but he was still too sunk in grief to worry himself over his absent son's activities.

Natalya's parents would certainly have wanted to know, and they would both have been shocked to have witnessed their daughter's unrestrained behaviour whilst away from their parental boundaries. It was true that Natalya's life, in contrast to Alexander's, had been full of love and emotion. Stern and unyielding as her father was, he could not escape the histrionic passion inherent in his race. He loved as fiercely as he hated, and his love for his wife and daughter was almost as great as his devotion to the Party. He would have killed for either. Natalya's mother, born Margaret Webster, was the daughter of a wealthy Wiltshire vicar, but no pale English rose. Rather, she was a fiery, intelligent woman embracing the communist ideology as passionately as she would embrace her child and husband, leaving behind her liberal capitalist upbringing without a backward glance. So her parents' culture, whether inborn or adopted, would have had no place in it for Natalya's wild behaviour; it could not allow for perceived immorality. Her mother might have tried to understand the love that had grown between Natalya and Alexander, but her father would have had no hesitation in removing her immediately back home, back under his rigid control, away from Alexander, away from Oxford and away from the influence of Western capitalism.

Wisely, then, Natalya told her parents only what was necessary: Alexander was just a dear friend, and had agreed to come and stay during the next holidays. They were bound to love him, she was sure.

CHAPTER 5

Somerset
Friday 17th May, 1996
9.15 p.m.

Even though it was getting late now, it was still very hot and humid in Bath police station. Josie irritably pushed her short, dark hair back from her face (she must be looking as sweaty as she felt). What an oppressive atmosphere, not made any more comfortable by the overhearing presence of Detective Chief Inspector Roderick Harris. Well, if she felt hot and sticky, it was nothing compared to how *he* looked. Overweight, pink in the face and with his hair cropped close to his glistening skull, he looked just like a gross pig, she thought distastefully. The 'phone rang and she lifted the receiver to her ear.

At first, she couldn't make out what the voice on the line was saying, and then realisation dawned. "Ah, yes, one moment please," she said, holding the receiver out for Harris. "Interpol for you, sir."

Harris grabbed the 'phone unceremoniously from

her, listened intently to what was being said, grunted occasionally, but contributed almost nothing to the conversation, until he exclaimed, "But that's not possible! Are you sure of this?"

More grunts (yes, he was just like a pig, she thought, not just in looks, but in manners too).

He put the 'phone down, brow furrowed, lost in thought for a moment, looking down at his feet, wondering perhaps whether to share this information with her. *Considering whether I am important enough*, she thought bitterly.

"That was Interpol," he said finally.

Oh, really, she thought sarcastically, *as if I hadn't already told you that.*

"Yes, sir?" she said expectantly.

"Information from Spain following our investigations into the mysterious Spanish lady, Donna Francesca Gonzales. It would seem that Donna Francesca Gonzales, aged twenty-five, was killed in a road traffic accident in Barcelona on 24th December, 1965. Her baby son, Michael Alexander Hamilton, who was in the car with her, was also killed instantly, together with Donna's parents. She had no other living relatives."

"Sir?" she questioned.

Harris looked at her impatiently as if she were stupid.

"The child was just under two months old. He was born and registered in Oxford, England, as Michael Alexander Hamilton. His date of birth was 28th October,

1965 and his father was a young man by the name of Alexander Edward Hamilton, a student at Oxford University, better known to us as the late lamented Professor Alexander Hamilton."

"Then who—?"

He didn't let her finish. "Precisely. Get me Ravell again on the 'phone now, will you. Quickly please, before he leaves Miss Hamilton's address."

Josie dialled the number but the only reply was the unobtainable signal.

"I'm sorry, sir, I'm not able to get through now. There seems to be some fault on the line."

He looked at her sourly.

"Well, then I expect you dialled the wrong number. You spoke to him before, didn't you? Try it again, will you, and hurry up about it."

Josie tried not to glare at DCI Harris. Perhaps he wasn't aware that his arrogant attitude was producing sentiments in her liable to lead to grievous bodily harm, if not actual first degree murder.

"But, sir, I know it was the right number – the line itself seems to be out of order. It must be the storm. Of course – the line must have been brought down by the storm."

His colour rose alarmingly.

"Just do as I ask you. I need to speak to Inspector Ravell and I would like to speak to him immediately. The new information will be of more use to him if he's still at Miss Hamilton's house, rather than on his way back to the station."

"Yes, sir." Realising that there was no point in arguing, Josie re-dialled the number, getting once again the meaningless tone that told her there was no hope of getting through on that line for the present. She mentally cursed Paul. Why hadn't he remembered to take his mobile 'phone in with him?

"I'm sorry, sir, the line is definitely not working."

Harris scowled at her.

"Well, maybe he's already left anyway. We'll give him—" He glanced quickly at his watch: nine fifteen p.m. "We'll give him another fifteen minutes and then I'm going out to her house myself, late hour or not. I need some answers, and I need them soon. Get me a cup of tea, no sugar, there's a good girl. And then you can get me Graham Sutherland from Mayhims. There's got to be some reason Scotland Yard are moving in. I'll have a quick word with him. Maybe I can crack this case before they get their big feet stuck in."

"Big feet indeed. Talk about the pot calling the kettle black," grumbled Josie to herself as she went off down the corridor to get him his tea.

She returned with the cup of tea, handing it to Harris who took it from her ungraciously.

"Hmmm, now get me Sutherland, will you."

Too important to even make your own 'phone calls now, she thought resentfully, as she listened to the dialling tone. God, this oppressive heat was making her bad-tempered.

The 'phone was finally answered by an affected, refined voice. "Graham Sutherland speaking."

"Good evening, sir. I'm sorry to disturb you at this hour, but I have Chief Inspector Harris for you," said Josie politely and handed the 'phone to Harris.

"Well, good evening, Chief Inspector Harris, and how may I help you?"

He was just the type that Harris despised: impeccably polite in a sardonic way, and disdainful and superior because he had the background and wealth that had given him privileges from birth. *Some of us have to work our way up the ranks*, he thought aggressively, *but we do get there*. He took a long swig from his cup of tea, cursing silently as he burnt his lips. Bloody polystyrene cups. He glared at Josie as if it were her fault before replying.

"Mr Sutherland, I wonder if you would be kind enough to give me some more information."

"What now? Chief Inspector, it is somewhat late, you know." Sutherland paused, allowing his voice to take on a shade of annoyance. "You are surely not suggesting that I come to the station at this time in the evening? I am rather busy at the moment."

"No, sir, that won't be necessary. I just wanted to confirm something on the telephone with you. I understand – strictly from a layman's point of view of course – that the project Professor Hamilton and his son, Michael, were working on involved the development of a culture that would be beneficial in the treatment of

AIDS. A revolutionary breakthrough, I understand."

"Yes, that is correct. But I can hardly see what it might have to do with Professor Hamilton's death."

"Well, maybe not, but could you just tell me, sir: was this project funded or sponsored by a particular medical research company, or were Mayhims going to develop the culture and then look for a suitable buyer?"

"Inspector—"

"Chief Inspector, if you don't mind, you pompous bastard," muttered Harris sullenly to himself, his hand over the mouthpiece.

"Inspector, I really do not understand what this has to with the case. I understood that your job was to find Professor Hamilton's killer. As far as I am concerned, it would seem to have been a rather pointless, violent break-in. I've already told you that our eminent Professor, brilliant as he was in his work, was somewhat absentminded, and quite likely to have been rather lax with security," replied Graham Sutherland lazily, his voice sounding weary, as if talking to a recalcitrant child, before continuing rather more briskly.

"And really, I do think you might be better employed trying to find that intruder, rather than concerning yourself with the details of Professor Hamilton's work, which was really rather specialist and perhaps best left to the experts, don't you think?"

"Maybe, sir, but as you know, at the moment we are rather concerned with finding Michael Hamilton and we are naturally interested in the work he was doing—"

Sutherland interrupted rather sharply. "I can assure you that Michael can have nothing to do with this unfortunate incident. Michael is a very clever young man, with as great a future – if not greater – than his father had. I happen to know that Michael and his father were very close, and he would never have done anything to harm him. I really do think you are barking up the wrong tree, Inspector."

Harris gritted his teeth; the man was deliberately lowering his rank to insult him.

"But you are aware that the evidence we have so far indicates that Michael may well be implicated?"

"And what have you got, Inspector, a bit of blood? Well yes, admittedly it is of the same type as Michael, and yes, it is an unusual type, but you don't need me to tell you that Michael is not the only person in this country with blood type AB. In fact, Inspector, I myself am type AB. Are you now going to accuse me of murdering my friend, and probably one of the best scientists that I've ever had the fortune to meet, let alone have working with me?"

Are you indeed? thought Harris, ignoring the sarcasm. *We slipped up there, didn't we? So convinced that the blood was Michael's, we didn't even check the bloody managing director's blood type.* But then why would they? Sutherland's alibi had checked out completely.

He answered as politely as he could.

"Well, sir, that is interesting, but there is also the

matter of the computer data. My men have spoken to Jason Tyrrell, your employee who returned from holiday early this morning. As you know, not being aware of what had happened, he arrived at work as usual and went to add some information to a file that Michael Hamilton had asked him to research, and found that all the computer data on the project had been scrambled, effectively destroyed. He told my officers that only Michael or his father would have been able to do this. Apart from Mr Tyrell's prints, forensic testing has found only Michael's prints on the keyboard and mouse so it couldn't have been Professor Hamilton. We also found Michael's prints on the telephone that was used to call the police."

Did he imagine it, or was there an imperceptible pause before Sutherland replied with exaggerated patience?

"Well, yes, but indeed, Inspector, you really should try to get your facts right. The computer data was merely scrambled, not destroyed." A long drawn-out sigh. "Oh, I do wish you had spoken to me before jumping to ridiculous conclusions. Of course Michael's prints have every right to be on the keyboard. I myself gave him and Professor Hamilton the authority to scramble the data on a random basis. It is merely a security precaution that we take from time to time. I can assure you that they always store a full backup of the data on an encrypted tape that is then kept securely in our safe. It was merely an unfortunate coincidence that it happened at this time.

Michael did a routine scramble of the data on Tuesday and of course with the upset over the Professor's death, we haven't got round to installing the backup data yet. I grant you that it does seem that dear Michael might have been a tiny bit lax; we do have a strict cleanliness protocol at Mayhims, and he should have thoroughly cleansed the keyboard and the mouse after use. I'll personally take great delight in reprimanding him myself when I see him next." The playful note that had entered his voice suddenly disappeared. "But really, and I must stress this, Inspector, there is absolutely no point in you talking to the lab technicians. You should discuss these matters with me. After all, there would be little point in taking such extravagant security measures if we then broadcast them to all and sundry, now would there, Inspector?"

Bugger, why hadn't that incompetent Ravell checked this out? Was he going to look a total fool when bloody New Scotland Yard arrived in their smart new suits to look down their arrogant noses and pick holes in all his evidence?

But Sutherland hadn't quite finished.

"I'm so sorry but this is getting very tedious. I can assure you that Michael has full authorisation to be in that laboratory to do whatever he wants, whenever he wishes. I'm afraid it never occurred to me that you would jump to the ludicrous conclusion that he had murdered his own father just because his fingerprints were found on the very computer that he used almost exclusively, far more so than dear Alexander who much preferred the practical side of their research."

Harris was really beginning to sweat now, and it wasn't just the humidity.

"Well, we're actually not accusing him of murdering his father. But, sir, as I said, his prints were also found on the telephone that was used to report the death of Professor Hamilton and we still haven't managed to locate him. Does it not seem strange to you that he hasn't been seen since the day before his father was killed?"

"Oh dear." A sarcastic note entered Sutherland's silky voice. "Michael certainly didn't ask my permission to use the telephone. And not to have cleansed it either – what a very naughty boy he's turned out to be! I suppose we must then assume he's also guilty of murder." He paused, before continuing brusquely. "Has it not occurred to you, Inspector, that any person who is capable of killing another person in cold blood is also capable of taking the simple precaution of wearing gloves before using a keyboard, mouse or telephone, knowing that the first thing the police will do is check for prints? Just because you found Michael's prints doesn't mean that another person hadn't been there. And as for Michael being missing – if indeed he is. I have to say, I think you are really making some rather large assumptions here. I agree it is regrettable that no one seems to know where Michael is, but he just might have decided to take a holiday and even now be unaware of what has happened."

"Without telling you or his family, not answering his 'phone, and leaving his car parked at his flat?" Harris wouldn't give up that easily. Like a dog with a bone, he couldn't let go.

"Well, there are such things as taxis, you know. I personally never use my car unless I have to, and maybe Michael just needed a break away from everyone. He certainly did not have to justify his actions to me. Both Michael and his father were free to take time off as and when they chose. Perhaps he did tell his father. I'm afraid we can't ask him now, can we?"

"He didn't mention a holiday to his sister."

"No, and that does seem rather strange, I must admit, but these brilliant types, Inspector, sometimes take it into their heads to act a little more impulsively than we plodders. I will perhaps get a little more worried myself if Michael doesn't turn up in a day or so."

Harris smarted under the casual phrase 'plodders'. He knew very well that it was meant to refer to himself only. He wasn't getting anywhere with this arrogant man and he was losing credibility even with himself. He decided that this was not the time to mention the extra information from Interpol. Sutherland had already dismissed Michael's missing childhood as just another idiosyncrasy of the brilliant. "A man has a right to his privacy," he'd said when first informed of the discrepancy, arguing that if Michael and his father had together chosen to fabricate some of Michael's background, then they had obviously had a good reason and it was not for him to question it. After all, as he'd pointed out, Michael's work spoke for itself. What did it matter if Professor Hamilton had chosen to reinvent some of the details of his youthful philandering? Michael was still his acknowledged son, albeit illegitimate.

Harris had no doubt that the supercilious bastard would shrug off the most recent evidence from Interpol in pretty much the same way. *Well, yes, of course, Inspector, I remember now, Professor Hamilton did tell me that there had been some mix up and that Michael and his mother were actually reported as being killed in that car accident when he was a baby. He thought it was really rather amusing. But really, Inspector, these Spanish police are incredibly stupid, can't get a thing right you know. He and his mother actually survived that crash – it was only her parents who were killed. That was the reason that the girl returned to England with the baby and Professor Hamilton took it upon himself to support her.* He could almost hear the amused tone as if it was true, and Sutherland was actually saying it. He'd keep that information to himself for now.

"Well, thank you, sir, for your time. I mustn't keep you any longer. I am sorry to have troubled you," he said instead, with as much politeness as he could muster.

"Anytime, Inspector, anytime. I'm always ready to help our boys in blue."

Harris released some of his frustration by slamming

the receiver back on its rest after Sutherland had hung up, realising too late that he hadn't had much of an answer to his question about the commercial activities of Mayhims.

Josie, who had been listening intently, really thought Harris might have exploded several times during that conversation, so red had he become, but she'd tried to keep her eyes averted whilst he was on the 'phone, allowing herself only the odd furtive glance, instead pretending to be occupied reading through the file. But it gave her no pleasure now to witness his discomfiture. She watched him covertly as he stood up, glancing in her direction, satisfying himself that she appeared preoccupied.

His bluster had gone. He seemed subdued and pensive, but then glancing at his watch absently, he gave a start.

"Good, God, it's nine forty-five p.m. and Ravell still isn't back! It must be about three-quarters of an hour since you spoke to him. How long does it take to drive from Stratton-on-the-Fosse to here?"

"About twenty, twenty-five minutes at the most, I would have thought, sir."

"Well, try the number once more and if there's still no reply, I'll go out there. No, we'll both go out there. It is after all a lady we'll be disturbing at this late hour. Go and tell DI Formby where we're going and then meet me by my car. Hurry now."

Five minutes later, they were in his car, leaving the

police station and travelling down the busy rain-swept roads towards Anna's cottage, windscreen wipers working furiously, the beam of the headlights hardly able to pierce the torrential rain.

CHAPTER 6

Somerset
Friday 17th May, 1996
9.20 p.m.

Anna cried out as Michael collapsed. Paul dropped to his knees beside him, feeling with practised fingers for the pulse in his neck. He looked up at Anna.

"It's OK, I think he's all right, he's just passed out. Exhaustion, by the look of him. Could you give me a hand? We need to try to get him off the floor."

Don't let her faint on me now, he thought. *Christ, she looks near enough.*

But she didn't. Silently, she knelt down beside him and together they gently rolled Michael over so that he was lying on his back, Anna trying desperately to control the shaking that seemed to have taken hold of her body. This couldn't be true, this couldn't be happening. This couldn't be Michael lying here unconscious on her floor, as white and motionless as a waxen dummy.

"Look, could you manage to lift his feet," grunted

Paul as he strained to lift Michael under the arms. "I think we should try to get him over onto your sofa."

God, he thought, *I must be losing it, I can't even lift him. He's a damn sight heavier than he looks.*

Somehow they managed to half-carry, half-drag Michael across to one of Anna's sofas and drop him none too gently onto its cushioned seat. Neither of them noticed the gun that had fallen from his hand as he collapsed, and now lay hidden under the bookcase by the door.

Paul stood looking down on him, muttering.

"He does look pretty awful and his jacket is drenched." Turning to Anna, standing silently beside him, seemingly numb with shock, he said briskly, "Do you have anything warm? A sweater or something? I think we should try to take that wet jacket off him at least."

Glad to have something useful to do, a physical activity to obliterate the numbness she was feeling, she ran upstairs to her spare room, full, it seemed, of Michael's clothes strewn untidily across every available area of space, all left on various occasions, sometimes lent to her when the evening turned unexpectedly chilly; one jumper used, she remembered, to wrap up the cat on a visit to the vet – not to keep the cat warm, but to protect Michael from its vicious claws. Where was Brian anyway? Stupid name for a cat really, but he did look and act like the fictional snail he was named after. She hadn't seen him since before she fell asleep. Probably hiding somewhere from the storm. Brian always was scared of thunder and lightning. Grabbing the first sweatshirt that she found, Anna hurried back downstairs. Michael still lay motionless on the sofa, but Paul had managed to pull his jacket off his shoulder and was leaning closely over him. He looked up quickly as she came back into the room and motioned for her to come over.

He spoke distractedly, almost to himself, not looking at her but poking around Michael's left shoulder, pulling the torn and drenched shirt off his shoulder, exposing the angry-looking flesh, red and swollen, surrounded by bluish green bruising.

"Of course, I should have remembered: the blood in the laboratory. He was there when the bullet ricocheted off the pillar. That's what we thought. It's no wonder he looked so awful. It doesn't look as though he's had it attended to at all."

He pulled the shirt and jacket back over Michael's shoulder, forgetting about the sweatshirt that Anna had dropped on the floor by the sofa. "We need to call an ambulance. It looks very inflamed, and he's running quite a fever."

Anna was calm now despite the sight of Michael lying there, quieter than she'd ever known him, no longer her support, and no longer the brother who'd burst into her life filling it with happiness and love. This was a stranger on her sofa. But of course it wasn't; it was still Michael. She bent over him and gently smoothed his bedraggled hair away from his eyes. But the thought wouldn't go away that this was a stranger. This was, in all probability, the person who had killed their father. She touched him again; his forehead hot under her touch, sweat glistening on the ashen pallor of his skin.

Paul continued. "Yes, call for an ambulance and I must 'phone the station." He debated for a moment whether he should go out to his car and get that wretched mobile 'phone. No, it was still pouring with rain. Two minutes wouldn't hurt. He really must remember in future to tie it round his neck.

But he was wrong: two minutes can hurt, for two minutes could perhaps have made a difference, two minutes can be the difference between life and death.

Anna picked up the 'phone and dialled. She waited for what seemed like an age. And then, like WPC Josie Grimley before her, all she heard was the unobtainable tone. *The storm*, she thought, *the bloody storm*.

"The line must have come down in the storm. I can't get a dialling tone."

"OK, I'll go out and get my 'phone from the car," said Paul, and then they both turned as Michael stirred on the sofa, muttering unintelligible words.

"What did he say?" asked Paul.

"I don't know. Michael, what did you say?" She moved across to him, bending over him, willing him to wake up. His eyes flickered open, dark pits in a white face. He looked at her, recognition in his eyes, but then he turned his head away.

"Michael, tell me, what did you say? Please, talk to me!" she said, desperation in her voice now.

Paul moved across to join her. "Michael, we can help you, please—" He didn't get the chance to finish his sentence. Neither he nor Anna had heard the door open quietly behind them, preoccupied as they were with Michael.

Suddenly the room was full. Three men had entered, faces hard and unsmiling, gloved hands holding guns, footsteps muffled by plastic overshoes.

"Just move away from him. Let me see your hands and then keep them by your side," one of them said in a hard voice.

Anna didn't have time to react. Paul quickly pushed her behind him, holding out his arms to show his empty hands. They were not armed – Avon and Somerset Constabulary – certainly not for a routine interview of a possible suspect's sister. He hadn't even got his bloody mobile 'phone.

The one who had spoken moved forward and smiled grimly at Michael whose eyes were fully open now.

"Hello, Michael, so very nice to see you again."

He then roughly searched Paul. He found nothing of interest except his warrant card, which he examined carefully and then put back.

"Please, do sit down, Detective Inspector." He motioned to the other sofa, pushing Paul roughly so that he fell backwards onto it.

Anna fared no better. She stood still, too shocked to move, staring at them, unable to take in what was happening. One of the other men came up to her.

"Sit down next to him," he snarled venomously.

She obeyed, still too shocked to think coherently, sitting down next to Paul without a word, incapable of speech, and not even daring to look at him. One of the men stood behind them, gun in hand.

"Check him out, Carl," said the first man, tilting his head towards Michael who had by now raised himself up on his good elbow, and was watching, eyes sharp now – fever or no fever. But he hadn't spoken yet. He just sat there, watching and waiting. He didn't have to wait long. The man referred to as Carl leant over him.

"Well, Michael, you bastard. Not looking so clever now, are you?" Michael didn't reply. Instead he looked away, across the room to Anna, his eyes filled with a deep sadness.

Carl wasn't having that. He bent over, grabbing Michael's face violently in his free hand and twisting it towards his own, ignoring his look of distaste, his attempt to recoil.

"Look at me, you fucker, you've caused us enough trouble already."

"Carl, leave it, just leave it be for the moment. You'll have your chance later."

The first man spoke softly but with cold authority in his voice. Carl released Michael roughly, drawing back reluctantly, but still glaring at him. Michael stared back silently.

The first man spoke again. He seemed to be the one in charge, thought Paul; the others certainly seemed to defer to him.

"Right, Mark, cover the girl. Carl, cover the filth. John, you can give me a hand with Michael."

This last said to the man who had quietly entered the room just a few seconds ago, a short stocky man, slightly out of breath.

John walked quickly across to Michael and stood in front of him, gun in hand, as one on duty.

Paul sat quietly, his muscles tensed for action, as Carl and Mark moved behind himself and Anna. No amateurs here. These two looked like they knew how to handle those guns in their hands. He'd have to wait for his chance, and it wasn't yet.

Anna had taken a good look at the one referred to as Mark. She couldn't quite think of them as people. He was actually quite young, probably around her own age, presentable but not good-looking; his pinched and spiteful expression ruining any chance of that. But he was the type of man she could have met on any occasion other than this and would have thought normal, and normal was not a word she would have used to describe her present situation. At least he did look reasonably human, unlike the one called Carl who, with his flattened face, aggressive manner and his short, thick pugnacious body, looked like a boxer straight from his final bout, a boxer who was the victor at that. She looked across at Michael. Whilst the middle-aged, well-dressed man she'd mentally christened 'No-name' had been speaking, Michael had managed to pull himself up further and had swung his legs round and down onto the floor. 'No-name' blocked her view for a moment as he bent over him, leaning close.

"Michael, you've caused us a fair bit of trouble these last few days. We don't like that very much, you know. We like a quiet life. We just want you to help us now. You know what we want from you, don't you?"

Before Michael had a chance to reply – if indeed he had any intention of doing so – there was a quiet bleep. 'No-name' frowned and stood up, pulling out a mobile 'phone from his pocket. The others turned to watch and listened in silence.

"Yes, how long ago?" He looked at his watch, and then turned his attention back to his 'phone. "OK, well, we can be finished here in a few minutes. If they do come round, they won't find us here. Yes, we've been careful, we've taken every precaution. There won't be any trace of us."

A long pause as he listened intently, nodding occasionally, interrupting only once to say, "Oh, I don't know, hang on," and then turning to John. "What state is he in? What medical attention does he need?"

John leant more closely over Michael, pulling his jacket and his torn and bloody shirt away from his shoulder, poking with rough fingers, ignoring Michael's involuntary exclamation of pain, and then replying.

"His shoulder's a mess, needs cleaning up, a dressing put on, probably a strong injection of antibiotics, heavy duty painkillers. That's all, I should think."

Michael pulled his shirt and jacket back over his shoulder, pushing himself as far back on the sofa away from John as he could. *Probably wondering what further indignity they're going to subject him to, poor devil*, thought Paul with sympathy. Whatever Michael might have done, he was obviously not enjoying the situation he'd found himself in, and he really did look unwell. *But then again*, he thought, trying to ignore Carl's aggressive presence behind him, *I'm not enjoying this much either*.

The original speaker relayed the information given by John and finished the call.

"OK, we'll see you in a short time." He nodded across to the others. "Slight change of plans. Nothing to worry about, but we need to move a bit faster than we'd planned. We'll have to sort things out elsewhere now."

He turned to Michael, his voice soft.

"We'll be leaving soon, Michael, and you'll be coming with us. We'll get that shoulder fixed up for you in no time. All we need from you now is a promise that you will help us."

Anna felt the menace in his voice; soft though it was, the tension filled the whole room. Michael met his eyes defiantly and sat up straight, holding himself upright on the sofa, by whatever effort she couldn't imagine.

His voice, when he spoke, was hoarse, as if he hadn't

spoken for a long time.

"I know what you need, Richard. I have it, but it's not here. I'll come with you, I'll help you." He paused and looked across at Anna and Paul. "But not unless you promise that Anna and this police officer are left here unharmed. You can do what you like to me, I don't care, but this is nothing to do with them."

Anna frowned in consternation. What was he involved in? They all seemed to know him, and now it seemed that he knew this man's name. Had they been friends? How was he to help them?

Carl snorted from behind her and Paul.

"For fuck's sake, let me talk to him. I'll talk some sense into him!" But Richard waved him into silence, concentrating again on Michael who had now turned his head away, leaning wearily back on the sofa, closing his eyes and dismissing them all.

"Michael, listen to me, you are in no position to bargain with me and you know it. It will be much easier for you if you do it willingly. Don't make us use force. We can be friends."

This time when Michael spoke, his voice was perfectly controlled, the hoarseness gone. It was the old Michael who spoke. But he didn't look at Richard as he spoke; he kept his eyes half closed, his face averted.

"Don't you understand, Richard? Just hear me out. I will not help you unless you promise not to hurt them. Put your guns away, just take me and leave them here. Or kill me if you like. I don't care."

There was silence for a moment. Paul looked furtively around him; all attention for the moment was on Richard and Michael. Adrenaline pounding, thoughts racing, he wondered if he had a chance of jumping them.

Don't even think about it, he told himself firmly, *there are four of them. What chance do we have? Me, a slip of a girl and Michael, weak and...* Well, he had to admit, he was confused about Michael now. He obviously knew these men, and knew what they wanted, but he was at least trying to bargain for his and Anna's safety. But he just didn't know who Michael really was, or where he fitted into this scenario. He'd just have to go along with it for the moment. He looked at his watch surreptitiously: 9.50 p.m. What time had he spoken to Josie? Surely it must have been nearly an hour ago? He had said he'd be leaving soon, and if it hadn't been for Michael's unexpected arrival he would have done, and been back at the station long ago. Surely even Harris would have realised he should have been back by now? Why weren't they here? But then why should come here, why should they worry; they didn't even know that Michael had turned up, let alone this assorted crew of roughnecks. Did anyone have any idea how complicated this case was? Had he known? No, not at all. Scotland Yard – they must know, which is why they're coming in on this.

Richard smiled gently and his whole, creased face lit up with his smile. It was the most unpleasant smile Anna had ever seen in her life.

"Michael, it won't be you that we kill. You're far too valuable – for the moment, at least. But you *will* help us, you know, just wait and see." And he looked across to where Anna and Paul were sitting. He studied them for a long moment and then he looked behind them at Mark and Carl. He nodded, just once.

Anna felt a cold sensation on her neck. She didn't need to look to know it was a gun being pressed against her flesh. She repressed a shudder and tried to stay upright. Not so Paul, as the cold barrel of the Glock pressed against his neck. With no warning, the trigger was depressed and released, a loud *pop*, and there was Caitlin, her arms open wide, smiling now and welcoming him, the dead baby in her arms.

"We're together now, Paul. This is all you ever wanted – your family, the family you loved and thought you'd lost – together now for eternity."

Anna screamed a scream that lasted a lifetime, as Paul fell heavily against her, his blood spraying across her, a crimson tide of life coursing down her t-shirt and jeans.

Looking back, she was never really clear what happened next. She was vaguely aware of Michael somehow getting to his feet, struggling to get to them, shouting words that she didn't understand, fighting off Richard and John who were trying to hold him back; Carl going to their assistance and striking Michael hard across his face; Michael reeling backwards against the wall, almost falling but being caught by John. And then

Michael being held back, still shouting, blood dripping from a cut on his mouth, and all the time Mark said nothing, standing calmly behind her whilst she still screamed, holding his gun steadily to the back of her neck.

And then it was all over.

Richard dusted himself down and, smiling calmly, said reprovingly to Carl, "Carl, you didn't have to hit him quite so hard. That was unnecessary." He turned to Michael. "Michael, I would advise you to be quiet. You don't want your sister to have the same treatment, I take it? No? Then calm down." His attention reverted to Anna. "And as for you, you're not hurt, so shut up." Then, looking behind her, he said, "Mark, you can put the gun down now. I don't think she'll give you any trouble. Pull him off her, will you."

Mark moved around the sofa and, leaning across Anna, pushed Paul roughly so that he fell sideways over the other arm of the sofa, his unseeing eyes gazing blankly at the scene in front of him. Anna's screams subsided but she couldn't look across at Paul. Instead, she leaned down over her knees and buried her head in her hands, her whole body shaking with silent sobs.

All the fight was gone from Michael. Far from restraining him, John was almost holding him up. Michael gave one last futile attempt to break free of his grip but, finding himself unable to do so, he looked wearily at Richard and said in a defeated tone through bruised lips, "Richard, I will help you. I will do anything you ask. I copied the data onto a tape. I'll take you to it. Just please let Anna go, leave her alone. She has nothing to do with any of this."

"Oh no, my friend, she comes with us. She will guarantee your co-operation. We don't trust you, you see, but as long as we have your little Anna, I think you will help us."

And then, brusquely, over his shoulder as he moved quickly down the hallway, he said, "Remember to keep your gloves and shoe covers on. We can't leave behind any trace that we've been here. Mark, take the girl. John, help Carl with Michael. Get them both outside. I'll get the car. I'll be outside in just a couple of minutes."

Mark dragged Anna up from the sofa, grabbing the sweatshirt she'd brought downstairs for Michael, indicating to her to put it on. Still trying to suppress her sobs, she complied, allowing him to march her out of the room and along the hall, trying not to look behind her as she heard Carl speaking roughly to Michael.

"OK, pretty boy, can you walk? Good, now get going. Don't try anything clever." And then, "Oh fuck, give me a hand! Catch him, John, he's falling!"

The worst of the storm had abated now, but it was still warm and the rain's enthusiasm had not yet fully expired. Mark hurried Anna outside. She was in a daze, pulled along by him, trying desperately to ignore his silent presence as she attempted to regain control of herself. In her desolation, she realised she hadn't been able to communicate with Michael – it had all been so sudden that she hadn't really had a chance talk to him, or maybe he hadn't even wanted to – and now she was about to be pushed into some car and driven some place by these men who had just shown themselves to be capable of cold-blooded murder. Oh, God, Inspector Ravell! No, she couldn't think of him, but yet, how could she not? His blood, everywhere, all over her, his face with eyes wide open, unseeing, dead.

Mark led her unresistingly down the path. Behind her she heard her front door close reluctantly with its usual protesting squeak. She glanced behind her. Carl was almost right behind them, short and squat, staggering slightly under his load, Michael slung over one shoulder like a long sack of coal, arms hanging limply down. The car drew up almost immediately, a large dark saloon. She had no idea what make it was as it was too dark to see. Richard leant out of the driver's window.

"Quick, get them in. Put the girl in the front with me, and Mark, sit behind her and keep your gun on her. Carl, put Michael in the back and get in with him. John, have you checked that we haven't left any traces behind?"

John nodded in assent, his bald head gleaming in the rain.

"Just the dead cop, Richard. They won't be able to connect him to any of us – the bullet will be too similar to the one that killed Hamilton."

"Good," Richard continued. "You'll have to walk to where you left your car. Keep out of sight and drive carefully. Don't attract any attention to yourself. The filth might be here soon and you don't want to run into them. You know where we're going, we'll meet you there."

And John was off, walking briskly down the lane, into the gloom of the night, out of sight within seconds.

Mark pushed Anna into the passenger seat. Climbing into the seat directly behind her, he whispered gently into her ear, brushing her hair with the cold metal of his gun.

"Sit quite still, sweetheart. Just look like you're going for a ride with some friends and don't try to attract any attention."

It was the first time she had heard him speak. It could have been a pleasant voice, light and well-spoken, but it was ruined by a petulant inflection that she suspected was habitual. She felt the car shake slightly as Carl, panting, dumped Michael onto the back seat and heaved himself into the car next to him, grunting at Mark.

"Move over, Mark. Just give me a hand to get him upright. Make it look as though he's just fallen asleep."

"Do it yourself, you fat oaf," replied Mark sullenly.

Did people snarl? Anna wondered. They must do because that was the only word she could think of that could best describe Carl's response.

Richard looked behind him irritably.

"For Christ's sake, sort yourselves out in the back, will you. Is he OK?"

"Yes, he's all right, he's just passed out. Do you want me to bring him round?" Carl sounded as if he might relish the idea.

Anna shuddered to think what sadistic methods he might employ to achieve this aim.

Richard obviously had the same thought, for he replied hurriedly, "No, leave him be. At least he's quiet."

The car drew quietly away down the lane, pulling out to pass by Paul Ravell's car parked just beyond the bend. Richard turned onto the main road that ran through the village of Stratton-on-the-Fosse. Here was an exercise by Somerset County Council in traffic management: little peninsulas butting out into the road, scarcely enough room now for even one car to get through with ease.

Traffic calming, my arse, thought Richard as his foot instinctively hit the brakes rather suddenly at the oncoming headlights, trying to work out whose right of way it was from the sign.

"Red arrow, his right of way," he muttered, braking completely now.

The unmarked police car drove slowly past them, WPC Grimley and DCI Harris both peering ahead beyond Richard's dipped lights, squinting through the sheeting rain to find the turning to the lane that led to Anna's cottage. So engrossed were they in this attempt, that neither of them paid much attention to the dark blue BMW that had stopped to let them pass; neither of them noticing Anna's white face gazing bleakly ahead, ghastly in the beam of their lights. There was really no reason that they should have paid it any attention, not having any concept of what they were about to find. Premonitions, unfortunately, do not always come to order. In hindsight, however, they were both to remember the car. Josie would even recollect that it was a dark-coloured car and would wonder at its significance, wishing from the depths of their souls that they had at least noted its registration number. But of what use is hindsight? It couldn't have helped Paul now.

CHAPTER 7

**Somerset
Friday 17th May, 1996
10.05 p.m.**

Harris and Josie turned the corner into Anna's lane, seeing Paul's car parked by the side of the road.

"Bloody hell!" exploded Harris. "Ravell's still here." He lifted his hand from the wheel, twisting his wrist in an attempt to read his watch. Josie gripped the side of the seat as the car swerved slightly. "I can't see my watch. What time is it?" he barked at her.

She managed to get a quick look at her watch by the light of the dashboard as the car straightened up from its erratic course, narrowly missing one of Paul's wing mirrors.

"Just gone ten p.m., sir."

"Well, he'd better have a bloody good reason for still being here at this time. He should have left ages ago. He's got some explaining to do," he mumbled irascibly as he slowed down and parked right outside Anna's gate.

I do hope he has, thought Josie. Poor Paul; she hoped he wasn't going to get himself emotionally involved with this girl that he'd been sent out to interview. She hadn't spoken to Aiden herself but apparently he'd told Glyn Jones that Paul had seemed pretty keen to go out alone to question her again.

The car stopped. Harris jumped out immediately, impatience oozing from every pore in his body. Josie followed more slowly, her thoughts still on Paul. He'd never really got over that tragedy. How could she forget that day? She'd only been at the station for a few weeks, hardly known him really, but he'd come bursting into the office, eyes aglow, hugging her in his excitement.

"Josie, I'm just off to the hospital. Could you tell old Harris for me please? Should be soon now and then I'll be a dad!"

And, as excited as any child on Christmas morning, he had gone rushing out to perhaps the worst day of his life.

Josie snapped out of her reverie. Harris was standing impatiently by the gate.

"Come on, get a move on," he grumbled, standing aside to allow her to pass. "You'd better go first."

She reached Anna's front door with Harris one step behind her, admiring the quaint stone cottage softly illuminated by the dim light showing through the curtains. She reached up to ring the bell, almost letting out a screech as a dark shape leapt from the bushes to land by her feet. There was a deep purring sound, and a warm body wrapped itself around her legs. *A cat, Josie,* she told herself firmly, *it's just a cat. Get a grip! You'll have to do something about your nerves.*

No answer and no sound from within.

"Ring again," said Harris testily.

When there was still no response, Harris pushed past her impatiently, hammering with his fists upon the door. He waited for only a moment and then tried the handle. It wasn't locked. The door stuck at first and then opened with a protesting squeal. The cat ran swiftly between their legs and then disappeared through an open door at the end of the hallway. Harris and Josie followed more slowly. There was an unnatural silence inside the cottage that penetrated even Harris's thick skin. Looking around him, he stopped halfway down the hallway and called out.

"Miss Hamilton? Ravell! Are you here?"

Silence answered him. He moved forward, briskly now, pushing open the door to the sitting room and then came to an abrupt halt on the threshold. Josie almost walked into his broad back, so suddenly did he stop.

"Wait, hold back now, I think you'd better prepare yourself for a shock," he said in a grim voice, as she tried to peer around him. He moved slowly into the room, allowing her to follow.

The room was a picture of cosiness: cushions and rugs, comfortable sofas and tasteful bric-a-brac carelessly arranged. Then Josie screamed, forgetting her training, forgetting everything except the sight of Paul

Ravell, slumped sideways on the sofa opposite her; Paul lying with his sightless eyes turned towards them, the lower part of his face unrecognisable, blood everywhere, the life-blood that had drained from him now staining the white sofa cushions red.

Harris was standing over him, looking grim. He wouldn't be the one to forget his training. He turned to look at Josie.

"Are you all right?" he asked her gruffly, in the kindest tone she'd ever heard him use. "Don't touch anything, but sit down over there if you need to."

But Josie was in control of herself now. Screaming wouldn't help Paul. Nothing could help him now.

"Sorry, sir, it was just… Just the shock," she managed to say.

Harris had moved behind Paul's body and was peering at it closely. "Poor devil, shot from behind, right through the back of his head." He looked at Josie, his heavy face expressionless. "He probably wouldn't have felt a thing."

The grey and white cat had perched himself on the back of the other sofa and was looking intently at them through his green eyes.

Harris looked almost at a loss for a moment, the unexpectedness of the situation almost cancelling out the shock of what he was seeing: probably his best officer, lying dead in front of him, brutally murdered. And he had been going to censure Ravell. Recriminations started up in his mind. Why hadn't he come over earlier? Could he have prevented this in some way? But what the hell had happened? Ravell had given no indication to Josie on the 'phone that there was any trouble. And where was the girl? Oh, God, the car they'd passed earlier! He looked at Josie grimly.

"That car we passed on the way here. Did you notice the occupants? Do you think that it might have been connected to this?" He waved his arm towards Paul.

Josie looked at him almost in panic. She hadn't paid any attention to the car as she'd been too busy trying to see through the teeming rain to make sure they didn't miss the turning.

"I didn't look at it really, sir. I don't know... The rain – it was so dark – I'm sorry. I think it was a dark saloon car but I didn't notice anybody in it. Oh, if only I'd looked. If only we'd been a bit sooner, we might have prevented this!"

"Well, we don't know if there was any connection," he said sternly. "It could have been anyone." But deep in his heart he had a feeling that perhaps that car did hold the clue. No point in recriminations now though.

"Are you able to stay here whilst I check out the rest of the house?" he asked Josie.

She nodded wordlessly, unable to take her eyes off what was left of Paul.

Harris was gone for only a couple of minutes. Anna's cottage was not large: two bedrooms, a kitchen, a bathroom and the sitting room were all that it comprised.

"There isn't anyone else in the house and nothing seems to have been disturbed, although her spare room looks a bit like a second-hand clothes shop, mainly men's clothing. Do you know if she had a permanent boyfriend?"

"I don't know, sir. Not that I know of. DI Ravell knew the most about this case. He did discuss it, but he seemed only concerned with finding her brother."

Harris nodded. "Ah yes, the brother, our friend Michael Hamilton, who doesn't appear to exist. He holds the answer. I wonder if he's responsible for this." He looked around the room. "We'd better get some help here. Call the station. Don't use her 'phone – we'll need to get forensics on that. Here, use my 'phone."

Josie took the 'phone numbly, remembering Paul's sheepish admission that he'd left his 'phone in his car. She wondered if remembering it would have saved him. Could a life hinge upon such a fragile omission? The 'phone call to the station was unpleasant. Paul had many friends there, and Josie couldn't handle the shocked disbelief that greeted her news. She handed the 'phone wordlessly back to DCI Harris. This was, after all, his duty. He was her superior; this was what he was paid for.

She listened as he barked orders down the 'phone. She was still unable to take her eyes off Paul, expecting that any moment he would stand up and laugh at them.

"Haha! Fooled you that time."

But he didn't.

Harris placed the 'phone back in his pocket. "We'll have to wait here until forensics arrive. I can't let you touch anything, not even make a cup of tea, I'm afraid." He tentatively pushed back one curtain with his finger, peering into the wet gloom outside. "I'm not going to even attempt to look around outside yet. They'll bring strong torches. They can look."

The cat jumped down and strolled across to them, arching his back and rubbing against their legs. He was obviously interested in what was going on, his curiosity not quite getting the better of his hunger though. These humans didn't seem to understand that his friendliness was merely a ploy to be fed. His own human would have done, but she wasn't here. He gave up after a couple of minutes and then noticed the one lying on the sofa. Might as well go over and have a look. Perhaps it might wake up and feed him.

Harris watched the cat with disinterest until he showed signs of jumping up onto the sofa where Paul's body lay. Suddenly realising his intention, Harris bent down quickly to pick him up but not quite getting a firm hold because with a yowl the cat spat at him in surprise, leapt upwards into the air and landed with a thud by the door. He looked balefully at Harris for a moment and then, seemingly distracted by something, he lay down on his belly and began to poke his paw under the bookcase by the door. Josie knelt down by the cat, intrigued by his activities, glad to have something to take her mind off Paul. Then she saw the metal gleaming under the bookcase.

"Sir!" she said excitedly. "There's something under the bookcase. I think it might be a gun."

Harris squatted down next to her, breathing heavily as his paunch compressed. He had some difficulty in getting low enough to see the gun without losing his balance, but he somehow managed and then smiled with grim satisfaction.

"Looks like the murder weapon all right. When we get the prints on that, we'll have Ravell's killer." He heaved himself upright, finishing harshly, "And Professor Hamilton's murderer too. I have no doubt."

CHAPTER 8

Somerset
Friday 17th May, 1996
10.05 p.m.

DCI Roderick Harris and WPC Josie Grimley might have been too preoccupied to have noticed Richard's car and its occupants, but not so Richard. He'd smothered a violent curse as the other car had cruised slowly past them, glancing quickly at Anna to ensure that she hadn't tried to communicate with the passing car in any way. He needn't have worried; she still sat silently, eyes fixed straight ahead of her. Richard engaged first gear and the car slid smoothly forward through the narrow gap, past the traffic islands on both sides. Of course he had no idea who the occupants of the other car might have been (it was only his own paranoia that made him think they might have been the police) but as he glanced in his rear-view mirror, he suppressed a shudder as he saw the car turn down into Anna's lane.

"Did you recognise them?" he asked of his backseat passengers.

"No, but they looked like the fuzz," grunted Carl from the corner.

"Well, they've turned into her lane. We can't take any chances so we'll have to change the plates when we get there. Mark, you can do that," continued Richard.

"Honestly, Richard, I do think you're getting paranoid," complained Mark. "If you're going to think that every car we pass is looking for us, we might as well get out right here and walk."

"Shut up, you ponce," growled Carl. "Don't talk such crap."

"Not as much crap as comes from your big arse, sweetie," replied Mark.

Richard suppressed a sigh. The sooner he could separate these two the better. Why the hell he'd selected them as part of the same team he just couldn't imagine. And yet, maybe there was some logic. Chalk and cheese they might be, but both had their own merits: Mark, devious and clever, devoid of conscience, the coldest, most hard-headed accomplice he could ever have asked for, would never lose his head whatever the circumstances and Carl, as impulsive and hot-headed as Mark was cold, capable of almost mindless physical violence. Between them, they had enough sociopathic and psychopathic traits to keep any psychologist or psychiatrist in full-time employment for a whole lifetime.

Silence reigned in the car for a while as Richard drove on, keeping well within the speed jurisdictions (getting pulled up for speeding now would be a disaster). Several cars passed them, but Richard ignored his inner worries. Maybe Mark was right: maybe he was getting paranoid. He drove towards the centre of Bath, concentrating on the roads. The driving rain wasn't helping and visibility was almost nil. It was hard to think the rain could continue at such force, but at least the worst of the storm had passed.

Mark and Carl had subsided into an incompatible silence. Richard suspected that, left to their own devices, they wouldn't even bother to communicate with each other. It was only the presence of others that provoked their bickering. Anna had still not spoken or even moved from her frozen position. Richard risked another quick sideways glance at her. He felt a grudging respect for her as Christ knows she'd been through enough in the last hour or so. Most women would probably have been hysterical by now, but she seemed to have control of herself, which was something he admired in a woman.

It was just as well that he couldn't see inside Anna's head. Her mind was buzzing with a cacophony of confused thoughts. So much had happened in the last few days – particularly in the last two hours – that she couldn't absorb. She needed more time to assimilate all the recent occurrences. She sat motionless; her mind engrossed in trying to sort out what was happening. She was conscious of Richard glancing across at her every now and then, but she didn't react. What she really wanted to do was to look behind her to reassure herself that Michael was all right. But she daren't. Her mind was too full of the vivid recollection of Mark, gun held against her neck whilst Carl had calmly pressed the trigger that killed Inspector Ravell. Suppose that by turning round to look at Michael she prompted the same response, and either she or Michael were killed instantly? She didn't know if he'd regained consciousness. There was occasional movement in the back, as if bodies were shifting about slightly, but who it might be, she had no idea. She couldn't even tell by listening carefully if he was still alive. She could hear breathing from the backseat, sometimes heavy, sometimes lighter, but she had no way of knowing where the sounds were coming from. She gave a slight start as Richard addressed her.

"Are you feeling all right, Miss Hamilton? You are very quiet. I do apologise that you are being put through this inconvenience. I very much hope that it won't be for long. We have just a few rather important matters to clear up."

He could have been addressing a board meeting, Anna thought. She couldn't believe that this was the same person who had so recently nodded calmly, a ruthless nod that had sent Inspector Ravell to his death. She didn't reply; there seemed little point.

He looked across at her again briefly, accepting her silence. *So be it*, he thought, *the lady doesn't want to talk.*

They were in the centre of Bath now and Richard concentrated on the road. He knew it well but this rain was making driving very difficult and there were a lot of cars around now, with couples returning from the theatre and friends making their way back from an evening in the pub. Of course, he realised with a jolt, it was Friday night. Naturally there would be all this social activity. He took the road towards Claverton Down. Not far now. He decided that he would make Mark change the plates. Paranoia or no paranoia, there was nothing to be lost by playing it safe. After a few more turnings they drew up outside the gates of an impressive house.

Anna sat up and took notice now. She hadn't really allowed herself to wonder where they were being taken and was surprised they'd stopped so soon. She knew Bath as well as anyone, and she certainly knew this house. Her thoughts went into overdrive.

Richard drove along the long drive to the large house at the end. He stopped the car, pausing for a moment to sigh in relief. So far, so good. He looked behind him.

"OK in the back there? It's all very quiet."

It was Mark who replied. "Oh yes, we're all very fine here, no problems. Our friend's still asleep and Carl is still as uncommunicative as ever. I really must say, Richard, sometimes I do wish you'd tell me in advance who I might be working with. I would like—"

Carl interrupted him, as of course he'd known he would. "Shut up, you little fucker. Richard, I might need a hand to get him out of the car. He's still out cold and he's a bloody sight heavier than he looks."

"Yes, that's no problem. Mark, take care of the girl. Carl, wait for a moment and I'll be back to give you a hand with Michael."

Richard climbed out of the car and walked up the steps to the door, whilst Mark, who was out of his backseat almost sooner than the door could have opened, pulled open Anna's door and was motioning for her to get out. This she did, allowing herself now a quick glance at the backseat. Carl was sitting in the far corner and Michael was slumped in the middle. She got out of the car with as much dignity as she could muster, pulling away from Mark as he tried to take her arm.

The front door of the house opened onto a long, illuminated hallway, from where a short, slight, but imposing figure emerged. Richard grabbed Anna's arm and pulled her up the steps to meet the figure, rapidly instructing Mark to stay behind and help Carl with Michael.

"Well, hello, Richard. And Anna too. How lovely to see you. Please do come in. This is indeed a privilege."

It wasn't a shock, Anna had known from the minute they'd turned onto his drive, but she still couldn't comprehend that Graham Sutherland was a part of this. Perhaps he wasn't. Perhaps they were safe now, with this friend, this man who had spent so much time at her home, with her father and Michael.

His next words repudiated her hopes. He looked beyond them at the car and then fixed his gaze back upon Richard.

"Where's Michael?" he said sharply. "I assume that you've got him in the car? Take her inside. Quickly now."

"He's in the car, passed out. Carl and Mark are with him. Did you get a doctor?"

"Yes, that's not a problem. Just get her inside. I'll go and help them. I'll be with you in a minute," replied Sutherland, going down the steps towards the car.

Richard hustled an unprotesting Anna through the open doorway and down the spacious hallway. She tried to look around; it was all so beautiful. She'd been here before, of course, on several occasions, and had never failed to be impressed by its ornate decor. It could so easily have looked pretentious, but somehow just missed: rich velvety colours and expensive paintings, dark wood panelling half lining the walls, and beautiful antique furniture arranged tastefully on the sumptuous carpets.

Without hesitation, Richard took her into the room she knew as the study. A man was sitting in the chair by the roll-top desk, a dapper man, dark-suited and unsmiling, who stood up on their entry, but not before Anna had noticed the black case lying by his feet. *A doctor?* she wondered. Her thoughts were confirmed by his opening words.

"Good evening. I understand I am to treat a patient. I am in quite a hurry. Perhaps you can tell me where this patient is?"

He'd obviously decided that neither Anna nor Richard were candidates for his Hippocratic care.

We mustn't fit the bill, she thought hysterically. *And I bet it's a large bill.*

He must suddenly have noticed the bloodstains down Anna's jeans as before Richard had a chance to reply, he spoke again.

"Are you all right, miss? I can't help but see that you—" He didn't get the chance to finish before Richard interrupted him peremptorily.

"There is a person who needs your attention. He will be brought in shortly. The young lady is fine. She's just had rather a shock, that's all." Silence ensued. Richard indicated to Anna that she should sit down, which she did, without demur, watching the door anxiously, willing the others to come in because then she might at least see Michael again. She was doomed to disappointment, however. After a few minutes, Graham Sutherland entered the room, smiling and debonair as ever.

"Good evening, Doctor. I am so sorry to have kept you waiting. If you will just come this way, please."

And without further ado, he and the doctor left the room, leaving Anna and Richard alone.

Silence fell again. Richard seemed to have no desire to engage in conversation, and sitting himself down on one of the leather chairs he gazed absently into space, one leg thrown carelessly across the other, apparently at peace with his thoughts, whatever they might be. She watched him furtively. She felt she should know him, but couldn't place him.

Michael had certainly known him, but then she no longer knew what Michael was mixed up in. The events of the last few hours had left her incapable of rational thought. Every time she tried to analyse events, all she could see was Inspector Ravell, lying on her sofa, blood everywhere, eyes open, looking blankly, accusingly, at her. But what could she have done to help? He had seemed a nice man, she thought sadly, forgiving him the discomfort he had subjected her to. And then, irrationally, she remembered Brian. She hadn't fed him tonight. He hadn't been in the house. Where was he?

The door opened again and Graham Sutherland re-entered the room, smiling urbanely.

"Sorry to have left you. Had to get Michael attended to. Now, are you hungry, Anna?"

She looked at him dumbstruck. How could he even mention food? "No, thank you. But, Mr Sutherland, I really would appreciate an explanation of what is going on! Where is my brother, and why have we been brought here in this manner?"

He looked faintly surprised that she had the energy to respond so positively. She didn't dare imagine what she must look like. She knew that Inspector Ravell's blood stained her clothing, and she had been dragged out into the car in the pouring rain, which probably hadn't done much for her appearance. She didn't care. Bedraggled or not, she wanted an answer.

"Anna, my dear, I am so sorry, but, well, it is quite late now. I can assure you that Michael is in the best of hands. We'll have him fit and well in no time at all. I think the best idea is for you to go to bed now and get some rest. You will be my guest tonight and then you shall see Michael tomorrow. Now, come along with me and I'll show you to your room." Then, turning to Richard, he said, "Richard, I'll be back shortly."

Graham Sutherland waited by the door as Anna reluctantly got up from her chair to follow him. He led her back through his panelled hallway and paused.

"Anna, I know there are many questions that you would like answered. Believe me, I do understand, but these are complicated matters. I hope those men weren't too rough with you. They don't have a lot of common civility, I know, but unfortunately it was necessary for them to behave as they did. A good night's sleep and things will seem a lot better in the morning, believe me."

Dumbly, she followed him up the stairs to the first floor, through a door that led to a winding staircase, and up the staircase to a dark corridor. There were two doors leading off, one of which he opened. The room was small but cosy, with an adjoining door left slightly ajar. A bed, a chair and a chest of drawers were all it contained. The window was dark, the shutters closed.

"Now please, do make yourself at home here. I'm sorry that we haven't been able to bring you a change of clothing. We'll sort that out tomorrow for you. There is an en suite bathroom there," he said, indicating the half-open door. "Now, it wouldn't be a good idea for you to come downstairs until we call you in the morning. I'm sure you understand me, but I'll lock the door, just in case."

And with another smile he was gone, leaving Anna alone in the room. She heard the key turn in the lock as the door closed behind him.

Sutherland walked quietly across the corridor and entered the room where they'd taken Michael. The doctor was just packing up his bag while Michael lay motionless on the bed, a large white bandage wrapped over his left shoulder and secured around his chest. Carl and Mark stood by the window, silent for once.

"How is he? Did he give you any trouble?" he asked.

The doctor looked up. "Well, he came to, got a bit feisty, so I've sedated him. He shouldn't give you any trouble for a while. I've cleaned him up a bit, but haven't been able to get the bullet fragment out as it's in too deep. I'll need to operate in a sterile environment. It's starting to look quite infected so I've pumped him full of antibiotics, but we shouldn't leave it too long. 'Phone me tomorrow and we can sort something out. Meanwhile, there's some painkillers on the table over there. They're quite strong so just give them to him when he asks."

"Thank you, Doctor, I appreciate what you've done," said Sutherland smoothly. "If you'd like to go down to my study, Mark will show you the way. I'll be down in a couple of minutes to settle up with you."

As the door closed behind Mark and the doctor, Sutherland turned to Carl.

"Operation? I don't think so. I'm not throwing good money after bad. Now, have you got your gun?"

Carl nodded and produced his gun from his pocket. Sutherland took it and carefully wiped it clean with a cloth, and then he motioned to Carl to hold up Michael's right hand. Holding the end of the gun carefully with the cloth, he wrapped Michael's fingers around the gun, pressing hard, but taking care not to accidentally depress the trigger.

"There," he said in a satisfied tone as he placed the gun in a plastic bag. "Now we have that policeman's killer. Come on, Carl, let's go join the others, and I need to pay off that crooked quack."

And with one last look at Michael, he followed Carl out of the room and locked the door.

CHAPTER 9

Somerset
Friday 17th May, 1996
10.15 p.m.

Harris and Josie didn't have long to wait before they heard the unmistakable sound of the sirens screeching along the quiet lane towards them. This was followed by doors banging and heavy footsteps thumping up the path, squelching through the puddles.

Before long, Anna's small cottage was full of white-suited men; deep voices and exclamations of anger and distress at the pitiful sight of Paul Ravell.

The pathologist went straight to the body. He had his work to do, though the fact that he'd known and worked with Paul made his job all the more difficult for him.

The forensic team started their painstaking duties, carefully examining every object in the minutest detail, filling their plastic bags carefully. Not a scrap of evidence must escape their eagle eyes.

DI Aiden Formby, Paul's closest friend, had arrived with the forensic team. He pulled Harris to one side.

"Sir, do you have any idea who is responsible for this?"

Harris took a moment to answer, seemingly lost in thought. "How much did Ravell tell you about this case?" he asked eventually.

"Well, not a lot. I know he was very anxious to find Professor Hamilton's son, Michael. It seemed like there was some discrepancy in his background details, and he thought perhaps the daughter might be able to give him more information," Aiden replied slowly.

"I can't tell you much more than Ravell probably did. I was waiting for his final report before this," Harris gestured towards the sofa, then continued, "before this happened. But I think once forensics have finished, we may well find that Michael Hamilton is implicated very heavily."

Aiden didn't reply for a moment. "The sister: she was obviously here when Paul called. Do you have any idea where she might be?"

"No, vanished without a trace. And yes, she was here. WPC Grimley spoke to Ravell earlier but he gave no indication that there was anything amiss."

He was interrupted by PC Glyn Jones shouting from the door.

"Sir, I've just been looking around outside and the 'phone line has been cut."

"Ah," said Harris as he and Formby walked over to the door. "That at least explains why we couldn't get through the second time."

"But didn't Paul have his mobile 'phone?" Aiden Formby asked sharply, looking at Josie who had just joined them.

Josie cringed. Poor Paul, that one mistake had cost him dearly.

"No, I'm afraid not. He said he'd left it in his car," she replied quietly, not able to meet his eyes.

Aiden pursed his lips, frowning.

"Well, this must have happened very suddenly; his car's parked nearby. It would only have taken him a couple of minutes to go and get it. He couldn't have thought he'd need it."

"Maybe he didn't get the chance," suggested PC Jones. "If he was caught by surprise, perhaps he wasn't able to leave the house." Turning to Harris, he continued. "There's not much in the way of footprints out there. The rain has been so heavy and any imprints have been washed away. But we've found quite a few muddy footprints on the kitchen floor. Some of them are quite clear: trainers, about size eleven or twelve we think. They're just measuring them now. Whoever left those prints was having quite a problem walking straight for whatever reason, and some mud has been trampled into the sitting room from the kitchen, probably by the same person. Oh, and DI Ravell's jacket is hanging over a chair in the kitchen. Looks like he put it there to dry out."

"Thank you, Glyn, well done. Please take the jacket back to the station when you leave," said Aiden, and then turned to Harris. "Sir, I'll get someone out to Michael Hamilton's flat. They can check his shoe size."

Harris merely grunted, and then turned his attention to DS Sean Adams who had now come up to speak to them.

"What else have you found then?" he asked testily.

DS Adams spoke precisely, careful not to allow his dislike of his superior to show in his voice.

"There are two empty glasses. One has contained whisky, one has contained water. We're checking for fingerprints now."

He pointed over to the coffee table, where a white-suited figure was busy dusting.

"We've got the gun and the bullet casing – ballistics will check that out – and we will need the bullet to make a match. There's a small splattering of blood on the wall by the kitchen door. It might be DI Ravell's but it's unlikely. It's too far away from the sofa where he was—" He paused, finding it hard to say the word. "Killed. There are also some clear footprints—"

Harris interrupted him. "Yes, yes, we already know about the footprints. Can't be Ravell's or the Hamilton girl's. We'll be sending someone out to check Michael Hamilton's shoe size. What about the rest of the house? Have you found anything?"

"Nothing untoward. The whole cottage indicates one female resident, although there is quite a bit of male clothing in the spare room. The girl's boyfriend maybe, or her brother? And they've also checked the cottage opposite. It's empty and doesn't look as though it's been occupied for a while, although PC Jones seemed to think the floor might have been recently swept. But they couldn't find any real evidence to support that."

Aiden thanked him as Harris turned away without a further word. DS Adams nodded, raised his eyebrows at Aiden and went back to his team.

The pathologist came across, his gruesome work done.

"I think he would have died instantly, Roderick. Bullet penetrated the base of his skull. The only blessing is he wouldn't have known a thing, poor devil. I'll do a postmortem as a matter of course, but I don't expect to find anything else – unless there's anything in particular you think I should be looking for?"

"Nothing else at the moment that I can think of," replied Harris grimly. "Thank you, James."

And the pathologist was off, leaving others to cover the body and arrange its transport.

Harris turned his attention back to Aiden. "What do you think? Can you see any signs of a struggle? Anything to indicate that the girl could have been dragged off against her will?"

"Well, the rugs are scuffed up in places, and there is the blood on that wall—" He stopped in surprise, looking down at his leg. Brian had reappeared from the hiding place where he'd scuttled in fright at the activities of the forensic team, and was now entwining himself around Aiden's legs, purring loudly. "Bloody hell, it's a cat," he said, stating the obvious. "Looks like it's hungry. Can we feed it, do you think?"

Harris looked at him in surprise. Was the man soft in the head? He'd always had his doubts about Formby, no matter that the Super thought he was one of the best. He personally thought he was a wimp, too bloody good-looking for his own good. But maybe he had a point. The cat must belong to the Hamilton girl and if they neglected it, they'd probably have the bloody RSPCA on their backs as well.

"Yes, in a minute, if you want to. Looks like they're done in the kitchen. Just finish what you were saying first," he replied grumpily.

Aiden ignored the tone. "There isn't much more. Like I said, the rugs are scuffed in places," he said, indicating the spot where Michael had been forcibly dragged back. "And there's that bit of blood on the wall over there as well so could have been a bit of a scuffle there. There are impressions on both the sofas; looks like they've been sat on recently, but—" he paused doubtfully.

"But what?" Harris was getting even more impatient. Why couldn't the man just get to the point?

"Well, they've obviously been well used, these sofas, so it's hard to say for certain whether they're just not permanently flattened in places. It does look as though Anna Hamilton and Paul were sitting talking, having a drink. Looks like they were sitting opposite each other, one on each sofa, judging by the positions of the glasses on the coffee table."

"Yes, yes," Harris said sarcastically. "I think I could have worked that out for myself."

"But," Aiden continued thoughtfully, ignoring the interruption, "it also looks like someone was sitting next to Paul when he was shot, from the pattern of the blood. That person will have bloodstains on their clothes. See how it's marked the sofa to the side of Paul? So if that person was Miss Hamilton, she must have been told to move and sit next to Paul before he was shot, presumably by the person who surprised them: Paul's murderer."

"And that person was Michael Hamilton, of that I have no doubt," said Harris dismissively. "You might as well go and feed that cat."

Aiden mentally shrugged his shoulders. No wonder the man wasn't well-liked. Oh yes, and that reminded him. "There was a call just before I left the station, sir. Commander Lyons from Scotland Yard will be with you around seven tomorrow morning."

Ignoring Harris's black look, he went into the kitchen, Brian and Josie following closely on his heels.

"Does it take two to feed a cat?" shouted Harris after them, but they chose not to hear.

"Aiden, I just can't believe it," said Josie as they entered the kitchen.

She felt uncomfortable; it was the first time they'd been alone together since that night in his flat two weeks ago, the night of that dreadful row when she'd stormed out, vowing never to see him again. She'd been so hurt, and had done her best to avoid chance encounters since then, but now the circumstances were slightly different. To cover her confusion, she rummaged around for a tin opener, keeping her head down.

"Poor Paul, he didn't deserve this," she finished quietly.

Aiden seemed unaware of her embarrassment; his mind wasn't on personal matters. "What was he doing, forgetting his mobile?" he said pensively, and then, with concern in his voice, "Oh, God, I wonder who's going to have to tell his mother? She never got over that trouble with his younger brother. Paul said she couldn't accept it; she blamed the police for giving chase and causing him to crash. He used to worry about her so much."

"Well, at least there isn't a wife or children to inform," said Josie, and then went bright red with embarrassment at her tactlessness. "Oh, I'm sorry, Aiden, that was stupid of me."

Aiden turned abruptly to her, the remembered pain of Caitlin's loss showing in his dark eyes. "Had you forgotten, Jo, that Caitlin was my sister as well as Paul's wife?"

But his face softened as he looked at Josie; she looked so upset. He regretted that pointless argument that had caused such a rift between them. He missed her and wanted to try to put it right, but Josie had been avoiding him since that night. He shook his head slightly to dispel the thoughts. Now was not the time.

He smiled at her and spoke more gently. "It's OK, Jo, no one can hurt Paul and Caitlin now. Let's just hope there is an afterlife and perhaps they can be together again. And let's hope we find the bastard who did this to Paul. Now, let's feed this cat before it completely savages my leg."

Josie was feeling more relaxed now, and they stood watching in comfortable silence as Brian devoured the entire tin of cat food in about two minutes flat, before sitting back contentedly licking his chops, regarding them solemnly.

"Do you think we should leave him here?" asked Josie doubtfully. "I could take him home with me. I don't like the thought of leaving the poor thing in an empty house."

"I see no reason why not. Take him. At least if the girl turns up again, her cat will be safe," replied Aiden absently.

They returned from the kitchen, Josie carrying the now contented cat, her pockets bulging with tins of cat food. Harris was standing waiting impatiently for her.

"Come on, WPC, get a move on, we can't do any more here now. I want to get back and sort things out for tomorrow. It's gone eleven thirty and I've got to be up at the crack of dawn. I'll drop you back home. You're surely not proposing to take that thing in my car, are you?" He said the last words almost in horror as Josie showed no signs of putting the cat down.

"Please, sir, I can't leave him here," she almost pleaded.

"Oh, all right, but if it craps in my car, you can bloody well clear it up."

And he strode off, leaving Josie to smile ruefully at Aiden, catching his wink behind Harris's back, before hurrying to catch up with him, a purring Brian held firmly in her arms.

CHAPTER 10

Somerset
Saturday 18th May, 1996
7.30 a.m.

It was dark in the room but so very warm. He curled up and then allowed himself to stretch out luxuriously. The bed – for it must be a bed on which he was lying – was so comfortable, and apart from the gnawing pains in his stomach that told him how hungry he was, he couldn't remember the last time he had felt so good. And then as consciousness began to slowly dawn, poised on that deep level somewhere between animal comfort and human awareness, he wanted to retreat and to return to whatever state had given him so much pleasure, or at least back to oblivion, but he couldn't. The memories started to intrude: that night in the laboratory, the days and nights out in the open, the rain, the cold, the pain, the sight of that police officer being shot before his eyes. And Anna. He sat up with a start.

"Good morning, Michael," said a smooth, familiar voice.

His eyes tried to accustom themselves to the gloom but didn't need to for long. The shutters were thrown back and bright morning light filled the room. He looked around him: a small room, bare, but with enough amenities to satisfy; a bed, on which he was lying, a small table, a chest of drawers and a chair by the bed, a chair in which Graham Sutherland was now sitting, having returned to his place of watching.

"That's not my name and you know it," he said, lying back on the pillows and turning his head away.

"I know, dear boy, but it will have to do for the moment. How are you feeling?"

"Where's Anna?"

"She's fine. You can see her soon, no need for you to worry – now. How are you? How's your shoulder?"

Michael considered these questions. He didn't really know the answers. He felt numb and lightheaded, the pain of the last few days a blur now. He looked down to see a large white bandage covering his left shoulder, crisscrossing his chest under his shirt. He frowned, he couldn't think straight. He couldn't remember enough; it was all so patchy. He didn't know how he had got here. He tried to think back, the events of last evening seeming like a dream. Perhaps it had been a dream? But that policeman – that had been no dream.

"That policeman – they killed that police officer in cold blood."

"Michael, don't concern yourself with my problems. All I want is for you to feel well again. You've had a bad time." Sutherland was looking at him intently, eyes narrowed, trying to assess him. He continued but with less sympathy now. "Michael, I can't pretend I'm very happy about what you've done. It was clumsy and you've caused me a fair bit of trouble. Now we have to sort out this mess that you've got us into, and you know I need your help."

At first Michael didn't answer. He appeared to be engrossed in his thoughts, and then his face darkened as the memories came flooding back. "I said I wouldn't help him. He told me what you both did, what you are doing now. You are as much a part of this as he was—" He didn't get the chance to finish as Sutherland interrupted.

"Enough, Michael. I can't begin to understand what possessed Alexander to talk to you about any of this." He looked shrewdly at Michael. "But he obviously did, and it seems he told you way too much. For now, we just need to reinstall that data, and then you and I can have a little chat about what he said. And about our future."

"There is no future. I have no future with you."

"Look, my dear boy, you know as well as I do that with Alexander dead, and with what you did, you are the only person who can help me at the moment. I think you owe me that, at least. After all, if it weren't for you, I wouldn't be in this mess. And I don't think you're in any position to throw moral rectitude at me, are you? You are going to produce that tape – yes, Richard has told me what you said – and you're going to reinstall the data, like it or not. I've already covered it up by telling the police that your action in scrambling the data was merely a routine security precaution. So now we need to prove the truth of that lie, don't we, dear boy?"

Michael didn't reply. His thoughts were too busy trying to make sense of things, trying to evaluate the events of the past few days, but they wouldn't run straight and he couldn't clear his head. He couldn't rid himself of the sight of Paul falling across Anna, his blood covering her.

"Why did that police officer have to die?" he asked. He couldn't really remember much after that, everything became a blur. Christ, he felt so weak. And where was Anna?

"Where is Anna?" he demanded.

Sutherland sighed. "Look, the police officer just got in the way, but now he'll serve a useful purpose. And I just told you that Anna is safe, she's here. You'll see her very soon. I'll do my best to answer your questions later, but you are going to have to help me, you know, and soon." He looked expectantly at Michael for a couple of minutes, and then, when he still received no reply, he spoke impatiently, the softness gone from his voice.

"Listen to me, Michael. I can't condone what you've done, but I'm trying to understand. I appreciate that whatever Alexander told you must have come as a shock. I would very much like us to continue to be friends. There's no reason why we can't have a long and mutually beneficial relationship. I'm sure once you've had time to think things over you'll agree with me. However, our relationship doesn't necessarily have to be friendly or even last that long. Your indispensability is not unlimited. Just remember that as far as the police are concerned you're guilty of one murder, and now, with the police officer, we can make that two. They don't like to have one of their own killed, you know." He allowed himself a slight smile. "I told you he could serve a useful purpose—"

"Please, Graham," Michael interrupted. "Just let Anna go. I promise I'll help you then. I'll do anything once I know that she's safe."

Sutherland ignored him, rising lithely from the chair and moving across the room, pausing only at the door to speak, all softness gone now as the room filled with the menace in his quiet voice.

"My dear boy, don't waste your breath. You really have no negotiating power with me. I've got you and I've got Anna. I hold all the cards. Just consider for a moment. The police aren't very clever, you know. All they want to do is to find the person who killed Alexander and their officer. I could provide them with all the evidence. You've made that very easy for me, I must say. The newspapers will love it, you might even make the front page, just imagine the stories: Brilliant young research scientist, working way too hard, has a breakdown and goes on a killing spree. First he murders his father, then a police officer, then his sister and finally, in remorse, commits suicide. It all sounds very plausible, now, doesn't it? I can just see myself fighting back the tears when I get the news that they've found the bodies – yours and Anna's. I shall blame myself, of course, for not noticing how close to the edge you were getting."

He paused for a moment to let his last words sink in, before continuing. "And it wouldn't have to be that quick, Michael. I think our friend Mark has got quite a thing about your little Anna. You, my friend, are without any options at the moment." Then, more briskly, "Now, I suggest you get off that bed and put your shoes on. I'm sorry I can't offer you any clean clothes. We'll get some for you later... perhaps. There's an en suite bathroom through that door over there, and there is a glass of water and some painkillers on the table here. Just take a couple if you need them. I'll send Carl to bring you downstairs in a few minutes." And without waiting for a response, he was gone, locking the door behind him.

Michael stayed still for a moment, cursing the weakness that had taken him to Anna's cottage. He should have known that of course they'd be watching. Why hadn't he just stayed away? If he'd stayed away, that police officer would still be alive. He didn't even know his name. Had he been told his name? And then Anna wouldn't be involved in all this. But no point in recriminations. He had to find a way of getting her out of this mess. He had to co-operate for the moment and get his strength back. He gingerly moved his arm a fraction, surprised to find that it didn't hurt too much. It was stiff and numb, but that dreadful pain had gone. He swung his legs slowly down onto the floor and then stood up carefully. He felt dizzy and lightheaded and his thought processes were still too slow. He wondered what concoction of drugs they might have pumped into him. He decided that taking more painkillers wouldn't be a very good idea so he just took a long gulp of the water and splashed cold water over his face when he was in the en suite.

Careful not to disturb his shoulder too much, he managed to shrug himself into his jacket that at least had dried out. His trainers presented more of a problem. Leaning down made his head swim and his left hand was more or less useless as he had hardly any feeling in his fingers. He swung himself back on the bed and by leaning backwards and contorting his body he somehow managed to lever one foot inside its trainer. He was struggling with the other foot when he heard the key in the lock. The door opened to admit Carl.

"How the mighty are fallen," he sneered, standing by the bed with his arms folded, enjoying the sight of Michael almost doubled in two attempting to sort out his laces.

Michael ignored him, still concentrating on his laces, before rolling sideways off the bed and managing to pull himself upright.

"OK, Carl, shall we go?" he said with no inflection

in his voice. The last thing he wanted to do at this time was to provoke Carl. His memory might be rather haphazard (he still couldn't remember how he had got here, or indeed much of the events after the policeman at Anna's had been shot), but nonetheless he knew what Carl was capable of. *A sadistic thug*, he thought. *As big a bully as he's ugly*.

Carl felt slightly peeved – no excuse for a fight here – but he took some pleasure in the sight of Michael. He might look a bit better this morning than he had last night (it would be quite difficult not to) but his mouth was still bruised. Carl smirked at the memory; he'd enjoyed that. And bandaged or not, he still looked pretty awful, white and drawn under that stubble. He didn't waste his breath speaking to Michael again. He had his orders, and he motioned for Michael to follow him as he led the way downstairs. Michael looked about him as they walked down the corridor. He'd worked out that they must be in Sutherland's house, but although he'd been there before on countless occasions in the past, he'd never before been beyond the sumptuous ground floor. This must, he guessed, at one time have been the servants' quarters. They were high in the house; he suspected he must have slept in an attic bedroom although he hadn't had the chance to look out of the window. The corridor down which he was being led was dark and narrow, terminating in a narrow staircase. There were two other doors opening off the corridor but he didn't get a chance to look further before Carl was off down the flight of stairs. Michael followed him slowly.

Anna had slept fitfully. When Sutherland had left her, she'd been too upset to even consider the thought of sleep. She'd tried the door, which of course was locked (not that she'd expected anything different) She'd rattled and twisted the doorknob, though she knew it was a waste of time – she'd heard Sutherland lock the door, but she had to try – before walking through to the adjoining en suite bathroom. The window there was locked and shuttered like the one in the bedroom. She'd gone back into the room to sit on the edge of the bed, trying to clear her thoughts, trying to work out what was going on. Everything had happened so quickly that she hadn't really had a chance to think.

But now she did. Her mind was in turmoil, going back over all that had happened from the moment on that dreadful night, last Wednesday, at eleven p.m., when that policeman had stood on her doorstep, solemnly saying, "Miss Hamilton, may I come in? I'm afraid I have some bad news for you."

He'd proceeded to tell her gently that her father had been found dead in the laboratory at ten thirty p.m. that evening. The kind policeman wasn't able to give her much more information, not even how he had died. The police were at the scene now, he'd said, but they would be sure to let her know all the details as soon as they were able. She'd shuddered at those words.

He'd then said that someone would be over to see her

the next morning and did she want anyone to stay with her for the night? She'd blindly shaken her head, the shock of what he was saying not really sinking in, needing time alone to absorb the news. He'd got up to leave, asking her gently again if she would be all right. She'd nodded. And then, almost as an afterthought, he'd asked her if she'd seen Michael that evening. The police had tried to contact him as well, to let him know what had happened, but they hadn't been able to find him. He wasn't at his flat, wasn't answering his mobile 'phone, and hadn't been at work that day.

She'd shaken her head dumbly. The first thing she had planned to do when the policeman left was to 'phone Michael but now it seemed that she couldn't even do that. *Where was he?* she'd wondered. But then he didn't have to answer to her. Why shouldn't he be out? But why not go to work? Then again, he'd always done the odd disappearing act and no one had questioned it before. When the policeman had left, despite what he'd said she'd still tried to 'phone Michael, but there had been no reply, just an empty ringing. But about five minutes later, her 'phone had rung. She'd got up reluctantly to answer it, dreading some faceless official giving her more information about her father's death over the 'phone, wishing now that she'd been stronger and had insisted on going over to see his body for herself so as to convince herself that he was really dead.

But it was no official – it was Michael, desperation

in his voice, telling her that something terrible had happened, that he couldn't get to her yet, that she mustn't tell the police that he'd 'phoned her, that someone was after him and that he'd be in touch when he could. He hadn't allowed her to speak with him. He'd ended the call with no goodbye, and that had hurt the most. And yet she'd still believed in him, until the facts, relayed by Inspector Ravell, had finally seeped into her consciousness. And she'd denied him; she'd said that Michael must have murdered their father. Michael had come to her for help but had only heard what she'd said. He'd heard her betrayal and had had no chance to tell her what had really happened, unable to give her his side of the story. And then those men had arrived, to kill Inspector Ravell, and to bring her here to Graham Sutherland's house. Why? Anna's thoughts ran round in circles. She had to get some sleep. She was reaching that point of despair – the knowledge that things won't be better in the morning; a dark, hopeless feeling of emptiness.

Michael was implicated heavily in this in a way she couldn't even imagine, and that poor Inspector Ravell, shot dead as he sat next to her. It must be late. She was frightened to think anymore, and she hadn't slept well these last two nights. Despite her doze this afternoon, she still felt so tired. She lay across the bed, fully clothed, her head heavy. She closed her eyes, seeing blood: blood spurting across her, blood everywhere, everyone she knew and everyone she loved covered in blood.

Someone was shaking her shoulder, disturbing her, breaking into the oblivion into which she had buried herself. *Leave me alone, go away,* she thought. She turned over and, raising herself up, saw Mark. Reality, sharp as a dart, pierced into her; Mark, the gun held against her, Michael shouting in some strange language, the journey here, and Sutherland. Where was Michael?

"Where is Michael?" she demanded, recoiling from him.

Mark smiled lazily at her. Smiling was not his strongest point, but he smiled at the pleasure of seeing this young woman emerge from sleep. She was attractive, with her hair tousled and her eyes heavy with sleep. Then reality intruded. His instructions were to take her downstairs. *But if there was a chance later*, he thought, looking at her and taking in the curves of her body as she straightened herself out… He shook his head. *Later, hopefully later, but for now just get her downstairs.*

"I need to use the toilet," she said.

"Fine," he said. "And then we'll go downstairs."

As he stood waiting outside the door for her, Anna relieved herself and then stood in front of the small mirror trying to make some order of the disarray that had affected her appearance. Conscious of his presence outside the door, and without any implements to enhance her looks, she had to make do with running her fingers through her bedraggled hair and splashing water over her tense, tired face.

Mark led her back down to the study. Pushing open the door, he motioned for her to precede him. She entered with trepidation, not sure of what she might find. Michael was leaning back in the leather chair by the desk, his eyes closed. Graham Sutherland was standing by his side. Richard was lounging in the chair by the window. Neither Carl nor John were in the room. As the door opened, Michael looked up and his eyes met hers. He looked at her with an expression she couldn't read and pulled himself up out of the chair.

"Anna, are you all right? Have they hurt you?" he asked, coming up close and putting his arms around her, holding her tight. She stood, resisting for a moment, at first not able to return his embrace. He tried to look at her face but she kept it hidden, and then, with a heavy sigh, she buried her head in his shoulder, feeling the padding beneath his shirt, smelling the clean antiseptic smell, fiercely returning his hug, releasing all the pent-up emotion of the last few days.

"Very touching," said Mark sarcastically.

"Shut up," said Michael over Anna's head before turning to address Graham Sutherland. "Graham, may I at least have a moment alone with Anna, please?"

"Sorry, dear boy, not possible yet, we've got too many things to sort out. Let's have a cup of coffee and perhaps a bite to eat. You two must be absolutely famished. Mark, go and get some coffee and croissants."

Mark looked like he might refuse but with a brief

sullen look he flounced out, slamming the door after him. Richard rose and followed him with a wry grimace. Sutherland motioned for Anna to sit down on the chair opposite the desk. Michael hugged her tightly and then released her. She sat down in the chair as instructed, reluctant to let him go, but waiting to see what was going to happen next. The situation was making her feel increasingly uneasy. Michael dropped back into his chair again. She studied him for a moment. He looked considerably better that he had the previous night, but he was still gaunt and haggard, his face unshaven and with dark shadows under his eyes, his mouth bruised. At least that doctor had attended to his shoulder.

There was silence for a moment and then Michael spoke to Sutherland again.

"Graham, please, I beg you, let Anna go. I will help. I guarantee I will co-operate with you. I'll help you all I can."

Sutherland sighed. "Michael, don't be tiresome. Let's not play games. You know as well as I do that Anna's presence here is probably the only leverage I have over you. So just forget any ideas of trying to persuade me to let her go. She stays, and you will help us."

"What is going on, Michael?" Anna suddenly burst out, looking from one to the other. "Mr Sutherland, I think you at least owe me an explanation of what is happening, and why I've been brought here against my will."

As she spoke, she realised how trite her words sounded. Anger built up within her. It was only a few hours since Inspector Ravell had been shot dead in her home and here she was, being offered coffee and croissants.

"Answer me!" she demanded, as they both looked at her in silence. "For God's sake, tell me what is going on!"

Michael opened his mouth to speak, but she interrupted him before he could utter a word.

"And as for you, Michael, where have you been? What happened in the laboratory? Were you there?" She couldn't bring herself to mention their father by name. "Did you kill him?" She looked across at him but he was looking down at the floor now, not meeting her eyes. "Michael!" she demanded. "I want an answer."

Sutherland had remained silent. He was watching intently now, his eyes on Michael.

"Yes, Anna. Yes, I was there." When Michael spoke it was with reluctance, as if the words were being dragged out of him. "I didn't mean for it to happen, but yes, I killed him."

"But why?" She almost wailed as her world came crashing down around her. "How could you? Why would you kill him, murder him? I thought I knew you, but it seems I didn't. The police told me that you've lied about your past. Everything you've ever told me was a complete lie."

"Anna, it's so complicated. I will explain everything

to you, but I can't, not like this, not here, not yet. Please, trust me," he begged.

She turned her head away from him, refusing now to meet his eyes.

She'll understand, he thought. *She will, when she knows the truth.* But deep in his heart he wasn't sure; she was going to have a lot to forgive. He shook his head sadly. He'd have to worry about that later. For now, he just needed to get them both out of this awful situation.

Sutherland's ears had pricked up at Anna's mention of the police. *Hmm,* he thought, *they'd managed to get more information than he'd expected.* He spoke up briskly.

"Now, Anna, I told you last night it would all be explained to you, but at the right moment—"

The door opened to admit Richard carrying a tray, the smell of steaming coffee and hot croissants filling the room.

"Ah, just what we needed," Sunderland finished brightly.

I shan't eat, she thought, *I think I'd choke. But I will have some coffee.* And she accepted the proffered mug of coffee, shaking her head at the offer of food.

Michael had no such qualms. He was starving, looking apprehensively across at Anna who was still painstakingly ignoring him. He accepted a mug of coffee and took a croissant, biting hungrily into it. *Food,* he thought, *real food at last. And the coffee is so good.* He had to force himself to eat slowly. His stomach had been empty for so long that he was afraid it might reject the food. *If I survive this,* he promised himself, *I shall never go hungry again.*

Sutherland smiled benignly as Michael took another croissant. *Let him eat,* he thought. *Let him get his strength back. He's no good to me half-dead.* And he turned to Richard, asking, "Where's Mark?"

"I've sent him to change the plates on my car. We'll take John's."

As if he had heard his name, John chose that moment to enter the room.

"Are you ready?" he asked. "I've parked the car outside. Here, take the keys, Richard."

Richard nodded and took the keys from him.

Sutherland turned back to Michael. "Have you eaten enough?"

Michael nodded.

"Good. Now, I want you to go with Richard and Carl, and collect the tape. Anna will stay here with John and myself. She'll be quite safe, I assure you, so long as you behave yourself." Turning to Richard, he said, "He'll show you where it is. Try to be as inconspicuous as you can. Oh, and be careful when you get back. I'm not expecting any visits from the boys in blue, but if they've found their friend, you never know what they might do."

Michael had stood up as he was speaking. "It might take some time. It was dark when I hid it," he said.

"Well, I'm sure it won't take you too long to remember. I expect you'll want to be getting back as

153

soon as possible, just to make sure that Anna is all right," replied Sutherland smoothly.

With a last backward look at Anna, who still kept her head averted, Michael allowed Richard to escort him out through the door. Anna heard Carl's voice in the hallway outside, and then the slamming of the door as they left. She was alone with Graham Sutherland and John. She looked at them defiantly.

"My friends will be missing me. They'll contact the police and the police will find the dead inspector, and then they'll come looking for me."

"I know, my dear, but the police won't think to look for you here. They'll assume you've been abducted by Michael – if they think anything at all. I think it's probably best if you return to your room for now. I've got more important things to do. John, take her back upstairs."

John smiled at her. She hadn't really studied him before. He seemed to be the quietest one, bald and stocky but otherwise nondescript in appearance. She stood up to leave with him just as the brass doorbell gave a loud clang.

"Damn," said Sutherland. "Now, who can that be? John, go and check. I'll stay here with her for the moment. If it's the police, take them into the drawing room and tell them I'll be there in a moment. If it's anyone else, get rid of them." Turning to Anna as John left the room, he continued. "Don't even think of making a sound."

After a couple of minutes, John was back. "It's the law."

Sutherland looked displeased. "Who? That fat idiot, Harris?"

"No, it's some bod from Scotland Yard. Commander Lyons. Said he knew you," replied John.

It was the first time that Anna had seen Sutherland even remotely ruffled.

"Lyons? Bloody hell, let me think. Did you tell him I was here?"

John looked hurt. "Yes, you told me to. I've taken him to the drawing room."

"OK, I'll go and see him. Take her upstairs. No, take her into the kitchen. If you have any reason to think that we may be moving round the house, take her out the back and bloody hide her – in a shed, in a bush – anywhere." He paused at the door, looking pensive. "What's he doing here? Surely he can't suspect anything?" And he left the room.

John gave him a few minutes and then opened the door quietly and peered out. The hallway was empty; Sutherland had closed the drawing room door behind him and his unwelcome guest.

"Come on," he said, producing a gun from his pocket and pressing it into Anna's ribs. "And keep quiet."

She walked unresistingly down the long hallway, then they turned to the left, down the corridor that led to the kitchen. *It really is an enormous house*, she thought, trying to rack her brains to remember its geography.

They walked past the downstairs cloakroom and she suddenly stopped.

"I need to use the bathroom," she whispered to John. "It's my period," she said, smiling sweetly at him.

He looked embarrassed, as she'd known he would. She'd accurately summed him up; this was no new-age man.

"Well, be quick. I'll be waiting right outside," he whispered back, his discomfort at being privy to her bodily functions showing clearly in his face.

She went into the room, closing the door firmly behind her. Excitement rose within her. Yes! The top window was open. Climbing onto the toilet seat, she slid carefully through the window, jumped lightly down onto the grass on the other side and ran towards the laurel hedge faster than she would have thought possible, her heart pounding so loudly she thought it must be heard by Sutherland in the drawing room at the other end of the house.

CHAPTER 11

Somerset
Saturday 18th May, 1996
9.00 a.m.

Graham Sutherland paused for a moment outside the drawing room door to adjust his tie, glancing briefly at his watch: nine a.m. He pushed open the door, his smile already fixed in place.

"Alistair, my dear old friend," he said effusively to the smart, dark-suited middle-aged man who had risen on his arrival. "This is indeed a pleasure."

"Hello, Graham, how nice to see you again. It's been a long time. How are you?" Commander Alistair Lyons replied gravely as he moved forward to shake hands, without waiting for a reply. "But this is a bad business, Graham. I'm sure you've guessed why I'm here."

"Well, yes, poor Alexander, you've obviously heard," said Sutherland. "Such a tragedy. But I hadn't realised that you were involved in the case. I thought it was just the local force in Bath. I didn't realise that you'd even kept in touch with Alexander."

"Well, I hadn't really kept in touch – just a card at Christmas, and my wife dealt with that. But I heard about this by chance whilst the officers here in Bath were making some enquiries, and because it was Alexander, I decided to have a look into the matter myself. I expect they've told you pretty much what they've found so far, but I felt I should come to let you know of more recent developments, and to warn you to be careful. One of our local officers was killed yesterday. This case is turning out to be a lot more serious than first thought."

At the word 'warn' Sutherland's heart had almost missed a beat. But no, Alistair couldn't suspect him. Why should he? He smiled suavely.

"Alistair, would you like some coffee? I've just made a fresh pot."

"No thank you, Graham, I've just had two cups down at Bath Police Station whilst they updated me on recent events. But do have one yourself – don't mind me."

Sutherland shook his head; he had to get rid of this man as soon as possible. He felt very uneasy with Anna in the house. John seemed competent, but he wasn't the quickest thinker in the world.

"Well," said Lyons. "What have they told you so far, Graham?"

Sutherland considered for a moment to make sure he only said what he'd been told. He knew that Alistair was nobody's fool. It was that razor-sharp brain of his that must have enabled him to climb the ranks so rapidly.

158

"Well, old chap, as you probably know, at first I thought that dear old Alexander had been a bit careless in re-setting the security system at the lab. He was always so absentminded, you know."

Alistair nodded in recollection. "Yes, that sounds like old Alexander. Did he often work late in the evening?"

"Oh yes, common procedure. You see, that's what I thought," Sutherland relaxed slightly. "I thought that perhaps someone had been watching the lab and perhaps noticed Alexander working late on several occasions, and seized their chance. But the local police didn't seem to think that was what had happened."

"No. They did consider that possibility at first, and might have continued thinking along those lines, but there was the matter of Alexander's son, Michael, going missing."

"Ah yes, dear Michael. Has he turned up yet?" asked Sutherland innocently.

"No, but we have strong reason to believe that he may have been to his sister's house last night. You must know her, I'm sure – Anna, I believe she's called. Well, she has now disappeared too. The inspector on the case was found at her house, shot dead, and Michael's prints were found all over a gun discovered in her house. There were also several footprints, which match Michael's shoe size, and traces of his blood type on the wall. And I think you know already about the blood in the laboratory. Strange coincidence, you sharing the same blood type. There's also the matter of the data being scrambled, although I have been told that that was done with your knowledge."

At the mention of the gun, Sutherland's ears had pricked up. *What was this?* He'd forgotten to ask Michael what he'd done with the gun. He'd just assumed he would have hidden it with the tape. So the young fool had kept it on him, damn. And they'd already discovered the dead police officer. Yet he had complete faith in Richard: he wouldn't have let his men leave any traces behind.

"Oh yes, I myself authorised Michael to scramble the data. It was a standard security precaution. The blood I can't explain quite so easily." He gave a brittle laugh. "I suppose you're not suspecting me?"

"No, of course not. Your alibi for the night of Alexander's murder checked out completely. But what do you think of the other evidence?" replied Lyons.

"Was it the same gun that killed your man?" Sutherland asked innocently.

"Well, it's the same make, a Glock, and it's definitely the same gun that killed Alexander, no doubt about that. But ballistics aren't very happy about the bullet match with the shot that killed the inspector last night. However, the coincidence is so great, and the gun was fired at very short range, making it quite difficult to be sure. They're re-checking now."

"But it couldn't have been Michael. I mean, Alistair, I know him, remember. He wouldn't have hurt his father. Anyway, what possible motive could he have had?" Sutherland let his voice die down on a note of pained disbelief.

Alistair didn't answer for a moment, seemingly lost in thought, and then, as Sutherland looked at him expectantly, he smiled disarmingly.

"Do you mind if I smoke, Graham?"

"Haven't given up the filthy habit then, Alistair?" asked Sutherland indulgently, almost glad of the distraction as he took an ashtray out of the cabinet.

"No." Lyons smiled ruefully as he lit his cigarette. "No, it's got a hold on me, I'm afraid." He paused and took a deep lungful of smoke. "But, Graham, one of the reasons I wanted to speak to you myself..." He paused again, looking abstractedly at the blue smoke curling up around his fingers, obviously finding it hard to find the right words. "Look, I know it was a long time ago, but do you think this has any connection with, well, you know, what happened at Oxford? You see, there's this thing about Michael—"

Graham interrupted him sharply. "Alistair, why should there be any connection? As you say, it was a long time ago. None of us are involved now, are we?"

"Well, I'm certainly not, although I've kept up a couple of friendships. But there's this problem about Michael. I mean, I thought it strange at first when the local police told me about this son of Alexander's, but then I put two and two together and worked out what must have happened."

Too clever by half, thought Sutherland, as Lyons paused again to drag on his cigarette. *But hopefully not that clever.*

"Anyway, I figured that Donna must have stayed in touch with Alexander. He was supposed to have been supporting them so they must have been in touch. And when she died a few years ago, it seems Alexander and Claire took the boy in, and he came to work with Alexander at Mayhims. Seems like he's a chip off the old block."

Sutherland nodded. "Well, yes, that's what Alexander told me. You'll remember that he and Donna split up while she was pregnant, but maybe you didn't know that when the baby was born, she went back to Spain. Alexander said he felt responsible for her. He'd openly acknowledged that the child was his, after all, and he got in touch with her after a while, brought them back to England and supported them. Used to visit them too (not that he told Claire at the time). But then Donna died. She had cancer, you know, and he had this guilt thing, something about his mother having died of the same thing before he could get to see her. Anyway, when Donna died, he confessed everything to Claire, and she was the one who said that Michael must come and live with them. At least he'd have one natural parent, she said."

"Yes, yes." Lyons looked rather intently at Sutherland for a moment, as if he was trying to see through him, and then his expression became bland again. "Yes," he repeated, lighting another cigarette. "But, Graham, it seems Alexander was lying. We've got proof – indisputable proof – that Donna and her baby, Michael, were killed in a car crash in Spain, a month after she returned." He paused to let his words sink in. "Michael Hamilton has been dead for nearly thirty-one years."

Sutherland carefully composed his face into lines of disbelief. *Shit, so they'd found that out. What else did they know?*

"Alistair, you must be mistaken. I've worked with Michael, remember? I know him. He's Alexander's son."

"Well, he can't be the baby that Donna and Alexander had, that's for sure. That baby definitely died in 1965, and this recent Michael has been using that baby's birth certificate, with Alexander's knowledge, and, I might add, with a totally fictitious background, also endorsed by Alexander. This is why I think it's got something to do with our days at Oxford. Alexander has been lying, and whoever this Michael is, I'm sure he's connected to that time. Now, tell me, how old is he? What's he like?"

Sutherland pretended to think. "Must be about thirty – the right age – tall, about six feet two inches, dark hair. Doesn't really look much like Alexander, but then lots of children take after their mother, and I remember Donna as being very dark. He's got Alexander's brain anyway, slight foreign accent, nothing you'd really notice but apparent sometimes. There again, I put that down to his mother's influence. I assume he's bilingual. I haven't actually tested his Spanish – it never occurred to me to do so. I took his academic credentials on Alexander's word, never bothered to check, and he's proved himself anyway. Alistair, this is really rather a shock. I can't believe that Alexander would have lied to me."

"Could he be half-Russian?"

"Alistair, what are you saying?"

"Well, do you remember that girl, Natalya, who Alexander used to talk about? He'd been desperately in love with her, I seem to remember. I know she'd gone back to Russia when I met him, but Donna always believed that Alexander was only with her on the rebound from this Russian girl."

Sutherland paused for thought; better go careful here, Lyons could be dangerous.

"Well, I vaguely remember him talking about her. I don't know that I ever met her, but it was all finished, Alistair, and she went back to Russia. I'm sure she went off with someone else in the end, some Russian chap."

"Yes, maybe, but you knew of her. You were there at least some of the time that she was. Can't you remember her surname? I think I might just look her up."

Damn this man! Who would ever have thought he'd reappear like this? And damn Michael even more for creating this situation.

"Well no, I can't, sorry. She's probably married now

anyway. These Russian surnames aren't the easiest. Alistair, I do think you're wasting your time. I'm sure this has nothing to do with her. We were just kids then – it can't be connected."

"Not such kids that we didn't dabble in dangerous matters, Graham," Lyons replied sharply. "You might say in hindsight that we were just kids, but we believed in what we were doing, and if we made enemies then, why shouldn't they have long memories?"

Before Sutherland had a chance to reply, there was a tap at the door. He looked up in annoyance.

"Please excuse me a moment, Alistair."

Lyons nodded, lighting up another cigarette and gazing pensively out of the window, admiring the beautiful gardens. *Graham Sutherland had certainly done well for himself,* he thought. He couldn't pinpoint what it was that he so disliked in Sutherland. He'd never really taken to him. Even when they were young, he'd always had an uncomfortable feeling around him, always smiling that repulsively smooth, ingratiating smile.

Sutherland opened the door to find John standing there, red in the face and perspiring. He shut the door hurriedly behind him, pushing John unceremoniously in front of him into the study, closing the door carefully, then turning to him and asking furiously, "What the hell are you doing interrupting me! And where's the girl?"

"She's escaped."

"What?" he responded in total disbelief. "How? In

Christ's name, what have you done?"

John was sweating for a different reason now: Sutherland icily angry was one thing, but this blind fury was frightening.

"She fooled me, she said…" He still felt embarrassed to mention the details. "She said she needed the toilet, that it was, you know, her time of the month, so I let her." He looked pleadingly at Sutherland who was still staring at him in speechless fury. "She must have got out through the window. I waited for her outside the door, and when she didn't come out, I went in to look for her. She wasn't there, Graham, but the window was open. I've searched the grounds, I've looked everywhere. She's not here, I can't find her." His voice tailed off.

Sutherland's brain was working furiously. What should he do? He looked at his watch: nine fifteen a.m. She could be anywhere by now – he didn't live far from the centre of town.

"Take your car and go and look for her. Assume she'll try to make it to the city centre. And, John, you'll pay for this!"

"They've taken my car, and Mark isn't back yet with Richard's," mumbled John.

"Well, bloody walk then. No, wait!" shouted Sutherland in frustration, as John looked set to obey him. What incompetent idiots had Richard chosen? He was very conscious of Lyons still waiting in the drawing room. Suppose he took it upon himself to wander around the house and find them, or hear him shouting?

He lowered his voice, trying to regain his composure.

"No, wait. Take my car. But listen: if you find her, take her straight to your house. I'll contact the others to meet you there and I'll be in touch. If you don't find her in half an hour, go to your house anyway and just wait for further instructions," he finished angrily, turning abruptly on his heel and leaving the room.

He took a deep breath to calm himself and returned to his smoky drawing room. Lyons had lit yet another cigarette.

"So sorry, one of the men from Mayhims. I must leave soon, old pal, they need my help reinstalling the data."

"Yes, I am sorry to take up your time, Graham. I do appreciate how busy you must be, especially with two of your best men out, but I just need to ask you a few more things," said Lyons firmly.

Best men indeed, thought Sutherland viciously. *I'll enjoy killing Michael with my bare hands, when he's served his purpose.*

"I can't really help you any more, Alistair. I can't remember her name. I'd forgotten about the whole matter, you know. It's all such a long time ago."

"Yes, I know, but I can't help feeling there might be a connection. After all, we didn't do anything that would exactly endear ourselves to our Soviet friends, did we? And yes, I know USSR is now CIS, and I know that Glasnost and Perestroika have changed the political situation, but it's not that different, you know. The

167

Mafia have picked up where our old friends the communists left off."

He paused for a moment, and then looked directly at Graham. "Could the Russians have been interested in your work here? Is it possible that they sent this Michael over to obtain information? Maybe he had some kind of hold over Alexander. Supposing Alexander had a child with Natalya, and supposing this Michael is really Alexander and Natalya's son, come back for some reason, using the dead baby's name. He could have been blackmailing Alexander. Graham, I really feel there may be some connection."

Sutherland went cold inside. He fleetingly wondered if he could get away with killing Lyons. Had he shared his thoughts with anyone else? Had he told the local police? No, he wasn't thinking straight, he must stop panicking. Of course he couldn't kill him, not here in this house, not right now. But he had to get him out of the house and at least get the girl back. This was all going very badly wrong. Supposing she managed to get to the police station?

But Lyons hadn't quite finished.

"I can see from your face that you think this is just guesswork, and much of it is, but we checked Alexander's passport. He's made a fair few trips to Russia in the last few years. Did you know that?"

The last question was asked more sharply. Sutherland was beginning to wonder if Lyons was playing with him. The man was astute, no two ways about it.

"No, no, I didn't know where he went, he never told me, but he took a fair bit of time off. He needed it, he was a very hard worker, you know." Sutherland stood up, distracted. Would this man never get the message? Why wouldn't he just go now? He looked anxiously at his watch. She could be anywhere. He hadn't heard John come back yet.

"You look agitated, Graham," smiled Lyons smoothly. "I really do apologise for taking up so much of your time, but there are so many oddities about this case, and it seems such a coincidence that we all knew each other, doesn't it? Now, you have been very helpful, but before I go, I just need a little information about the work that you do at Mayhims. No one seems to know much about it – it seems very secretive," he finished blandly, his face devoid of expression as he calmly lit another cigarette.

Sutherland was fighting rising panic but he forced himself to sit down again, crossing one leg over the other, trying to look relaxed.

"Well, it's a bit technical," he began doubtfully (not much hope of fobbing Lyons off the way he'd dealt with that idiot Harris last night). "But I'll try to explain. As you probably know, we are a biomedical research centre, currently working on the problem of AIDS in the population. I expect you know as much as anyone about AIDS?" he questioned.

"Yes, I have a layman's knowledge," replied Lyons.

"Well, we are at present working towards developing a vaccine. The secrecy that you mentioned is vital to any research centre. We have to protect ourselves against industrial espionage, as you can imagine. We are making good progress, but as always we are working against time; another company could just as easily get there before us."

"Do you have government funding for this?"

"No, we are an entirely private concern. We could have applied for a research grant, but we have chosen to develop our work privately. I hate to sound mercenary, but there are greater profits to be made that way."

"Does this mean that you would sell your work to the highest bidder?" asked Lyons shrewdly.

Sutherland looked shocked. "Alistair, I know I mentioned profits, but you must understand that we are working towards defeating a major health threat to the human race. Yes, we would look to make a profit, but we would only market our vaccine through a reputable drug company, and we would put self-interest low down on our list of priorities. The common good is our major aim."

"Hmm," Lyons nodded, sounding sceptical. "And this is the only project that you are working on?"

"The vaccine is our major project, and as I said, we are making some progress, which is why this unfortunate episode has caused me so much trouble. Both Alexander and Michael were highly instrumental in working on developing a vaccine. But, of course, you understand that a vaccine would only help those who haven't already been infected with AIDS, and to vaccinate the whole country could only fulfil a long-term goal. We are also looking into how the mechanism that re-activates the viral genes that cause the virus to kill the host cell can be made dormant. If we can maintain this dormant state, then a cure is possible for those already hit by the virus," Sutherland finished, thinking, *now will you go away?*

At first Lyons just smiled blandly, showing no signs of moving for a moment but then he rose to his feet, moving across to shake Sutherland's hand again.

"Well, thank you, Graham, you have been most helpful. I can see how important this young man must be to you. I promise you we'll redouble our efforts to find him – whoever he might be. I'll leave you to get on with your work now."

He moved towards the door, followed closely by Sutherland who managed to get in front to lead him to the front door. Here, Lyons paused on the top step, looking penetratingly at Sutherland.

"Have a think about what I was saying about our past, Graham. You see, the more I think about it, the more I'm convinced there must be some connection. Just think how useful your vaccine would be in the hands of some unscrupulous country: Russia, for example." And then he was in his car and driving away, waving cheerily, before Sutherland had the chance to reply.

Sutherland stood on the doorstep, undecided for a

moment before turning on his heel and re-entering the house. *Remove all traces.* What had they left? Thank God he'd given his housekeeper the weekend off. He had to think. If the worst had happened and Anna had got to the police station, the local police might be over soon. But they couldn't prove anything. Even clever Lyons couldn't prove anything, not unless he found evidence, and without Michael it would be her word against his. But he must stay here, he must appear innocent; flight being the resort of the guilty. And he must contact Richard. Oh yes, and stop Mark coming back here.

Sutherland checked the house quickly. No, nothing remained. That crooked doctor who had charged the earth but been suspiciously speedy in his ministrations had at least cleaned up after himself. He smoothed down the covers on the beds until they no longer looked as if they'd been slept on, and quickly washed and dried the cups and plates, leaving only his to be found on the table. Taking out his mobile 'phone, he punched out the numbers to contact Mark first. Mark answered after a few rings in his normal sullen tone. He would be back soon, what was the panic? He listened impassively as Sutherland quickly explained that plans had to be changed, agreeing (without asking any questions) to keep away, and to meet the others at John's house. Sutherland immediately punched out Richard's number. At least here was one person who might be able to think constructively.

"Hello?" said Richard guardedly.

"Richard, it's Graham. It's urgent, we have a problem. I need to speak privately. Can you talk?"

There was a pause at the other end. He could hear faint voices in the background. Richard was obviously trying to move away from Carl and Michael.

"Graham, what is it? We're close to the place where he says he hid the tape. We were just about to go and get it, then we'll be straight back."

"Don't come back here. Take Michael to John's and leave him there with Carl, John and Mark, then go to your house and wait there for me."

"For Christ's sake, what is going on? Why are we changing plans now?" demanded Richard, sounding annoyed.

"Look, I can't say much. I don't trust these 'phones, but the bird has flown. Don't let Michael know."

"What, she's escaped?" almost shouted Richard. "What the fucking hell has happened?"

"Ssh! Keep your voice down, he mustn't find out yet. Look, I can't leave here yet. Don't let Michael suspect there might be a problem – make up any story you like. And, Richard, keep Carl off him for the moment."

Sutherland ended the call before Richard could say any more.

CHAPTER 12

Somerset
Saturday 18th May, 1996
9.05 a.m.

Anna had only one thought in her head: get away. She knew that she had minutes, at the most, before John would discover that she'd escaped so she had to get away from the house as soon as possible. She figured he'd be too embarrassed to go into the cloakroom at first, but once he did… She shuddered at the thought, remembering that gun in his hand.

She ran across the freshly-cut lawn and into the shelter of the laurel hedges as fast as she could. Panicked, she fought through the unforgiving tentacles then emerged onto the main road, confused for a moment. Which way to go? To the left, the road led towards the university, to the right she could get to the city centre. It might be quicker to get to the university but she decided to risk the city centre. She'd been brought up in Bath – she knew it like the back of her hand – but she wouldn't need to keep to the main road for long. She ran, keeping close to the walls and hedges, trying to look like a jogger out on a morning run. Thank God it wasn't as hot as yesterday had been. It was an average mid-May morning, warm but fresh. She came to the turning she was expecting, nipped down the narrow path and turned sharply left, over a gate, and then she was on familiar territory. Shielded by the trees, she moved cautiously now; no point in being given away by rustling bushes.

John had reached the end of the drive and looked out onto the road. Panting, he stopped, looking left and right. Which way had the bitch gone? The woman sitting in the blue Metro that was parked across the road outside the rugby ground tried to signal to him. His daughter had gone right, she wanted to tell him, but he didn't notice her gesticulating. He stood undecided, breathing heavily. And then he turned and ran back down the driveway, disappearing from her view.

The woman shrugged her shoulders. *Family argument,* she thought, *they'll make it up later I expect.* She made a mental note to tell her husband about it when he came back to the car after finishing sorting out the under fifteens' kit for tomorrow's game. It was quite amusing, really, seeing first the young woman appear out of the driveway, looking just as if the hounds of hell were after her, and then a few minutes later the man appearing, looking just like the hounds of hell himself. She frowned. The girl had actually looked frightened. Perhaps it hadn't been a family row after all. She craned her neck to see if she could still see the man but he'd disappeared out of sight. She leant across the car to look at the name of the house. *Quite impressive*, she thought, *quite a long driveway*. She couldn't even see the house from the road, but it didn't seem to have a name.

Oh well, none of my business anyway. She went back to her Mills and Boon novel where her heroine nurse was leaning forward into the young doctor's strong arms, pursing her rosy red lips as his strong mouth came gently down towards her. She sighed with pleasure and turned to the next page, and forgot all about the girl and the man. Thus, yet another potential Good Samaritan metaphorically walked on the other side of the road.

Anna didn't stop. She'd already decided what to do: if she didn't run past a policeman, she'd go straight to the police station itself. She was getting tired now. She wished she'd had something to eat, but then she might have got a stitch. She wasn't used to running like this.

She was getting closer now, down Ralph Allen Drive; so steep it was hard to keep up her pace, and she nearly tripped over her feet several times. She forced herself to slow down a bit and at the bottom stopped to get her bearings. Yes, she must head towards the railway station. It wasn't that much further from here.

Passers-by were looking at her curiously. *I must look a sight*, she thought, panting and dishevelled. At least the sweatshirt covered Inspector Ravell's blood on her t-shirt, but there were visible bloodstains on her jeans. She looked down. *It could be paint,* she thought, *no one*

176

would expect it to be blood. Yet she was hardly the usual sight to be found in sedate Regency Bath on a Saturday morning. She decided to walk now and mingle as best she could with the other pedestrians. She resisted the urge to look behind her. If John had alerted Sutherland, they might be out in a car by now, and with a bit of luck they'd get tangled up in the one-way system. But if he'd run after her in the same direction, he could be right behind her! She didn't really want to know – she was frightened enough.

She was at the railway station now. It was teeming with people; a train must just have got in. She looked enviously at these people: students, couples – ordinary people with ordinary lives. She'd been like that once. *Don't stop, keep going!* On she walked, briskly, heart pounding, avoiding the aimless shoppers. Getting closer, she could see the police station now, she was almost there. Then she was right outside it, up the steps and in through the door, relief welling up inside her, safety, a haven at last.

She went up to the desk, aware that the desk officer was regarding her with interest.

"Please," she said breathlessly, her words coming out so quickly that they fell over each other. "You have to help me! I was abducted last night from my home. I've got away but they'll try to find me. They've got my brother. I don't know where they are but they shot Inspector Ravell," she said, bursting into tears.

A young WPC passing by heard her words and

stopped in astonishment. She came over before the stunned desk officer had time to collect her thoughts.

"Would you be Anna Hamilton?" she asked gently.

"Yes," said Anna, too distraught to even question how her name should be known. "Yes, I'm Anna Hamilton. Will you help me, please?"

Josie Grimley took Anna's arm gently. *The poor girl is in a terrible state,* she thought. *She's shaking.* She led her towards a private room, saying soothingly, "It's all right, you're safe now."

Anna allowed herself to be guided along the corridor and into the small room. Once there, she sank gratefully into one of the chairs, still trying to regain her breath. Josie looked down on her with concern.

"Will you be all right for a moment? I'll be right back."

Anna nodded wordlessly, and Josie ran down the corridor to Harris's office.

"Sir," she almost shouted as she burst into his office, ignoring his look of fury at her unannounced advent. "Anna Hamilton has just arrived at the station. She's—"

He almost leapt out of his chair. "What! Where is she?"

"I've put her in the counselling room. She's very shaky."

"You've left her alone? Come on, take me to her."

Aiden Formby intercepted them as they hurried out of Harris's office.

"Is it true what Jane has just told me? Is Anna

Hamilton here?"

"Yes," replied Harris shortly, not slowing down his pace.

"I'd like to see her. May I be present at the interview, sir? As you know, Paul and I were close," asked Aiden, lengthening his stride to keep pace with Harris while Josie followed behind them.

Harris pondered for a moment. Friends, yes, but now that he remembered, they were more than friends: it had been Formby's sister whom Ravell had married. Bad business that, the poor girl. Killed instantly, hadn't stood a chance, baby too. Just about to be born and it had been snuffed out like a candle. He'd gone to the inquest himself, mainly to assess how badly they might be affected – two of his best men hit by one single tragedy.

That stupid neighbour (a friend she'd called herself) who'd been giving the wife – what was her name, Katy? No, Caitlin – a lift to the hospital. Silly girl had waited until the baby was almost due before agreeing to go, and the friend had panicked, or so she'd said at the inquest, panicked when Caitlin had had a strong contraction, and she'd shot straight through the red light, straight into a lorry. The friend had been lucky, got away with a few broken bones. The lorry driver was in shock, but the girl and her unborn baby never even made it to the hospital. Dead on arrival. Ravell had never really got over it, he mused. He'd blamed himself for not driving her himself although everybody knew that she'd left it so late that he wouldn't have had time to get home first. He'd had no option but to go straight to the hospital and that had meant that he was there when the ambulance arrived with its sorry load. Poor Ravell, he hadn't had a lot of luck in his short life.

Aiden mistook his silence for a refusal. "Please, sir, it is important to me."

Harris regarded him solemnly. "Yes, of course you may sit in," he said gruffly. "Commander Lyons from the Yard has asked me to continue to help with this case, Formby. In fact, I'll keep you on the case as well, but try to keep personal issues out of this. We all feel bad about Ravell's death."

He was uncomfortably aware that he should really attempt to inform Lyons that the Hamilton girl had turned up. But the man had hardly listened to the evidence they'd collected so far before he'd gone rushing off after the briefing, muttering something about following up on some of the leads. Well, if that self-important bastard was going to re-do all the work he'd already done, he could wait. Perhaps Harris could crack the case before he came back.

"And WPC Grimley," he continued. "I will need you too, but get us some coffee first. Get some for the girl as well, will you."

He opened the door to the counselling room. Anna sat huddled in the corner, looking up with fear in her eyes as the two men entered. Aiden felt a wave of sympathy wash over him. This was the first time he'd seen her. She was a pretty girl but she looked like she'd just been through a bad time. Her blonde hair hung in rats' tails around her face, her clothes were stained and her face was white – with tiredness or shock – probably both.

"Good morning, Miss Hamilton," he said kindly. "I'm DI Formby and this is DCI Harris. We're just going to wait for WPC Grimley. She's going to bring us some coffee and then we'll take a statement from you."

Anna looked up at him and her eyes widened in shock. It could almost have been Michael standing there speaking in this kind voice, looking at her with concern. Except, no, of course not. This man was shorter and more compact, and his dark hair was cut short above his ears, but it was a similar face, lean and intense, and a wave of sadness washed over her as Michael's face flashed before her eyes. And then she thought about what he'd said. *He's getting me coffee. The last cup of coffee I had was at Sutherland's house, and Michael was there, and now I may never see him again. Maybe they'll kill him because I escaped. And I didn't even say goodbye to him.* She burst into tears, her whole body shaking.

Harris looked at her glumly. *Oh, God, where was that WPC?*

Aiden sat down by her side, putting his arm around her shoulders. "It's OK, you're safe now," he said gently.

"Michael," she sobbed. "Michael."

He stiffened slightly. *Oh yes, Michael, who'd killed Paul.* "It's OK, we'll find him," he said firmly.

"Oh, I hope you do," she sighed, totally misunderstanding the emphasis in his voice, raising her eyes to his and smiling tearfully. "Please find him soon. I don't know what might happen."

Josie entered the room, not looking entirely pleased to see Aiden sitting with his arm around Anna Hamilton's shoulder. He removed it rather hastily, remembering their conversation earlier that morning when they'd agreed to give their relationship another try.

Harris had his job to do and had no time for over-emotional women.

"Right, Miss Hamilton, if you feel up to it, we'll take a statement from you now and we'll tape it – if you have no objection. You're not under arrest. You have every right to refuse my request. I only ask because it will make things easier for us to record the details. Do you have any objection?"

"No," said Anna. "I don't mind what you do – just get Michael for me."

Harris smiled pompously. "That is indeed our intention, Miss Hamilton. Now, WPC Grimley, could you set the cassette going now, please."

Josie switched on the tape player. The moment of jealousy she'd felt when she saw Aiden with his arm round Anna's shoulders had immediately disappeared to be replaced by a deep feeling of sympathy for her. She spoke routinely.

"The time is ten fifteen a.m., Saturday 18th March, 1996. The interview with Miss Anna Hamilton is about to commence. Detective Chief Inspector Harris and Detective Inspector Formby will question Miss Hamilton."

Harris went straight to questioning. "Miss Hamilton, can I ask you, did your brother, Michael Hamilton, come to your house yesterday evening?"

Anna looked apprehensively at Harris, slightly intimidated by his formal manner.

"Yes, he did."

"Could you give me all the details of his visit, right from the moment that he arrived?"

Anna looked confused. This could take a long time, and she had no idea what was happening at Sutherland's house. For all she knew, he might have got whatever it was he wanted from Michael and have killed him by now.

"Is this really necessary?" she asked doubtfully. Harris mistook her confusion for hesitation.

"Yes, I'm afraid so, but in your own time, Miss Hamilton," he said firmly.

They have no idea, she thought. They might be the police, but they could have no conception of what she'd experienced in the last few hours, the danger that she'd been in, the danger that Michael was still in. She must make them understand.

She started to speak quickly. "Well, Inspector Ravell

came to my house last night. It must have been about eight o'clock. I'm not sure of the exact time, I'd been asleep." She stopped; she couldn't help herself. They were just sitting there, watching her intently. Did they not think it strange that she'd just woken up at eight p.m.? Maybe they heard such strange things in their profession that they were immune to the idiosyncrasies of the human race. What the hell, she just needed to tell her story and then they could go and get Michael. The sooner the better.

"Inspector Ravell came to see me, to tell me that you'd found things that might implicate Michael in the murder of our father, that you couldn't find any trace of his background, that he'd lied to me. I found it hard to believe." She paused, the memories clouding her face.

Aiden had nodded in sympathy as she was speaking. He really felt quite sorry for her.

Anna continued urgently; she mustn't waste time. "I told him that Michael had 'phoned me after our father's death," she said, her tone becoming defensive. "I hadn't said before because I didn't know what to think, but I told him in the end. Then he took a 'phone call from somebody at the police station, or maybe it was before, I can't remember."

Josie nodded. How well she remembered that call, her last conversation with Paul, but he hadn't mentioned that Michael had been in touch with Anna. She was sure he would have done had he known at that time.

Anna was still speaking, her words falling over

themselves.

"And then he gave me more evidence that seemed to show that Michael had killed our father, and I agreed. I agreed that Michael must have murdered our father, and then Michael came in – he looked awful – and he heard me." She stopped, and buried her head in her arms.

Silence for a moment, and then Harris said (gently for him), "Miss Hamilton, we're here to help you. Don't distress yourself."

"Sorry, yes, then Michael came in. He didn't look like himself – he looked so desperate, so ill, and then he collapsed. He'd been shot, you see – his shoulder, it was really bad. We couldn't 'phone for an ambulance because my house 'phone had stopped working and Inspector Ravell had left his mobile 'phone in his car, so the inspector and me, well, we tried to help him, and then… And then three men came in and they had guns. They made us sit down, and two of them stood behind us."

Her audience was on full alert now. She'd deviated from the story they'd expected to hear.

"And then Michael came round and he said he wouldn't help them unless they promised not to hurt me and the inspector, and one of them, the one called Richard, he just nodded, and then the one called Carl shot Inspector Ravell."

She looked up at them, the remembered terror fresh in her eyes.

"And then they took us away in their car. Michael

185

had passed out again – Carl had hit him, you see – but he'd wanted to help, he really had, but they'd held him back. He spoke in some strange language – I couldn't understand, I didn't know what was going on, but Inspector Ravell, they killed him, his blood... His blood, it went everywhere. They just shot him. Look, his blood, it's on my t-shirt, my jeans."

And in front of their horrified eyes she pulled off Michael's sweatshirt to reveal her bloodstained clothes. No one spoke for a moment, and then Aiden tried to pick up her thread of thought.

"Miss Hamilton, may I call you Anna? You're doing very well. This is obviously very painful for you, but you are helping us tremendously. If you could just manage to keep going. You said they took you away?"

"Yes, yes, of course, sorry, they took us to Graham Sutherland's house."

She didn't hear the sharp intake of breath, or see the involuntary look that passed between Harris and Formby.

"He'd got a doctor waiting there, to look at Michael, but they wouldn't let me see Michael. Mr Sutherland made me go to bed and then this morning he took me downstairs, to the study, and Michael was there, and he told me that he had killed my father, but he said he could explain, and I wouldn't listen and now they've probably killed him..." Her voice tailed off on a note of desperation, and she looked from one to the other of them, needing reassurance. But they just stared at her, still trying to process what she'd said.

It was Harris who broke the silence.

"Miss Hamilton, you've just made a very serious allegation about Mr Sutherland. You also mentioned 'they'– can you be more specific? Did you know these people? Can you describe them?"

"No, I've never seen them before, but Michael seemed to recognise them. There was one they called Richard. He was middle-aged, about medium height, smart, wore a suit. I don't think I've seen him before, but I'm not sure. He seemed to be the one in charge until we got to Sutherland's house and then he took over." She paused, but they nodded for her to continue.

"And there was one called Mark. He was younger, about my age, short brown hair, quite tall and thin, wore jeans and a sweatshirt. He was so cold. He stood behind me with a gun." She remembered with a shudder his gun held steadily against her neck. "And another one arrived, he was called John, middle-aged, bald and short—"

And then she stopped abruptly, putting her hand to her mouth. "Oh no, my cat, Brian. He'll have gone home and I'm not there. He'll be hungry." She looked imploringly at them.

Josie and Aiden exchanged an amused glance. Brian, that cat was called Brian, and Josie had christened him Worms because he always seemed so hungry!

"It's OK, Anna, your cat is fine. I took him home with me," said Josie.

Anna looked at her in total surprise. She hadn't even realised these people had been to her cottage, let alone befriended Brian and taken him away. She supposed she should feel grateful, but she didn't. She felt that her life was no longer her own. It had been intruded upon by strangers – friendly or not, they were still intruders – and now they'd even taken Brian away from her. She wished she could move time back three or four days, to when life had at least still seemed relatively normal.

"Oh, thank you," she said stiffly. "Have you fed him? He's always hungry, you know."

"Yes," smiled Josie, trying to put her at her ease. "I've noticed. And yes, I've fed him. I took the liberty of taking some of your cat food. I don't have a cat of my own, you see. I hope you don't mind."

Harris interrupted before they started talking about bloody cats all day.

"Yes, yes, let's continue. Miss Hamilton, you mentioned someone called Carl earlier? You said he was the one who murdered our inspector?"

"Carl was a brute. Fortyish, short, stocky and really strong. Yes, he was the one who shot Inspector Ravell, but it was Richard who told him to. Well, he didn't actually say 'kill him' – he just nodded in this sinister sort of way, and Carl shot him, and he fell against me… His blood went all over me."

"What about Michael – did he have a gun?" asked Aiden, as she lapsed into a faraway silence, remembering the horror of the night before. She gave a slight start and then shook her head, trying to concentrate on what he was saying without the sight of Inspector Ravell constantly intruding.

"Yes, I think he did, when he first came in. No – it was when Inspector Ravell went towards him, just before he collapsed, he pulled this gun out of his pocket, but I don't remember what happened to it." She frowned, trying to remember. Michael had collapsed, and they'd managed to get him onto the sofa, but what had happened to the gun? "No, I can't remember, I'm sorry."

"And you're sure it wasn't Michael who killed Inspector Ravell?" Harris was speaking now, his voice harsh. This wasn't at all what he'd been expecting to hear. This put a completely different slant on the case and he wasn't sure that he believed her. He certainly didn't want to believe her. She might be lying in an attempt to protect her brother. Her whole story sounded very improbable.

She looked at him in genuine surprise. "Yes, of course I'm sure. I know he didn't. Michael had collapsed but we'd managed to lift him onto the sofa that was opposite, but…" She paused doubtfully. "But they might have killed the inspector to put pressure on Michael – to make him help them."

"I see. And just how was Michael to help them?" asked Harris grimly.

"Well, I'm not really sure. They mentioned a tape. I didn't really understand what was happening, but this morning, at Sutherland's house, Richard and Carl took Michael off to find a tape or something, something he was supposed to have hidden somewhere, but I don't know where they went, and I… Well, I escaped just after they left."

"Ah yes, this escape. How exactly did you manage to escape?" said Harris again, not very gently.

She looked slightly embarrassed. "This man came to the door. I think he was from the police, but I can't remember his name."

Harris leant forward and interrupted her, his eyes narrowing. "Very convenient."

Anna looked flustered. "Anyway, Sutherland told John to take me to the kitchen – it's at the far end of the house, well away from the drawing room, and… And when we walked past, I said I needed to use the bathroom." She couldn't look at the others; just fixed her gaze on Josie. "I said it was my period. I knew he'd be embarrassed and leave me alone. I went in there and I climbed out of the window. You see, I'd been in the house before, with my father and Michael, and I knew he always left that window open at the top. I could just about squeeze through. I managed to get away from John. I made it here, to you. I thought I'd be safe here."

Josie silently applauded her, wondering if she would have been able to think so quickly in such circumstances. She hadn't missed the sceptical look on Harris's face. *I believe you,* she thought. *I believe you because no one could have made that up; it's too real.*

190

Anna stopped to sip her coffee, feeling the warm liquid flow through her body and revive her spirits a bit, hoping they'd finished with her and would go to Graham Sutherland's house and bring Michael back to safety. But they just sat looking at her. The young policewoman seemed friendly, but the other two looked so stern. Didn't they believe her?

There was silence for a couple of minutes and then Harris spoke, his voice ponderous.

"Thank you, Miss Hamilton. As I said before, these are serious accusations that you are levelling at Mr Sutherland. Is there anything that you want to change in your statement?" He hoped she would. The case had been a lot simpler when they were just looking for Michael – whoever he might turn out to be.

"No!" She was indignant now; to have gone through all of this and still not be believed! "You have to believe me! It's what happened. Why would I make it up?"

"Well, Miss Hamilton, I could think of one very good reason: you could be protecting your brother. Inspector Ravell explained to you that there is some mystery surrounding your brother and that his past doesn't check out. He lied to you about his past and you've admitted yourself that he told you that he killed your father. How can you trust him? How can you be sure that he wasn't also involved in the events that led to the murder of Inspector Ravell?" Harris's tone was getting harsher now.

"No, well, yes. I don't know. Michael is involved in

some way, but I don't think he really wanted to help them. He tried to bargain with them. He asked them to just take him and to leave me and Inspector Ravell behind. I don't know why he killed our father. It might have been an accident. He wanted to explain to me but Sutherland wouldn't let us be alone, and now he may not get the chance." Anna was getting even more confused and tearful now. Why didn't they just go and arrest Sutherland, bring Michael back and let him explain? "Why don't you just go out and arrest Graham Sutherland and those others?" she suddenly burst out. "Bring them all in, make them admit it, make them let Michael go, then he can explain to you himself. I'm sure he'll be able to explain it all."

Harris leant forward. "Because, Miss Hamilton, you haven't given us one shred of hard evidence that Mr Sutherland is in any way involved in any of this. All we would have would be your word against his. I don't know what you think you understand about police procedure, but I can assure you that we cannot, and indeed will not, bring Mr Sutherland in even for questioning on your word alone, never mind arrest him—"

He held up his hand as she tried to interrupt. "Wait, and please listen to me, Miss Hamilton. You've turned up here, covered in Inspector Ravell's blood, admitting that your brother came to your cottage last night when Inspector Ravell was with you, that he had a gun, and that he admitted to killing your father. Yet you expect us to believe that it was all actually a complicated plot masterminded by Graham Sutherland, your father's friend and colleague, and incidentally, very well respected in the local community." His voice softened a little as he continued. "Yet, improbable as your account seems to me, you do seem very convinced, and it's hard to see what you could gain (apart from taking the suspicion away from your brother) by making such serious accusations against Mr Sutherland. And you do seem very anxious that your brother is brought here to be allowed to tell his story to us."

Aiden spoke then. He'd been quiet for a while, trying to assess whether she was telling the truth. The whole thing seemed too incredible to be believed. And yet he had a hunch that she was being honest, although he had a feeling that her faith in her brother was misplaced. She might well be in for a rude awakening there.

"Sir, maybe we should leave Miss Hamilton with WPC Grimley and make another routine visit to Mr Sutherland? If what Miss Hamilton has told us is true, there may be some evidence to be seen."

"Hmm," grunted Harris. "Yes, we'll do that. Miss Hamilton, I do understand that you have been through a very stressful experience, but you have witnessed firsthand the death of one of my officers, so I'm afraid I can't let you go home just yet. For one thing, we will need to bag your clothes as evidence."

"Yes, of course, I'll stay here," Anna said with relief. Wild horses wouldn't have dragged her out into the streets again, not whilst she thought John, or even worse, Sutherland, might be out there looking for her.

"Good. If you could let WPC Grimley know what you'd like, she'll arrange for someone to go out to your cottage and bring back a change of clothing and anything else you might need."

"Thank you so much," said Anna gratefully. Maybe it would be all right; they were going to go out to Sutherland's and they'd find Michael there. They'd see that she'd told the truth, and everything would be sorted out.

Harris and Formby stood up to leave the room, leaving Anna in Josie's care. At the door, Aiden paused and looked back at Anna.

"Miss Hamilton – Anna – could you tell me... Do you think that Inspector Ravell died straightaway? Did he suffer?"

She looked across at him. "I'm so sorry, was he a close friend of yours?"

"Yes, he was my best friend," he replied briefly.

Anna felt ashamed. She'd been too wrapped up in her own distress. In her worry and fear for Michael, her own reaction to the recent events and the shock of Inspector Ravell's death, she'd forgotten that these people had feelings too. Of course he'd had friends, and probably a wife and children to grieve for him too.

"I think he died instantly," she said gently. "It happened so quickly, I'm sure he couldn't have felt anything, or even known what was happening. Please, tell me, did he leave a wife? Children?"

Aiden gazed at her bleakly. She didn't know the significance of what she was saying.

"No," he replied abruptly, and followed Harris out of the room without a backward glance.

Anna looked distressed. *What have I said to upset him?* She looked across at Josie uncomprehendingly. "Have I said something wrong?"

Josie tried to smile reassuringly. "No, but they were very good friends. He's just upset. Don't worry, they'll find your brother for you." Then she continued briskly, "You must be starving. Come on, we'll find you some food. It's pretty awful here – our canteen caters for basic need rather than taste – but I'm sure we can find you something palatable."

Anna followed her without speaking. Yes, she was hungry. She was safe for the moment, and they'd find Michael soon. Everything was going to be all right.

CHAPTER 13

Oxford
April, 1965

Donna stood gazing at herself in the mirror for a long moment, then pirouetted gaily. It hardly showed; no one could possibly guess yet. The baby could grow silently behind her strong, young stomach muscles for a while longer.

Alexander would come round, she was sure. Admittedly, he had been very angry when she'd first told him, but then, much as she loved him, she had to admit he was a strange person: remote, cold even, at times. But to have taken her to his bed (and for Donna, with her strict Spanish upbringing that had been a momentous event) must mean that he surely loved her. Obviously, with his English reserve, he found it hard to speak the words of love, but his passion spoke more loudly than any words could.

Donna smiled at her reflection. *I'll be a model yet,* she told herself. Not for nothing did her friends admire her beautiful body. 'You could be another Christine

Keeler and bring down the government' they laughed. But no Profumo for her – Alexander was all she wanted. And for him, she would put off her life of stardom for a year or so. She'd carry on working in that awful café for a while yet, or at least until the baby prevented her from doing so.

He would want the baby, she reassured herself. Of course he would. Fancy mentioning that dreadful word: abortion. As if Donna would even consider the thought. No, it had just been the shock that was all. She was sure that he'd always love her, and he'd love the baby too when he saw it. And then he would become a famous scientist and she would become a famous model. She patted her stomach, speaking silently to the unborn baby. *And you, my darling, will be proud of your accomplished parents.*

The year was 1965 and the month was April. Harold Wilson had been prime minster for about six months, and Alexsei Leonov had recently become the first man to walk in space. But these matters did not concern Donna, for her thoughts were firmly turned inwards. She had Alexander: her mentor, her beloved. She would have walked to the stars for him.

And now she bore his baby. Not for Donna, with her strict Catholic upbringing, to have any thoughts of contraception, and not for Donna to really consider sex before marriage. But she *had* for Alexander! She loved him and he must love her, which made everything all right. Surely, now that the baby was conceived,

197

Alexander would marry her? Of course he would. They would wait until the baby was born, and then she would stun them all as she floated down the aisle. She would be the most beautiful bride that anyone had ever seen, and Alexander would forget that Russian girl.

Donna frowned. She hadn't meant to let the memory of that girl get into her mind. She hadn't even met her, but she knew that Alexander had had a long love affair with her whilst they studied for their first degrees; that degree, she smiled proudly, that Alexander had achieved so effortlessly: the double first. Not that she'd known him then, but she still basked in his success.

But the girl, Natalya, had studied with Alexander, had loved him and had lived with him. Donna knew that, but Alexander had said that she'd been called back to Russia in July 1963, after Kim Philby had been identified as the 'third man', after Guy Burgess and Donald Maclean, and 'Russians under the bed' had become the contemporary paranoia. Natalya (so Alexander had said) had just completed her first degree when her parents had recalled her, fearing that Britain was no longer the best place for their daughter – not that they feared for her contamination; they would have sheltered Kim Philby themselves given half the chance. All they feared for was her safety.

Donna found herself scowling at her reflection. Now that the girl had entered her mind, she couldn't shake her off. The memories came flooding back. She knew that Alexander had followed the girl to Russia and had studied there at Moscow University for a while. She didn't want to think of that time. Suffice it to say that he'd soon returned, back to Oxford, to finish his MSc by a more conventional route, and later met her at the coffee shop where she was working whilst she waited to be discovered by a talent scout.

Donna's thoughts were rudely interrupted by a banging on her door. She looked once more at her reflection and tried a tentative smile. Yes, she looked good. She went to open the door. Alexander stood there, dripping wet. Donna hadn't even noticed it was raining.

"My darling!" she exclaimed as she threw herself into his arms.

"Donna," he said, or tried to say as he attempted to free himself from her passionate embrace, moving his head as her lips searched for his. "Donna, about this baby," he continued as he finally broke free and allowed her to usher him inside her small flat, fussing over his wet clothes and trying to make him comfortable. "Donna, if you really want this baby, then I won't fight you any longer. I am the baby's father and I will stand by my duty. I will give the baby my name—"

He didn't get the chance to finish. Donna had heard enough; her dreams had come true! This was a declaration of love from Alexander. He would marry her, their baby would bear his name, it would cement their relationship and they would be together for ever. Without waiting to hear any more, she threw her arms around him again, putting her fingers on his lips to silence him before hugging him tightly and burying her head in his shoulder.

Alexander held her stiffly in his arms, gazing unseeingly at the wall above her head. It had all been so easy with her. There was no effort or feeling required on his part; she just didn't notice. As long as her needs were met (and those needs were fairly simple) she was happy. She had no conception of his total lack of feeling for her. He knew he could never love her for Natalya had seen to that. His heart would always be with her. He pulled himself to the present quickly before Natalya's flashing dark eyes had the chance to reappear before him. *Forgive me, Natalya,* he thought, his mind refusing to blank her out, reliving again their last meeting, her desperate grief, her passionate tears, the fear in her eyes as she was dragged back by her father.

"You must leave now, Alexander. Thank you for bringing her to us but we will deal with her now as we think fit," he had said sternly, forcibly restraining his daughter and speaking calmly above her wild screams. "You have been our friend and you are still our friend, Alexander, but Natalya is our problem and she is out of control. Leave it all with me, now. I will sort out what must be done and I will meet with you again when this matter has been resolved."

And he had half-led, half-dragged Natalya, still sobbing, out of the room, leaving Alexander and Natalya's mother together. He turned to speak to her but she put up her hand.

"Please, Alexander, it is better that you go. I need to go to my daughter." And she had hurried off after her husband and daughter.

To see her beloved daughter in such distress was more than that kind and compassionate woman could bear. Her values were confused as she began to question, for the first time, her unswerving loyalty to her stern and unyielding husband since she'd married her socialist ideals to his Marxist fanaticism.

"Do you like my new dress, Alexander?" asked Donna coyly, breaking into his thoughts. He looked down at her in annoyance as she raised her eyes trustingly to his.

"Yes," he replied absently, thinking, *Natalya would never have worn such a tasteless garment.* Natalya had no need to conform to ridiculously unflattering fashion. Natalya's style had been all her own. She would have looked good in a sack if she'd chosen to wear such a thing. Forget Natalya, that time was gone, and yet... Maybe not.

He looked appraisingly at Donna. Her pregnancy had not yet begun to show much. Natalya would be at the same stage now. No, a month or so further advanced (if they had even allowed her to keep the baby). Well, he would soon find out. He was due to visit next week; he must make preparations for his trip.

"Donna," he spoke quietly, the lies coming as naturally to him as breathing. "I must go to visit my parents next week. You know that I told you that my mother has been ill? I really have to go to see her soon. She may die… My father says she is quite ill."

Donna hugged him tightly. "Oh, Alexander, but of course you must visit your dear mother. And she will get better soon, I know. And then you will let me also visit. You must tell her about our baby! That will make her get better. She will love our little baby. She will want to be the grandmother."

Alexander suppressed a deep sigh. He didn't really know how he had ever thought he could cope with Donna's naiveté. For a time, she had fulfilled a physical need, but how on earth had she managed to get herself pregnant so quickly? It was a mystery to him. Why in God's name hadn't she taken the correct precautions? Natalya had always been so sensible, until recently of course, but things were different with her now.

"I'd like a coffee, Donna." He didn't need to say any more. She was up and in the tiny kitchenette immediately, busying herself with the kettle, humming happily to herself.

Alexander sat down in the armchair and stretched his legs out in front of him, looking down pensively at his long slender fingers. Unconsciously, he pressed the tips together until the ends turned white. *Natalya,* he thought, *have you learnt yet that our destinies are forever linked? That we are as one and always will be?*

His thoughts turned to more practical matters. Graham had promised to arrange the tickets and meet him at the airport. Accommodation over there was never a problem as they could always stay with Natalya's parents. Perhaps he'd better give Graham another quick call in the morning before he left for the airport though. You never quite knew what might have happened or what might be required. Things changed so rapidly.

A little shiver of anticipation ran down his spine. The emotions that Natalya had stirred in him all those years ago had never dissipated. At times, admittedly, they had lain dormant, suppressed by external factors or occasionally even by Donna. He tried not to frown as she bounced back into the room carrying two steaming mugs. *Yes, Donna actually bounced,* he thought with distaste.

"There, my darling, coffee for you, chocolate for me. I don't quite like the taste of coffee now – our baby will not let me!" she cried gaily, patting her small rounded stomach proudly.

CHAPTER 14

Somerset
Saturday 18th May, 1996
11.15 a.m.

Harris and Formby left the room, heading with mutual assent towards Harris's office. Once there, Harris closed the door firmly behind him. He turned to look at Formby, before asking brusquely, "Did you believe her?"

Aiden considered the question for a moment. "I am inclined to think she that was telling the truth, sir, but there are certain things that just don't add up. I find it very hard to understand Sutherland's connection in all of this. I suspect that the whole issue is much more complicated than Paul had first thought. We're going to have to look closely at Sutherland and Mayhims now. Perhaps there is a connection there that we hadn't at first considered?"

Harris suppressed, with difficulty, a repressive reply. Ravell had obviously discussed this case with his friend more than he had with himself, his superior. But he held back his irate comments. He might yet need this man, and the case wasn't looking too good now. Ravell hadn't got anything from Sutherland when he'd interviewed him. In his report, the man was as clean as driven snow, and Harris hadn't picked up on anything suspicious in his 'phone call last evening.

Well, he had Commander Lyons from Scotland Yard to consider. In fact, he really ought to contact him now, to update him before they went to visit Sutherland. Bloody hell, it wasn't his fault that the fellow had buggered off after the early initial briefing this morning.

He reached for the 'phone but then realised he couldn't contact Lyons anyway as the idiot hadn't even left his mobile number, if indeed he had one. What was he to do, 'phone round the houses until he found him? Or should he just go to Sutherland's house and speak to him? Perhaps find the scene that Anna Hamilton had described? He paused indecisively, aware that Formby was watching him expectantly, and then he consulted the file, punching out the numbers that would connect him to Sutherland, not really expecting the call to be answered.

"Sutherland speaking." The prompt and crisp reply took Harris by surprise.

"Good morning, Mr Sutherland, Chief Inspector Harris here. I am sorry to trouble you, but we would like to come over to ask you a few more questions concerning the death of Professor Hamilton." *No need to mention Ravell's death yet.* "We would like to come over straightway, if that is convenient to you?" *And even if it's not,* he thought.

"Yes, certainly, Chief Inspector Harris," Sutherland said in a remarkably pleasant tone. At least he'd got his rank right this time. "I'm at home now, but I do have to leave to sort out the computer data soon, so if you could make it as soon as possible that would be more convenient," Sutherland continued smoothly, seemingly a man with nothing to hide.

"We'll be right over," responded Harris, replacing the receiver. "Come on, Formby. I don't think he's got anyone there – he's too cool – but we'd better go over and check."

Aiden privately thought they might have been better advised to have gone straight over without warning the man first, but then if Anna's story was to be believed, Sutherland would probably have guessed that she would make her way to the police station and he would be expecting a response, so of course he'd be prepared – he wasn't stupid. And if she was lying, Sutherland probably had nothing to hide.

"Do you want me to arrange some backup, sir?" he asked, an image of Paul's shattered head flashing before his eyes. They weren't dealing with amateurs here.

"No," said Harris decisively. Instinct told him that Sutherland, if he was guilty, would not be waiting with his thugs. The man was too subtle for that. He may, if the girl's story was to be believed, have been responsible for the murder of Ravell, but Ravell had been working late, conducting an interview, with little chance of summoning help, especially without his 'phone. This was a different situation, and he still mustn't forget that the girl might have been lying to protect her brother. After all, what did they have on Sutherland? Nothing really except the girl's word and a few vague suspicions, but they did have quite a lot of hard evidence that seemingly incriminated Michael Hamilton.

He stood up, Formby following suit, and together they left his office, pausing only to inform DS Adams of their intentions and to leave instructions that WPC Grimley should stay with Anna Hamilton. As an afterthought, Harris left a message for Commander Lyons should he return before they did, and then they made their way to the car park to drive Harris's car the short distance to Sutherland's house.

Formby drove. He hadn't been to Sutherland's house before but he knew its location. Despite himself, he was impressed at its magnificence. The man must be doing well in his business to have such a residence. He remembered Paul exclaiming over Sutherland's mansion, but he hadn't been prepared for the long, tree-lined drive, the ornate hedging and beautifully tended lawns, or the old Georgian-style house, with its stone mullion windows, which stood looking down on them impassively from its elevated position, the drive widening at the bottom to accommodate it. The house and grounds looked deserted. Harris wondered for a moment whether it might have been more sensible to have come in force, but shrugged off the thought.

A pair of grey stone lions gazed sphinxlike at them as they strode up the steps to the front door. Harris looked in vain for a knocker while Aiden smiled and pulled the ancient brass bell to the side of the door. The heavy oak door was opened within seconds. Sutherland himself stood there, smiling, debonair as ever.

"Ah, you must be Chief Inspector Harris. How nice to meet you in person. And this would be...?" He left the sentence open for Harris to introduce Aiden.

"Ah, Detective Inspector Formby, such a pleasure to meet you," he said warmly as Harris introduced Aiden, and he held out his hand, looking him up and down appraisingly. Aiden reluctantly took his hand. Sutherland's handshake was firm but he held his hand for a moment longer than Aiden felt was necessary. As Aiden rather abruptly pulled his hand away, Sutherland smiled urbanely saying, "Please do come inside, gentlemen."

He stood back to allow them to precede him into the spacious hallway. Closing the heavy door, he turned to face them, a questioning look on his face.

"And how can I help you? You said you wished to ask me more questions about dear Alexander's death. I really don't know if I can be of any more help, but I will certainly try."

"Perhaps we could go somewhere to sit down?" asked Harris, refusing to allow Sutherland's poise to disturb him.

"Oh yes, of course, how very remiss of me. I do apologise. Please, come this way."

He led the way to his drawing room, more in control than he'd thought he would be. These two together were less dangerous than Lyons. And the fact that Lyons hadn't returned with them could only mean that they didn't have much to go on. They couldn't have any hard evidence – not that he'd thought they had – but it was reassuring all the same.

Once in the drawing room, he gestured for them to be seated. The smell of cigarette smoke still lingered strongly in the room, causing Aiden to look around with quick interest. No ashtrays in sight, and Sutherland didn't look like a smoker, so who had been smoking in this room?

Sutherland inwardly smiled. *Good, this one was quick.* He'd challenge him on that and he'd enjoy playing with this young man.

"Oh, yes, I must apologise for the smell. An old friend was here earlier. Oh, in fact, of course you will know him – Commander Lyons. Dear Alistair, can't quite kick the habit, you know."

He turned to gaze blandly at Harris who was looking positively nonplussed.

"We go back a long way, Alistair and myself. We were at Oxford together." His attention switched to Aiden, whose sharp expression had not escaped him. "Probably before you were born, Inspector."

Damn the ponderous chief inspector for coming over at such an inconvenient time, but he might be easier to deceive than this eager younger inspector. He swivelled round to face them both, continuing before they had a chance to interrupt. Obviously Lyons hadn't told them of their earlier connections. Good – their ignorance was to his advantage.

"As I'm sure Commander Lyons will have told you, it wasn't just myself and Alistair who were together at Oxford University. Alexander Hamilton was also there. In fact, that's where we both met him. We were all such close friends," he sighed. "It's so hard to lose a dear friend, you know. I shall miss him so."

Then he allowed himself to lapse into a mournful silence, looking expectantly at them, trying to read their expressions. The young inspector had looked grieved himself when he'd mentioned the loss of a friend. He'd probably been friendly with the inspector who'd got in the way, whose name, come to think of it, he didn't know. It hadn't really mattered. Well, so be it. Perhaps his grief might distract him and dull his thinking.

Sutherland was right: Aiden *was* distracted, but it wasn't only the memory of Paul that occupied his thoughts. He was beginning to think that Anna might have spoken the truth. Those feelings, those instinctive senses that we call gut feelings (for want of a better phrase) were strong within him. It wasn't just pure dislike, although he felt that too, but deep within him he sensed that Sutherland was putting on an act; a clever act of deception that might be hard to break.

He admired Harris for his blunt response; Harris who'd had to recover quickly from the surprise at hearing of Commander Lyons's friendship with both Graham Sutherland and Professor Hamilton. So that was why he'd got himself involved in the case. Why the hell hadn't he informed Harris of his connection?

"Yes, sir, we do understand how bereft you must feel, but we have a crime to solve. I expect Commander Lyons has informed you that one of our men was brutally murdered last night? We also feel grief as we have also lost a friend, and we are as eager as I'm sure you are to find the culprit." Harris paused for breath, trying to formulate his thoughts. Like Aiden, he wasn't deceived by Sutherland, but he was also aware that he had to tread carefully, especially if the friendship that this man had laid claim to was valid.

He continued slowly, but firmly. "There have been more recent developments in the case that even Commander Lyons is not yet aware of. I have to ask you if you can tell me of your whereabouts last night and earlier this morning."

Sutherland looked at him with calculated disbelief; a hurt tone entering his voice. "Inspector—"

That's right, thought Harris. *Drop the chief now that it suits you.*

"Inspector, would you like to explain a bit more fully why you are speaking to me in this accusing way? I do understand that you have your job to do, and no one

211

could be more eager than myself to avenge dear Alexander's death. However, correct me if I'm wrong, but as I understood the situation from Alistair – and I do find this hard to believe – it would seem that Michael is rather more implicated in this situation than I had thought. In fact, I am beginning to realise that in all probability Michael must have killed Alexander and your inspector too. But I really cannot begin to comprehend what reasons he might have had. I really find it so hard to believe. I have been so deceived by him."

He paused for only a second before continuing, allowing a horrified note to enter his voice.

"And you are surely not suggesting that I might be implicated in this with Michael? I promise you that I would never have been a party to the murder of someone who I can assuredly tell you was quite my best friend."

Aiden watched him carefully, worried now that they had jumped in too soon. *Go easy, Harris.* They had nothing to go on; there was no evidence that he could see. The only real evidence of recent guests in this room was that of the commander from New Scotland Yard. And Anna's impassioned words would hold no sway in a court of law. They certainly had no proof as yet.

Harris continued in the same blunt tone. "Mr Sutherland, I am certainly not suggesting anything of the sort. I have a crime to solve and I have my job to do. I've lost a good man, and you are just one of many people I will be questioning in connection with this case. You are quite right, there is a great deal of evidence that suggests that Michael Hamilton killed his father, and he may well have been responsible for the death of my officer. I can only apologise if you felt that I was accusing you; that was certainly not my intention. It is merely that we are investigating a certain line of enquiry and we need to question several people who may be able to help us; people chosen, sir, not because they are suspects, but because they are involved, or may have been unwittingly drawn into this case. A crime, Mr Sutherland, very often involves the innocent as well as the guilty."

He paused for breath, just as the grandfather clock in the hallway struck noon.

"And I, Chief Inspector, have nothing to hide," Sutherland replied equably, leaning back in his chair and crossing his legs lazily, addressing Harris but looking sideways at Aiden.

"If it is really necessary to your enquiries, my whereabouts last night can be easily confirmed: I had dinner with a colleague, Richard Summers. He will confirm that we were together." *And he could give Richard an alibi in the process.*

"I see. And where did you meet for dinner, sir?" asked Harris unperturbably, trying not to react at the mention of the name Richard. *Good God, maybe the Hamilton girl's story had some truth in it.*

"Why here, of course." Sutherland looked surprised. "I am, you must understand, Chief Inspector Harris, a very busy man, and also," he smiled modestly, "a very good cook. I enjoy cooking a good meal for my friends." He allowed a certain emphasis to fall on the word friends while still keeping his eyes fixed on Aiden, who had also picked up on the name Richard.

"And Mr Summers will be able to confirm that he was here with you for the whole of yesterday evening?" asked Harris, trying to keep any inflection out of his voice.

"Indeed he can. I can supply you with his telephone number and address," Sutherland said with a suppressed smile.

Aiden Formby spoke quickly in an attempt to cover his own embarrassment. He really wished Sutherland would stop looking at him so intently.

"And this morning, Mr Sutherland – can you account for your whereabouts this morning?"

Sutherland looked at him appreciatively. His voice had a pleasant inflection, an almost imperceptible Irish lilt, in contrast to his rather less cultivated superior. He studied Aiden more closely. He had always been attracted to that type: the rigid adherence to external discipline, the hard exterior, the hidden vulnerability just waiting to be discovered. And he was so good-looking, with those dark eyes, that wide mouth, just like Michael… No, don't go there! He was genuinely upset that he was going to lose Michael but he mustn't allow himself those thoughts.

Instead, with a self-mocking smile, he looked

directly at Aiden, enjoying the moment when Aiden averted his eyes in discomfiture.

"Well, Inspector." He smiled gently, enjoying his game. "Last night my friend and I both had a bit to drink, and of course we wouldn't wish to breach the law or endanger the public, so naturally he stayed overnight, only leaving this morning just before Commander Lyons arrived. Mr Summers will confirm the time that he left this morning." He paused again, and then changed his tone slightly, allowing a slight hint of anger to enter.

"You yourself, Chief Inspector, 'phoned and spoke to me here yesterday evening, on this number." He gesticulated towards the 'phone. "I don't even know why we are discussing this. If you would like to give me more details, then perhaps I can be of more assistance, but I can assure you I have not left this house since approximately six o'clock yesterday evening when I popped out to buy some groceries."

He sat back, satisfied. He knew he was telling a partial truth and that they'd have a hard job to disprove it. They certainly couldn't implicate him in the murder of their policeman, and as for the cars arriving last night, well, the chances of his not-very-near neighbours seeing any late activity was so remote as to be laughable. There was nothing they had to go on. And now he'd given Richard an alibi, although he must make sure that Richard backed him up too. He smiled to himself. Anna Hamilton must have made it to the police station, and this was without doubt the resultant visit, but what credibility would her wild words hold with no evidence? He decided that he would offer to show them around the house, but before he could make the offer, Harris spoke.

"Thank you, Mr Sutherland, we will naturally have to check the information you have given us with your friend Mr Summers, so yes, we will need his address and telephone number. But first I would be grateful if we could just have a quick look around your house."

He waited for an indignant refusal – after all, he hadn't specified why they had called. He hadn't even mentioned Anna Hamilton's accusations and, as far as Sutherland was concerned, they had no real justification for being there. He continued quickly in order to forestall a refusal.

"Of course, you have every right to refuse my request but it would be helpful to our enquiries if you could just show us around your house."

"My dear Chief Inspector, you and your colleague," and he put as much emphasis on the word 'colleague' as he could, unable to resist another sideways glance at Aiden, "would be welcome to stay all day and even through the night if you so wished. But much as I would relish the idea, I'm afraid that I do have pressing commitments today. I will gladly show you around my home and then, if you are satisfied, I shall need to sort out a few problems that have arisen since the death of Alexander. You must understand, it's Sunday tomorrow and we really haven't had the opportunity to sort anything out since his tragic death on Wednesday evening. And with Michael still missing, I do have rather a problem as you can imagine. Two of my best men gone, and if Michael is involved..." Here he managed to look both disturbed and disbelieving. "If Michael is involved, I truly have lost them both, and I will have a lot more problems to resolve."

He stood up as he was speaking, inviting Harris and Formby to follow suit, which they did; no challenge to be faced, no bluff to be called for the moment.

Sutherland led the way to the door, the others following behind him, not even a shared glance to indicate how they each might be feeling. Aiden felt a heaviness in his heart. He knew they were going to achieve nothing here as Sutherland was too clever for them.

They were guided through the hallway, Sutherland throwing open each of the doors in turn, inviting them to look around, watching them with a sardonic expression, his arms folded. There was nothing to be seen, as Aiden had known; the study tidily arranged, the dining room empty, the kitchen sparkling as a new pin, an empty coffee cup left casually on the kitchen table, presumably Sutherland's, another one washed and left on the draining board by the sink. The window was there, above the toilet in the spacious downstairs cloakroom, just as Anna had described. Of course it would be – on her own admission, she knew the house, it didn't prove a thing – but the window was closed.

Harris didn't even bother to open it to look out. He satisfied himself with a quick glance that it would be possible for a slight person to climb out. That was all he required to know.

The 'phone rang just as Sutherland was about to take them upstairs. The slight frown that passed briefly over his face didn't go unnoticed by either Harris or Formby, who both stood close by as he picked up the hallway extension.

"Hello, Richard, my dear friend." His voice was effusive as he moved slightly away from them. "You got home all right then? How's the head?"

He smiled mischievously across at Aiden who was straining to try to understand what the metallic voice might be saying back. Aiden frowned and looked away, still trying to listen, but of course he couldn't make out any words. It sounded like a male voice; that was all he could tell.

"Yes, I'm fine, but you'll never guess: just after you left this morning I had a visit from an old friend, Alistair Lyons. He's a commander now at New Scotland Yard. Yes, it was about Michael and poor Alexander. It seems Michael has deceived us all, and it looks like he might have killed Alexander, probably a police officer as well. The local police are here now."

He lapsed into silence, listening to the voice on the other end of the line. Aiden wondered briefly if he could make an excuse and find an extension, but Sutherland had begun speaking again.

"I'll tell you all about it later. I'll be over shortly, and you'd better stay at home. The police may want to speak to you, just to confirm that you were here yesterday evening and stayed the night here. It was about eight thirty a.m. when you left this morning, wasn't it?"

He paused again, raising his eyebrows at Harris and Formby, holding the receiver slightly away from his ear as the voice rose in pitch.

"No, it's OK Richard, it's just routine enquiries. They aren't interested in our private lives, but they will need to speak to you. Look, I must go now. I'm just showing the police around the house and then I'll get a taxi and come over."

He replaced the receiver with a satisfied smile. Well, that had saved him the trouble of alerting Richard at least. Now Richard would go back home and be there if the police did decide to question him. He'd just have to hope that John, Carl and Mark between them could control Michael. His smile faded as he thought grimly that this was not going according to plan. First the girl escaping, now the bloody police on his back. But he could wait, he would have to wait. Richard had just said that they had the tape now and they still had Michael. His plans were merely delayed, not ruined.

He turned back to Harris and Formby who were watching him, both thinking that if this was an act, it was a very clever one, with neither one of them able to do anything to stop him as he had effectively substantiated his alibi in front of them and possibly warned his friend in the process.

The rest of the tour of the house was as fruitless as before. Sutherland showed them around the bedrooms on the first floor but there was no evidence of any recent occupancy apart from in his bedroom. Even there, the bed was immaculately arranged, silk pyjamas laid neatly across the counterpane. The huge spare rooms were as immaculate as Sutherland's bedroom, with no evidence of anyone staying. Why would there be? Sutherland was obviously an obsessively tidy person.

He led them up another staircase, through a door and up a narrow staircase to a small landing, then along the corridor, showing them the room that had been Anna's prison, and the adjoining bathroom, but there was no evidence of her recent stay. All the doors were unlocked now. Further along the corridor, he took them into the room where Michael had been held. There were no signs left of the doctor's administration to the patient; just a quaint and cosy room, bright light streaming in from the wide-open high window.

"Well, that's it, there's no more to show you, apart from the cellar," he said, glancing at his watch as he led them back downstairs. A quick cursory look around the cellar showed only dusty wine racks. *Nothing here,* thought Harris glumly, allowing Sutherland to escort them out into the midday sun.

"Do you have a car, Mr Sutherland?" asked Harris as they prepared to leave, noting the open doors, the empty garage.

"Yes, Chief Inspector, a white Mercedes. Richard borrowed it this morning to return home. He took a taxi out here yesterday as his own car was at the garage being serviced, but it should be ready today."

Not the car they'd seen last night then, thought Harris despondently. He and WPC Grimley may not have paid it much attention but it had been a dark car, definitely not a white Mercedes.

"Isn't that rather inconvenient for you, not having the car to use yourself?" asked Aiden curiously. "You have mentioned how busy you are. Surely your friend could have taken a taxi again?"

Sutherland smiled at him. "My dear Inspector, I myself find it easier to take taxis. So much more convenient, and I do like to help out my friend."

"Well, thank you for your assistance, Mr Sutherland," said Harris formally. "We have made a note of Mr Summers's address. It will be a mere formality but we will check the information you have given us with him. I'm sorry to have troubled you again."

Harris sat silently as Aiden negotiated his way out of the drive and onto the busy road. Aiden broke the heavy silence as he pulled up at the first set of traffic lights.

"I think he's lying, sir, but I don't know how we can prove it unless we can find Michael Hamilton, and Sutherland's obviously not stupid enough to keep him at his house now."

"Well, we'll have to go and speak to Summers but I

don't suppose we'll find Hamilton there either. Anyway, Summers will obviously corroborate what Sutherland said, although it might be worth getting Anna Hamilton to have a look at him. If she identifies him as one of the men she said was involved last night, it might be a help," replied Harris.

"Yes," replied Formby. "Do you want to go and question Summers now, or shall we go back to the station first?"

"Back to the station. I hope Lyons will be back by now. I do think he might have told me that he and Sutherland were old friends. It made me look a complete fool not knowing that," responded Harris grumpily. "I don't suppose he'll be very happy when he finds out that I've been harassing his friend." And on that he lapsed back into a gloomy silence, staring moodily out of the car window.

CHAPTER 15

Somerset
Saturday 18th May, 1996
12.15 p.m.

As soon as the car containing Harris and Formby had driven away down his drive, Sutherland went quickly back into his house. It was imperative now to get in touch with Richard who must be pretty confused after that disjointed conversation. He was beginning to feel slightly perturbed himself by the whole situation. It was fine to put on an act in front of the police but in reality he had to get things back on course. He debated 'phoning Richard first and then decided against the idea. Instead, he would 'phone for a taxi and go directly to Richard's house. That, after all, was what he had told Richard (and the police) that he would do, so he might as well act accordingly. He'd just have to leave Michael at John's house with the others for the time being whilst he consulted with Richard.

The taxi arrived almost immediately and Sutherland was outside Richard's house within ten minutes of

Harris and Formby's departure. His car was parked outside. *Thank goodness for that,* he thought.

Richard must have heard the sound of the departing taxi, for the door was flung open before Sutherland had even reached it. His face was black as thunder. Sutherland motioned for him to go back inside, looking apprehensively around him as he did so. Richard's house did not occupy quite the same privacy as his. (It was a quiet cul-de-sac of modern executive houses, and you never knew who might be looking out of their windows.)

Once inside, Richard could contain himself no longer. His voice rose in a crescendo of fury.

"What the hell is going on? I cannot believe the fucking mess that this is turning into! First, the bloody girl escapes and then you seem to be spending half your bloody life entertaining the police! And why the hell did you have to complicate things by saying I spent the night at yours? We've got enough to worry about without making things up and having to remember all your lies!"

Sutherland raised his hand. "Richard, I'm sorry. Just calm down, it's not as bad as it seems. Now, tell me, you've obviously spoken to John? I take it he didn't find the girl?"

"No, he bloody well didn't." Richard was still angry, but starting to calm down slightly. "He drove around Bath for a while but she was nowhere to be seen, so he followed your instructions and went to his house. We met him there and were going to hang on until you came round. That's why I 'phoned you, to find out when you were coming round. I didn't expect you to have the police round again."

"Well, I didn't exactly invite them for mid-morning drinks. I assume our little friend Anna Hamilton must have made it to the police station and spilled out her story. But calm down, Richard." This last as Richard's colour rose alarmingly. "They have no evidence. Her story must appear extremely farfetched, and so far all the evidence points to Michael. Speaking of whom, how is he? I take it he found the tape without any problem? You didn't let him know that the girl had escaped, did you?"

Richard shook his head impatiently. "Of course not, though he was standing right next to me when you 'phoned. But yes, we got the tape, it's here. You can take it now. It's on the table over there. I don't know how you're going to get Michael to help you though."

"Why, was he being difficult?"

"Well, not exactly, but he did keep asking where the girl was. I reckon he'll refuse to co-operate if we don't produce her."

"Well, we'll just have to make him, won't we? Do you think he'll be OK at John's? I suppose they are capable of keeping him there, not that he'll try to escape if he thinks we've still got the girl."

Richard looked defiantly at him. "I didn't leave him with them – I didn't trust them. I brought him here with me. It's OK, you don't have to look at me like that. I've locked him in my study upstairs, and unlike some people, I didn't leave any windows open. He was exhausted anyway, so he won't try anything."

Sutherland just stared at him in horror, speechless for a moment. Michael, here in this house, the police probably about to arrive any minute, and all that shouting when he'd first come in! Had Richard gone completely mad?

"You must be out of your mind," he said coldly. "Richard, I told you to come here because the police might call round. Surely you understood what I was saying?"

"No, Graham, I did not understand, and I still don't understand. First, you 'phone me when we're just about to get the bloody tape, with Michael standing right next to me, and you tell me that the girl has escaped. Then you tell me to come here and leave Michael with the others, and then I find that you have virtually told the bloody police that I spent last night in your bed." His voice was rising again, ignoring Sutherland's attempt to calm him with his placatory, outstretched hand. "You talked nonsense on the 'phone, but yes, I understood that the police were interviewing you, and you've managed to implicate me, presumably to give yourself an alibi."

Sutherland tried to interrupt.

"No, just listen to me, I haven't finished yet. Then you tell me the police might want to speak to me. Fine, OK, I'll lie: I'll say I spent the night at your house. But there was no way I was leaving Michael with those morons. He has more intelligence than the three of them put together, and if that bitch of a girl can outwit John within minutes of being left alone with him, I dread to think what Michael could do."

Richard paused for breath. His voice had risen so high when he was speaking that Sutherland was almost afraid the neighbours would hear him.

"Richard, calm yourself, keep your voice down." He looked nervously around him, glancing up the stairs. They were standing right at the bottom of them and he just hoped to God that Michael couldn't hear them. "It wasn't just that I had to give myself an alibi, although you're right they did put me on the spot. But listen, if the girl has spoken to the police, they may be able to trace you. She might have heard your name associated with mine, and if they start fishing around someone is bound to come up with a connection. The reason that I 'implicated' you, as you put it, was to give you an alibi as well. And the reason I wanted you to leave Michael with the others was to try to protect you in case the police came round here. They'll have no reason to know the identities of John, Carl and Mark."

Richard glared at him but when he spoke his voice was calmer. "Graham, I'm not happy about all this. I suggest the sooner we get that information back onto the computer, the better. I want the hell out of this, and I want Michael disposed of so that once he's served his immediate purpose, he can't point the finger at us, or make the connection with John and the others. You'll just have to find yourself some other puppet scientist to continue your project. This is all getting way too dangerous."

"OK, but look, it's a bit risky to take him to the lab at the moment. I'll need to take some equipment out of there without alerting suspicion and I can't bring it here or to my house at the moment. I'll have to take it to John's place. Oh, and by the way, can you move your car from outside your house? I told the police that you borrowed my car. In fact, I'll take yours to John's and swap them over. At least then my car will be here if they do call round. Can I leave you for a while? Are you sure Michael's all right?"

"Yes, of course he is. I told you, I'm not John, but don't be too long. We need to get him out of here just in case the police do come sniffing round," replied Richard irritably.

"Just don't answer the door if they do turn up here before I get back. I'll be back soon with the others. The three of them can take Michael back to John's house and keep him secure there for now, and we'll stay here in case the police turn up." Sutherland took the keys that Richard held out. "It shouldn't take me more than ten minutes at the most to get over to John's house, then I'll just help the others to sort out somewhere to hide Michael, and we'll be back." And with a quick wave, he left.

Richard shut the door behind him wearily, his anger spent. All he felt now was anxiety. He was so tempted to wash his hands of the whole business, but then he was in too deep. Without realising it, he was pacing the floor, so engrossed in his thoughts that when he heard a loud crash from upstairs, he almost jumped out of his skin.

Heart pounding, he grabbed his gun and ran up the stairs, coming to a halt outside the study door. He stood listening for a moment, trying to hold his breath, but there was no sound from within the room. The walls were paper-thin he knew (typical modern-built house, any sound would travel) but it was quiet. He silently unlocked the door and, opening it very slowly, he cautiously edged forward.

The room was in darkness – Michael must have closed the shutters. Suddenly, he was hit hard across the back of his head. He stumbled and almost lost his balance. He whirled round, feeling for the gun in his pocket, murder in his eyes, just as Michael threw the heavy brass Buddha paperweight straight at his face. This time, he did go down, falling heavily backwards, slightly dazed by the blow, giving Michael the only chance he needed.

Michael wasted no time. He ran out of the room, slamming the door shut behind him and sprinting down the stairs. He could hear the study door opening even as he pulled open the front door. He slammed it behind him as hard as he could and ran out into the road, looking desperately from right to left, trying to decide which way to go in this unfamiliar territory.

He started to run to the left, out of the deserted cul-de-sac towards the main road, but he didn't dare look round. He was panting now and his lungs felt like they might burst. The blood was hammering in his head; the pain in his shoulder almost unbearable. That small amount of effort had cost him dear. He could hear Richard's feet pounding behind him. He ran out onto the pavement by the main road and, without slowing down his pace, he allowed himself a quick glance behind. Richard was almost on him, one hand in his pocket. Michael had no doubt the gun was in that hand. He stumbled as his ankle twisted on the edge of the kerb and he lost his balance, falling heavily backwards into the road. He didn't see the car; all he heard was the screech of brakes, and then everything went black.

The traffic was crawling along so slowly that it would have been quicker to walk but George Simons didn't really notice. He had a lot on his mind: the promotion that had seemed such a godsend at the time had just made the situation worse. Mary couldn't complain about the lack of money anymore, but this was replaced by her protest that she never saw him. She was never satisfied. He sighed to himself. How different it had been when they'd first met, those first few heady years of love. It might have been different if they'd had a child, but that wasn't to be. He smiled wistfully as the memories came flooding back: Mary with the long golden hair, the look of discontent not yet formed, happy to live on love and not much else. His smile of reminiscence turned into a frozen mask of horror as the figure lurched in front of his car.

Despite its slow speed, his car skidded sideways as he slammed on the brakes and tried to swerve, his seatbelt jamming back and cutting into him as he was thrown forward. The car ground to a screeching stop. He sat motionless for a moment, leaning over the steering wheel, his heart pounding with adrenaline, time suspended.

Someone was knocking on his window. The car behind had stopped, the occupants jumping out quickly. Suddenly the road was full of people, waving at the oncoming traffic to stop.

George opened the door and slowly got out, walking like an automaton through the muttered sounds of sympathy to the front of his car. He looked down. A young man lay motionless on the road in front of his car. His stomach heaved and he turned to the edge of the road, the remains of his last meal coming up violently.

Gentle arms guided him back to his car and he sat down thankfully, closing his eyes, the shock overwhelming him and making his whole body shake uncontrollably. He was unaware of the activity outside as more passers-by appeared, more cars stopped, shocked people bending over the still form in the road, looking, not touching.

Help had been summoned as lights flashed and sirens wailed. Uniformed police and fluorescent-jacketed paramedics were on the scene within a few short minutes of being alerted, deft and efficient.

Traffic was directed on, unnecessary passers-by sent on their way, the little band of witnesses remaining by the roadside, all clamouring to be heard.

"Please, one at a time," said PC White, desperately wishing more backup would arrive soon. He and PC Ackroyd had been only a few blocks away when the emergency call had come through. The ambulance had responded in record time, but then the hospital was less than a mile away.

"I'll take a statement from you all, but one at a time, please." He glanced quickly at the silent occupant of the car. He'd leave him for the moment until more help arrived. The man looked as though he was in shock; perhaps the paramedics had better see to him as well.

"Now, madam," he continued, addressing the nearest bystander as the little crowd lapsed into silence. "Did you see the accident happen?"

"Yes, I was in the car behind. It all happened so quickly although we were moving really slowly. But the poor driver in front of me didn't get a chance to stop. That man, he just seemed to fall over, straight in front of the car. It looked as though he was being chased."

"Chased?" PC White questioned, looking around. "And is his pursuer still here?"

"No," replied another bystander. "The young guy seemed to be running away from someone who was getting quite close to him, but as soon as he fell in the road, the other man ran off. Is he going to be all right?"

PC White ignored the question.

"It was a man, was it? Can you describe him?"

But they couldn't; the shock of the accident wiping the earlier details from their minds. As they said, it had all happened so quickly. They didn't even know which direction the pursuer had taken when he ran off. The only fact they seemed to agree upon was that he'd been a man, older and shorter than his quarry, and smartly dressed.

PC Acroyd waited no longer. Off he went to look for this unknown pursuer. Not much hope of finding him but he had to give it a try.

One of the paramedics came up to PC White, looking puzzled.

"There's something not quite right here. We've got him stabilized in the ambulance. He's unconscious, possibly concussed, but as far as I can see there's nothing broken. I'm not even sure that the car actually hit him. But I don't want to examine him too much until he's been thoroughly checked over at the hospital."

"You said there was something not quite right?"

"Yes, well, he's already been in the wars. Looks like someone has knocked him about a bit. His mouth is cut and bruised, he's got a massive bandage on his left shoulder, and he's running quite a high temperature. Seems strange, that's all, together with the fact that it seems he was running away from someone."

"Hmm. Does he have any ID on him?"

"Yes, I've just checked: driving licence and credit cards in his wallet in the name of Michael Hamilton."

Jed White couldn't quite believe what he was hearing! "What? What did you just say? Michael Hamilton?"

The paramedic looked even more confused. "Well, er, yes."

Jed White poked his head around the open ambulance doors. Since Anna Hamilton had burst in so dramatically that morning, the whole station had talked of little else than the elusive Michael Hamilton. Good God – that must be him! Certainly looked like the description they'd all been given. He decided he'd take the paramedic's word on the ID. He didn't fancy rummaging through his pockets as he really didn't look very good.

Now he was speaking urgently into his crackling radio, being passed from one officer to another, until finally speaking to DI Formby.

"Yes, OK, sir, I'll accompany him to hospital and stay with him until you get there."

CHAPTER 16

Somerset
Saturday 18th May, 1996
12.30 p.m.

They were greeted back at the station by DS Adams.

"Commander Lyons is here, sir, waiting in your office," he said to Harris. "He said to tell you that he must see you as soon as you got back."

As Harris strode off in the direction of his office, he turned to Aiden.

"Lyons didn't look very happy when he found out that you'd gone to interview Sutherland. I wouldn't like to be in the old man's shoes unless you've got something positive to report. Have you?"

Aiden shook his head. He almost felt sorry for Harris. The case was complicated enough without Sutherland having friends in high ranks.

"Oh well, Aiden, I expect Harris can take it. Anyway, what's this I hear about you and Josie? You two back together again, are you? That's good news, she's a nice kid."

Aiden smiled. She was a lot more than just a nice kid. He nodded at Sean Adams and went off in search of Josie.

Harris entered his office briskly. He was not going to be intimidated by Lyons. If necessary, he'd drag the Super in on this. What right had this jumped-up prat from the Yard to come poking his nose into his case on personal grounds? His temper wasn't improved when he walked in to find Lyons leaning back in his chair, feet up on his desk, apparently engaged in some 'phone call to yet another old friend. His cigarette was burning away in a half-filled ashtray.

"Thanks, Jeremy. I'm sure Jenny would love to meet up with Gwen again sometime soon. It's been a long time, too long, but work and growing families keep us so busy, don't they?" He looked up briefly through the blue smoke-filled air as Harris entered, waving his arm at the chair in front of Harris's desk. "Ah, Harris, sit down. I won't be a moment." He picked up his cigarette, taking a long drag before turning his attention back to the 'phone. "If you could find out what you can and dig out those old papers, I'd be really grateful. If necessary, we'll go over there and find her. Look, I can leave now. It won't take me much more than a couple of hours. I should be with you by about two thirty, maybe three p.m. this afternoon, I should think. Do you want me to come to your house or to your office? The office? OK. Will they let me in? It is Saturday, after all. That'll be all right, good, righto, I'll see you soon then."

He replaced the receiver slowly, before swinging his legs down. Leaning forward, he rested his elbows on the desk, making a steeple with his fingers to support his chin as he looked thoughtfully at Harris, who was trying to contain his indignation having seated himself in the chair opposite his own desk.

"Now, firstly, whilst you were out visiting Graham Sutherland, I've been having a little chat with our Miss Anna Hamilton. Interesting story she tells, and I have to hold my hands up – if it's true. I think I was Sutherland's unwelcome visitor who unintentionally, but in hindsight, thankfully, set the scene for her rather impressive escape." He paused and took a long drag on his cigarette. "Having heard her story, I can just about understand why you went rushing out to interview Sutherland but, Harris, I wish that you had consulted with me first. I just hope no damage has been done. Would you please tell me what transpired from your meeting?"

Harris had been prepared for anger, for a fight, a showdown even. What he hadn't been prepared for was the man's calm manner. His bluster disintegrated as he recounted the interview, his anger only surfacing as he reached the part where he had learned of Sutherland's friendship with Lyons.

Lyons nodded apologetically, diffusing his anger.

"Yes, Harris, you are quite right. I'm sorry, I should have informed you. I would have told you but I was anxious to get on with my enquiries. I thought it might wait until later. I don't think any of us were quite prepared for Miss Hamilton's rather dramatic entrance, but please continue."

Harris finished, leaving out no small detail. At the end, Lyons leant back in the chair and, lighting another cigarette, sat silently gazing into space, lost in thought for a moment. And then he looked directly at Harris, who hadn't realised until then just how piercing his eyes were.

"Harris, I do owe you an explanation, but it will have to be brief for the moment, and it will have to be confidential. I hope I can rely upon you for that?"

Harris nodded. "Yes, sir, you have my word."

"I met Graham Sutherland when I went up to Oxford University in 1963. He had already been there for a couple of years and we did not become close friends, but we mixed in the same circles. It was a small community in those days, you understand. We were both studying for a business degree and we both had the intention to join the civil service – the corridors of power, you know. I met Alexander Hamilton later, in 1964, I think it was. He'd already been at Oxford since 1960, gained his first degree, and then had gone to Russia after he graduated in 1963 to continue his studies at Moscow State University. He'd been involved with some Russian girl, you see, a girl called Natalya. He only stayed there for a short time though, before returning to Oxford to complete his Masters and start his PhD. That was when I met first him, but he did continue to visit Russia on occasion."

Lyons paused; this was the difficult part.

"You have to understand the political climate at that time: the cold war was at its height, and Alexander had already been approached by MI6 when they learned of his intention to study in Moscow. Oxford and Cambridge were the breeding grounds for such approaches in those days. We were all being watched, and it wasn't very long before Sutherland was also contacted, and then, later, me as well." Lyons paused to re-light his cigarette.

"So, as I said, Alexander had agreed to work for them whilst he was over in Russia. Nothing too heavy – he was a scientist after all – but his brief was to learn what he could of their work over there and to report back. This he did. I have no idea how useful his information was; that was never my concern, but I admired him. I was young and zealous, and as anti-Soviet as it was possible to be, so I jumped at the opportunity to work for my country, and even when I'd completed my time at Oxford, I still spent several years doing just that. As far as I know, Sutherland felt the same way, and I would occasionally hear news of him, until he decided to leave to start up his own business, and then shortly afterwards I also decided to leave and enter the police force."

Lyons stopped for a moment to get his breath, and then to effectively remove it again by pulling heavily on his cigarette. Harris hadn't uttered a word so far. Lyons continued; he must get this over with and then be on his way.

"When Alexander returned from Moscow, he entered into a relationship with a Spanish girl, one Donna Francesca Gonzales."

He ignored Harris's sharp intake of breath.

"They had a baby, a boy, in 1965, but Alexander had decided he couldn't stay with Donna, not even for the baby, and they split up some time before the baby's birth. Donna still loved Alexander and tried to persuade him to go back to her, but after it was born, she finally realised that he didn't love her. She became depressed and left Oxford, left England, to return to Spain and to her parents. That baby was called Michael Hamilton. Alexander had at least given him his name. Now that is as much as I knew until recently. I didn't really keep up my friendship with Alexander except for the occasional Christmas card, and I certainly had no contact with Sutherland. When I learnt of Alexander's death, and the details surrounding the case, I at first thought that the Michael Hamilton involved here must naturally be that baby. However, we now know that that cannot be the case. There is no doubt that both Donna and the baby died in 1965. Whoever our mysterious Michael Hamilton is, he is not Donna's child. Which then made me think that perhaps Alexander had resurrected his relationship with the Russian girl as, after all, he often travelled to Russia, and perhaps he'd had another child – this time with Natalya. And for some reason he had brought this child to England, passing him off as

Donna's child. Why, I can't yet fathom. It could be that he was forced into it, or it could be that he did it willingly. Certainly we know that he lied about it. When you came in just then, I was speaking to an old friend who has remained with MI6. He is going to check back on some old files to see if he can shed any light on this and I plan to meet him later today to discuss the matter."

Harris, who had been staring open-mouthed at Lyons during these revelations, finally found his voice.

"Well, sir, I do appreciate your frankness. I can see that this case is more complicated that I had realised. But where does Sutherland fit into recent events? I have to tell you that I don't trust the man. I still can't see that anyone other than Michael Hamilton – or whatever his name really is – can be responsible for Professor Hamilton's death. However, I do have a strong hunch that Sutherland is in this up to his neck, and possibly the one accountable for Inspector Ravell being killed."

"Yes, I agree with you, which is why I didn't particularly want you putting the wind up him. I've never trusted Sutherland myself but I can't quite get my head around the implications. My only feeling is that it may be something connected with the work that is going on at Mayhims, which is why I took the time today to speak not only to Sutherland, but also with a few of his employees."

"And did you discover anything?"

"No, not really. The employees, mainly technicians, are pretty much in the dark. It seems that Michael and

Alexander were the brains behind the project. Sutherland, however, did give me a brief idea of the two projects that they are working on: firstly to develop a vaccine against AIDS and secondly to somehow engineer the body's metabolism in such a way as to slow down the progress of the virus in the cells to the point that it becomes dormant. Both of which are entirely laudable projects, until you consider the implications."

Harris was confused for a moment. He was afraid to show his ignorance to this man. He hadn't really seriously considered that the nature of the work that was going on at Mayhims might be of relevance. His only concern had been the funding of that work. He had wondered if perhaps there was some kind of commercial implication that could be connected with the case. Lyons's next words reassured him slightly (his thinking hadn't quite the refinement of the commander's but then he hadn't ever worked for MI6).

"You see, the problem, as I see it, is that whilst such research could benefit a worthy cause, it could equally be explosive in the wrong hands. Just consider: if you were a corrupt political state, how you could use such knowledge. We all know the threat that AIDS imposes, yet we are complacent; we all think it won't touch us. But supposing it became a major epidemic. What power would those who could control it have? That could be biological warfare at its worst. We need to find out more details of the work they're doing there. I don't suppose for one minute that Sutherland gave me all the information."

Lyons stopped for a moment. He glanced at his watch; he really should go now to meet Jeremy. He looked at Harris's heavy-jowled face. The man might look stupid but he was nobody's fool. He felt he'd made the right decision to share his conjectures with him. He continued quickly.

"Look, I know this may seem farfetched to you, but believe me, these things happen – I know that – and I do think we are dealing here with more than just a couple of random killings. It might be a little too easy to assume our friend, the elusive Michael Hamilton, is guilty of these crimes, and then find him dead with a label round his neck confessing to the whole thing, then we close the case only to find years later, to our cost, that we were very wrong. I need to dig back into history a little, and I may need a bit of time to do that. Can I rely upon you to continue your investigations with prudence? Don't alert Sutherland. Obviously, if he comes to the door with a neatly written confession, deal with it as you think fit. Maybe gift horses do exist, but I doubt it. He's a slippery customer and a very clever man, make no mistake about that."

Harris wished he didn't feel so provincial against this man's wider breadth of experience. His voice, when he spoke, was deferential.

"Yes, of course, sir, you may be assured that I will tread very carefully in my investigations until you return, and I promise that we will not jeopardise a satisfactory outcome in any way."

Lyons nodded in acknowledgement, getting up and gathering his papers to him.

"Good man. Thank you, Harris. I will keep in touch with you, and you can contact me at any time on my mobile 'phone. I've written the number down for you on your pad. But I may have to leave the country. It is just possible that if I can locate Natalya, I shall visit her. She may just hold the clue to all of this. If I do, I'll only be gone for tonight and should be back tomorrow."

He got up to leave, pausing at the door and lighting another cigarette.

"Oh, the forensic reports came back whilst you were out – over there on your desk. I took the liberty of reading them. The blood on the wall in the cottage matches Michael Hamilton, not DI Ravell, and there's a report from the pathologist as well. Whoever killed the inspector did stand directly behind him, and was, incidentally, left-handed. It does seem that some of Anna Hamilton's story is starting to add up. You could ask her if this Carl character was left-handed; not that she probably noticed. Ballistics say that the gun that was recovered from the cottage has Michael Hamilton's prints all over it. He's definitely right-handed. They've also found a couple of partial prints that seem to match Alexander Hamilton. They're not sure yet, but it seems that the two bullet cases found in the laboratory came from the gun that we found at the cottage, but the casing from the bullet that killed Inspector Ravell seems like it came from a different gun, although it was the same make: a Glock 26. Oh, and Sutherland's 'friend', Richard Summers, isn't an employee at Mayhims as such, but he is apparently contracted to be responsible for the commercial and marketing side of the company. He might well be the 'Richard' that Anna Hamilton referred to, but now that Sutherland has given him an alibi, there's no point in pursuing it for the moment and risk putting the wind up him. Let him wait until I get back now. I did try to visit him myself after I'd been to see Sutherland but there was no answer when I called, and there was no car outside the house so not sure what to make of Sutherland telling you that he'd lent him his car."

And with that he was out of the door and gone before Harris had a chance to reply, leaving only the acrid smell of his cigarette smoke lingering behind him.

CHAPTER 17

Somerset
Saturday 18th May, 1996
12.40 p.m.

Aiden could hardly believe what he'd heard: Michael Hamilton. They had Michael Hamilton! After quickly instructing PC White to accompany Hamilton to the hospital, keep him away from other patients and not let him out of his sight, he hastened to Harris's office.

Harris hadn't yet spoken to Aiden since Lyons had left; he was still debating how much information to disclose to him, and pondering over the next steps he should take.

Lyons's instructions had been clear: stay away from Sutherland, and this Richard Summers as well, until he got back. Perhaps it was time to allow Anna Hamilton to return home. WPC Grimley could stay with her, and a male PC as well, for protection, just in case anybody should try anything. He stood up heavily, just as Aiden came hurriedly into his office.

"Sir, there's been an accident, in Lansdown. A man,

possibly struck by a car. Apparently he fell into the road, straight in front of the car, and the driver didn't have time to avoid him."

"Yes, well? Get to the point, Formby."

"The man who was hit – seems he was being chased by someone and he fits Michael Hamilton's description," Aiden continued excitedly.

"Who, the one who was hit or the one who was doing the chasing?" Harris asked irritably, not really concentrating.

"The one who was hit. He has ID on him and he's been taken to the RUH. I've asked Jed, sorry, PC White, to go in the ambulance with him and to stay with him until we get there."

"What! Is he badly hurt? Is he able to talk?" Harris's bad temper evaporated. He couldn't believe his luck: to have Michael Hamilton fall into their hands like a gift from the gods! Wait, mustn't get too excited, it might not be him.

"Are you absolutely sure it's really him?"

Formby seemed to have no doubts. "Well, apparently he was unconscious when they took him off in the ambulance, but the paramedic told PC White that he thought it was probably just concussion. He's got bandaging on his left shoulder, and his ID confirms his identity." Then as an afterthought, he asked, "What did Lyons have to say? Has he learnt anything new?"

"Hmm, well, yes and no. He thinks he's onto something and has a feeling it's connected with

Mayhims. He wants us to lay off Sutherland and Summers just for now. I can't really tell you any more for the moment, but yes, I should go over. I'll take the girl – she'll be able to identify him soon enough. Did they get the man who was chasing him?"

Harris suddenly thumped his desk, making Aiden jump. "Aha! Didn't Sutherland say that Summers lived at Lansdown? Perhaps there's a link here!"

"Yes, I think he did, but no, they didn't get him. Apparently he ran off as soon as the accident happened, and White and Acroyd didn't arrive on the scene until a few minutes after and had to deal with it all on their own. The witnesses were a bit vague on description too. Seems it all happened very quickly and they were too shocked by the accident itself. Do you want me to go out there, rather than to the hospital?" Aiden tried not to let the disappointment show in his voice.

"No, there's no point. Even if it was Summers, we can't do anything until Lyons gets back, and we don't know why Hamilton should have a reason to be near Summers's house. You can come with me. We'll go straight to the hospital. Just give me a moment to 'phone Hill, tell Anna Hamilton, oh, and we'll take Grimley along. She seems quite sensible and can help with the girl if she gets upset."

As Formby left the room, Harris made the call to Superintendent Hill. He had to update the man – not that he'd been much help so far – but protocol had to be observed. Hill hadn't been at all happy when Lyons had got involved in the case, and had put pressure on Harris to try to get fast results ahead of Lyons.

Hill's reaction was as predictable as ever. "Fine, Harris. I suppose you'd better contact Lyons, tell him what's happened, but then get out to the hospital. If he turns out to be Michael Hamilton, you can arrest him. We already know from the girl's statement that he has admitted responsibility for the death of Professor Hamilton. Charge him with that murder. I know as well as you do that Lyons has some strange ideas. He might be out chasing his Russian spies, but have no doubt about this: Lyons can chase his spy in the sky, but here we want to see some results. If we have a self-confessed murderer lying in some hospital bed, then we will nail him, and if he then turns out to be a bloody Russian spy, well so be it."

Harris returned to his office to quickly contact Lyons on the number he'd given him. The call was answered distractedly, motorway communication clearly not the best, and despite the news that Harris relayed, Lyons did not appear to think it merited a stop on the hard-shoulder.

"Yes, good," his crackling voice replied. "Just go to the hospital and interview him." Static intervened, killing his next words.

"You're breaking up," said Harris impatiently, aware his words couldn't be heard.

Lyons's voice was back, but he sounded remote, concentrating on his driving, Harris an unwelcome distraction.

"Yes, well, see how he is. If he's badly hurt and has to stay in the hospital, leave him be until I get back. Just leave someone with him to make sure he stays there. But if he's well enough to be discharged, arrest him for the murder of Alexander Hamilton. You've got enough evidence to hold him for the moment. Look, my plans have changed slightly. I'm meeting my friend at Heathrow and we're going straight to Russia. The information he has is helpful, but we need more. Should be back tomorrow. And, Harris, remember: keep away from Sutherland and Summers."

The line went dead, leaving Harris staring resentfully at his silent receiver. He sat quietly for a few moments and then replaced the receiver gently, lifted his bulk from the chair and, pulling himself up to his full height, walked purposefully from the room. A stranger might have admired his self-possession, but the two PCs who encountered him in the corridor exchanged the briefest of knowing glances and prepared themselves for some withering comment.

But Harris walked past them without a glance. He was too preoccupied to concern himself with other people. His mind was busy turning over the brief conversation he'd had with Lyons. What did he possibly hope to find in Russia? He must have located the woman – Natalya? Yes, that was her name. He felt so completely impotent in the face of what Lyons had revealed to him earlier; these matters were beyond him.

And then determination grew within him. He would crack this case before Lyons got back. Michael Hamilton had the answers, and he had Michael Hamilton.

He strode into the interview room where WPC Grimley and DI Formby were waiting with Anna. Anna had gone white when they told her why they wanted her to accompany them, and Josie had put her arm around her reassuringly. The poor girl had been through so much recently, Josie almost hoped it wasn't Anna's brother at the hospital, or at least not if he was badly hurt. But she knew that her words of reassurance were just platitudes; she didn't even believe them herself. Whatever happened, Michael Hamilton was in deep trouble. There was too much evidence implicating him in the death of his father, and Anna herself had admitted his guilt.

CHAPTER 18

Somerset
Saturday 18th May, 1996
1.20 p.m.

The white Mercedes stopped outside Richard's house. It'd taken Sutherland a bit longer than he'd expected. John had been morose, trying to make excuses, still blaming himself for Anna's escape, and Carl and Mark had been at each other's throats, bored and quarrelsome. But eventually he'd got them organised and the house ready so that they could take Michael back with them and keep him secure. The others pulled up behind him in John's car.

Sutherland climbed out of his car and knocked on the door briskly, calling out to Richard to identify himself. He was totally taken aback by Richard's bleak expression when he slowly opened the door.

"What? What on earth is the matter with you?" he asked.

When Richard didn't reply but just stood, blocking the doorway, Sutherland looked closer.

"What's happened to your face? You've got a bruise! Is that a black eye forming? Richard, for fuck's sake, what's happened? Let me in the house! I can't stay out here on the doorstep." He turned and indicated to the others to stay in their car.

Richard turned without a word and let him enter the house, leading the way to his kitchen. He sat down heavily on one of the bar stools and, resting his elbows on the breakfast bar, he put his head in his hands and mumbled.

"He's gone, Graham. He got away."

"Who's gone? Richard? Oh, Christ, not Michael! Tell me you haven't let *him* escape as well." Sutherland ran out of the kitchen and up the stairs, staring in horror at the open study door and the empty room.

Slowly, he walked back down the stairs and into the kitchen where Richard still sat with his head in his hands, refusing to look up. Sutherland took a deep breath, trying to keep calm, but his heart was pounding and he could hear the blood rushing in his ears.

"Richard, I need to know, just tell me what happened. Where is he? Why are you just sitting here? Why aren't you out looking for him? Why didn't you 'phone me? I could have brought the others over sooner to help find him."

"Graham." Richard looked up almost pleadingly, all his earlier belligerence gone, words falling over themselves. "Graham, just after you left I heard a noise, a thump from the study. I thought he'd collapsed so I went up to check. He hadn't looked very good earlier, but he was behind the door, he had my brass paperweight, the room was dark. I didn't see him. He hit me on the back of the head with it. I almost fell but as I turned round, he threw it straight at my face and then I did lose my balance. I didn't think he'd be strong enough to even be able to lift it himself."

Sutherland just stared at him, speechless.

"He got out of the house, but I was right behind him. I had my gun, I could have stopped him, he was starting to slow down, he hadn't got very far, but then, well, then…"

Sutherland found his voice. "Then? Then what, Richard? OK, this is a total disaster, but I need to know what happened."

"He ran, well, fell, really, right in front of a car. I think the car must have hit him. I don't even know if he was badly hurt. I had to hide, there were too many people, and then there were police, ambulances..."

"Wait." Sutherland held up his hand. "Did they put him in an ambulance?"

"Well, yes, I think so. Yes, they did. I didn't dare get too close."

"OK." Sutherland felt eerily calm. "Did anyone see you? Could anyone identify you?"

"No, I don't think so. I kept out of the way. They were all looking at Michael lying on the road, and fussing over the driver of the car."

Still feeling strangely calm, Sutherland said, "OK,

they'll probably have taken him to the RUH – we'll need to try to find out. But if it was very serious, he'd have been taken to Frenchay. But we can't do anything right now. See if it's on the news later. Did he have ID on him, do you know?"

"No, well, I don't know. Maybe."

Sutherland's calm deserted him as he muttered to himself, "Oh shit, this is an absolute nightmare. I can't think straight." But he pulled himself together, saying more briskly, "Right, I'll send the others back to John's place. They can all stay there for now. Richard, you and I are going over to my house now – and I mean *right* now – and there we'll stay, for the evening, for the night in fact. If the police come looking for you here, they won't find you. If Michael does say anything, they won't be able to prove that he was ever in your house."

"But they've already got the girl and now they'll have Michael as well. They'll both tell them what really happened! We're finished, Graham." Richard's voice rose alarmingly.

"Calm down, Richard, and get a grip on yourself. This is totally regrettable." (And here he did glare at Richard.) "In fact, it's a major fucking setback, but we are not finished." He continued tersely. "It can only be their word against ours. Anna Hamilton could be lying to protect her brother, and he could be making the whole story up. There's no way that either of them can produce any solid proof of what happened, especially now that we've got the tape. And I've taken the precaution of putting Michael's fingerprints all over the gun that Carl used to kill the officer. And yes, I wiped Carl's prints off first. We know Michael's prints must have been on the gun that killed Alexander, and the police have got that gun too. We can arrange for Carl's gun to be 'found', if and when we need to. The police might be suspicious – indeed they'd be a bit stupid not to question the fact that Michael was in the vicinity of your house – but he could have been in this area for any reason. Maybe he came to threaten you. They can't prove anything, and the fact that Michael disappeared after killing Alexander doesn't bode well for him." He stood up and said sharply, "Now come on, pull yourself together and get an overnight bag packed. We need to get out of here. I'll just go and tell the others to go back to John's place and then I'll go and wipe any prints from the study. Did he go into any other room?"

Richard shook his head morosely. "No, but he would have touched the bannisters going up and down the stairs, and the front door catch." He stood up shakily and for the first time Graham saw the half-empty whisky bottle and empty glass on the work surface next to him.

"Oh, for God's sake, Richard, getting drunk won't get us out of the mess that you've got us into. You need to keep a clear head. We have to plan how to get Michael back as I do need him to re-install that data," he sighed heavily. "Well, I suppose I should be thankful that at least I've got the tape now."

CHAPTER 19

Somerset
Saturday 18th May, 1996
1.20 p.m.

Formby took the wheel on the short journey to the hospital. Harris's mood was changing already. His resolution and momentary euphoria were evaporating as he weighed the consequences of the day's events. So what if he did now have the man he'd been searching for? He still couldn't do much until Lyons returned. Well, he smiled humourlessly to himself, what was he worrying about? He'd been told to arrest Michael Hamilton if he was well enough. So be it, he'd do just that, and if the bastard was still unconscious, he'd just wait and arrest him later. But something just didn't feel right.

If the world was beginning to hang heavily on Detective Chief Inspector Harris, it was nothing compared to how Anna felt. Her whole mind was in conflict. She hoped beyond hope that it was Michael at the hospital, but then there was the anxiety that his being in the accident had created, and she didn't want it to be him, not if he was badly hurt. She couldn't separate her confused feelings.

Self-doubt pervaded her whole being: her father lost, a father she had loved but never really understood, a distant father who had never really returned the love she had given him and needed for herself, but somehow, despite that, she'd managed to maintain her sense of self- worth. She'd tried so hard to love him, always thinking that she understood his difference from other people, set apart by his brilliance. Now she had to face her own inadequacies, and now she had to accept that she would never have the chance to express her feelings to her father. He was dead, she could never question his remoteness, nor challenge his indifference. She was left to feel that her unquestioning acceptance of his behaviour towards her had been misplaced. She would never be able to express the deep hurt and anger that she now felt towards him.

And Michael, who had at least shown her what it could be like to love, who'd given her the chance to express the love she had within herself, had betrayed her even further and had deceived her. He had lied about his past, his present, and then, finally, admitted responsibility for the death of their father without any explanation. If he were to die, as their father had done (and Anna had to face that possibility) she might never know the truth; she might never be able to understand, and then her love for him might also die. Then she would be more alone than she had ever been in her life.

Josie looked at Anna with concern as they walked across the hospital car park. Anna's quietness and preoccupation worried her. After that initial moment of shock on hearing that Michael was probably the victim of the accident, Anna had shown little reaction. And that, Josie felt, was uncharacteristic. She felt she'd got to know Anna reasonably well during the short but intense time they'd been together, and she was pretty convinced that Anna was near breaking point. She wished she could talk to Aiden about it, but he was preoccupied; his attention concentrated on trying to fit the jigsaw pieces of the case together in his head. *Anyway*, she thought as she mentally shrugged her shoulders, *what chance of getting him alone to discuss anything? Harris was quiet too*, she thought, glancing across at his heavy profile as he marched between the cars. He hadn't even displayed any of his usual arrogance; even absentmindedly holding the door open for her and Anna to get out of the car.

They walked inside the foyer of the hospital, the clinical antiseptic atmosphere causing Anna to falter, to want to turn back. She stopped abruptly, looking desperately around. They'd entered via the casualty department – its neat orderly chairs full, it seemed, of sick and injured people sitting quietly – but then a child with blood pouring down his leg began screaming in his mother's arms as she spoke urgently to the calm receptionist behind the desk. An old man, spitting and cursing, being half-dragged, half-restrained by a neat orderly, tried to engage the other patients in his deranged conversations. She almost expected to see Michael lying in a chair, dying quietly in the corner for want of attention.

Josie took her arm and gently led her down the corridor towards the lifts, signs everywhere, all pointing to the various departments with the unpronounceable names, preoccupied doctors in white coats scurrying through doors and busy nurses in blue uniforms wafting briskly by. They reached the desk that served the ward where Michael had been taken. The nurse listened impassively as Harris announced their identity, and then immediately summoned a distinguished-looking, grey-haired man.

"Good afternoon," he greeted them politely, introducing himself as Henry Barnes. "I have been expecting you. If you'd like to come this way. I'd like to have a quick word with you before I take you to see the patient."

And without further word he led them to a small room at the end of the corridor, closing the door behind him and leaning his back against it as he motioned for his guests to be seated.

Harris spoke brusquely. "We will need to identify the patient. We don't yet know if he is the man we are looking for."

Dr Barnes spoke gently. "The man who was brought in had his wallet on his person, containing his driving licence and credit cards. There would seem to be no doubt that he is Michael Hamilton. Now, if I may ask, are any of you relatives?"

Anna nodded dumbly as Harris spoke on her behalf. "Yes, this is Miss Hamilton, Michael Hamilton's sister. She is his only relative. I am Detective Chief Inspector Harris, this is Detective Inspector Formby and this is Police Constable Grimley. As you are aware, we are very eager to speak to Michael Hamilton in connection with an urgent police matter. Could you tell me how he is please and then we would like to be taken to see him."

Henry Barnes hesitated. He looked from Anna's bent head to Harris's aggressive face and replied politely, but firmly. "Chief Inspector, I would prefer to speak to Miss Hamilton alone first, and then I will take you to see Mr Hamilton."

A small trickle of fear ran down Josie's spine. Michael Hamilton couldn't be dead, could he? Why was the doctor being so evasive? She glanced apprehensively at Aiden, who raised his eyebrows back to her as if to say, *I don't know any more than you do.*

Harris opened his mouth to speak, to protest perhaps, to bluster even, but before he could utter a word, Anna spoke in a flat emotionless voice.

"Doctor, you may speak to me with them here. I don't mind."

Josie moved closer to her, but Anna ignored her, sitting small in the chair. She continued to gaze down at her hands as Barnes looked across at her with some concern. He crossed the room and sat down opposite Anna, leaning forward and speaking to her averted face, keeping his voice low and controlled.

"Miss Hamilton, your brother was brought in to us as a result of a road traffic accident. He was unconscious when he was admitted, and he has not yet recovered consciousness." He paused, as if waiting for Anna to speak. When she remained silent, he frowned slightly and continued slowly. "Head injuries are very unpredictable. He is, as I said, still unconscious, but his automatic responses appear unimpaired. He is responding to stimuli, which gives me hope that he is just concussed and will recover consciousness in a short while with no lasting ill effects."

Barnes tried to smile reassuringly, and then paused again, obviously trying to choose his words carefully. He continued to look steadily at Anna but gave a slight sideways glance at Harris, Aiden and Josie, then took a deep breath before continuing.

"However, there is another problem. He has an injury to his left shoulder that we have X-rayed. The X-ray shows that your brother has what appears to be a fragment of metal lodged in that shoulder. Someone has made a rather clumsy attempt at cleaning and patching him up, but unfortunately didn't feel the need to remove the fragment itself that seems to be embedded in the tissue around his shoulder joint."

Harris could contain himself no longer, and leaning forward aggressively, he glared at Barnes. "Doctor, I have to tell you that this fragment of metal is actually a bullet fragment, and Miss Hamilton's brother is a person of interest in our enquiries into a very serious incident. We need to question him as soon as possible."

Barnes appeared to be completely unfazed at being told that his patient had a bullet wound. Instead, he looked squarely at Harris and replied impassively. "Chief Inspector, I quite understand that you have your job to do, and no doubt Miss Hamilton's brother can help you in some way with your enquiries, but I also have my job to do, and at the moment my priority is to get my patient better."

As Harris looked ready to argue, he continued repressively. "Whatever the rights and wrongs of the situation, that young man would be in no fit state to answer any questions even if he were conscious, which he isn't. I assume you would prefer to interview him—"

He stopped mid-speech and looked apologetically at Anna. Josie thought that he'd been just about to say, 'alive rather than dead'. But if he had, he'd obviously thought better of it for he continued carefully. "If you don't allow me to treat him, I doubt he will be in a fit state to answer any questions for quite some time to come." And then turning to Anna he said, "Miss Hamilton, the fragment of bullet in his shoulder has set up an infection, which in his present weakened condition could, I'm afraid, become quite serious if left unattended. Unfortunately, because he obviously did not get medical attention at the right time, the wound has closed over the fragment which makes it rather difficult to treat. I really would like your permission to operate and remove the fragment before the wound becomes any more infected. There is a risk attached – he is in a weak state now but he would appear to have been fit and healthy before this incident, so I think he'll be able to withstand an operation. Do I have your permission?"

Anna didn't reply immediately. She looked across at Josie. Never had she missed her friends so much; never had she felt more alone. If only she'd been able to call upon one of them to be with her now. If only circumstances hadn't forced her into that police station, away from her home, away from her life.

"Miss Hamilton," continued Dr Barnes gently, "it is likely that the trauma that your brother has suffered recently has contributed to his present coma. I've seen cases where, when the body has had enough, the mind just shuts down. I need to get that infection under control before it turns into something a lot more serious, if it hasn't already."

Anna was looking for support from Josie but she wasn't consciously letting her know her need. Josie had been watching her the whole time and she understood the unspoken appeal. She leant across and took one of Anna's cold hands within her own.

"Come on, let's go and see Michael. You can make your decision then."

Anna smiled gratefully at Josie. She didn't feel quite

so alone now. Standing up, she turned to Dr Barnes, saying, "Yes. May I see my brother now please?"

"Of course," he responded, relieved to see a spark of animation return to her. When she saw her brother, she'd understand the need for prompt medical attention. "Come this way."

Without specific invitation, the rest followed him as he led the way down the corridor towards the room where Michael had been taken. Police instructions had been to place him away from the main ward, and luckily a private room had become available after its previous occupant had unfortunately died before her treatment was completed.

Michael lay under the covers as peacefully as if he were sleeping naturally, a monitor bleeping quietly in the background, wires attached to his chest and a drip attached to one hand.

A young nurse, who had been deep in animated conversation with PC Jed White, came forward as they entered.

"No change," she reported to Dr Barnes, who smiled kindly at her and suggested she took a break for a while. Harris nodded at PC White and likewise dismissed him, staring across the room at Michael, his expression inscrutable. Aiden and Josie exchanged glances as they too gazed at the still figure in the bed. So, this was the man they'd all been so focused on finding. Somehow, it seemed almost like an anticlimax. He didn't look like he could be responsible for two murders.

Anna sat down in the chair next to Michael's bed and looked at him sadly. Her heart sank as she saw how much worse he looked than when she'd seen him just that morning. His eyes were closed, the dark shadows showing like bruises below his eyelashes, his cheekbones jutting out as his pale skin stretched tightly across his face under the dark stubble. She touched his hand gently, feeling its dryness, sensing a slight response. But she didn't speak to him. Instead, she spoke to Dr Barnes who stood silently watching.

"Yes, operate, do whatever is necessary. I'll sign the forms. I am his only relative."

"Thank you, Miss Hamilton," said Dr Barnes as he took a form out of the folder clipped to the foot of the bed. "And can I just ask: has your brother, to your knowledge, ever had an anaesthetic before? And if so, did he suffer any adverse reaction?"

"Er, yes, he has. He broke his leg quite badly some years ago, but no, he didn't have any problems with the anaesthetic. He had the treatment here so there should be a record of it somewhere," replied Anna as she took the form and blindly signed.

Harris suddenly came to life and pushed forward impatiently, leaning over Michael and breathing heavily.

"Michael Hamilton, can you hear me? Wake up! I have to talk to you about the death of your father! Can you hear me?"

Michael's fingers twitched slightly within Anna's

hold, but Dr Barnes had moved forward towards the bed. Looking at Harris, he spoke firmly. "Chief Inspector, please step back, you will stress my patient. He will be able to speak to you when he is well enough. At the moment, he is in my care and he urgently needs my treatment. I can assure you he isn't going anywhere right now, apart from the operating theatre."

Harris scowled but stepped back.

Then Aiden spoke for the first time. "Doctor, it would help our enquiries if we could examine the bullet fragment that you remove from him as it is vital evidence."

Harris shrugged his shoulders resignedly. Damn, why hadn't he thought of that? He frowned. He'd been so sure that as soon as he got to Michael Hamilton, he'd get all the answers. He was still sure of that, but the man had to be able to speak to him first. And Formby was right: they still had to consider the circumstances. It was so easy to lose sight of the facts. Even if Michael Hamilton had killed his father – no, not even *if* as it was a certainty that he had killed him – what reason had he had to commit murder? They were really not much further on with their enquiries, but one thing was for sure: arresting him now was hardly the answer. As the doctor had said, at the moment he wasn't going anywhere other than the operating table.

"I will certainly keep the bullet fragment for your examination," replied Dr Barnes. "And now, if you don't mind, I'd like to get on as soon as possible." He turned to Anna questioningly, holding his hand out for the form. "Miss Hamilton, with your permission?"

Anna stood up with a last look at Michael. "Yes," she said, handing him the form, "go ahead." And then her eyes filled with tears. "Please take care of him. Bring him safely back to me. I'll stay in the hospital until after the operation, if that's all right?"

Barnes smiled at her gently. "Of course, we'll take the greatest care of him." And then, more briskly, "There's a visitors' café, or there are vending machines where you can get a drink or snack, and take them to the waiting room. Just ask at reception, they'll point you in the right direction. I'll send someone to find you once your brother is back from theatre."

They were dismissed. As they walked out into the corridor, Harris spoke briefly to Aiden, having consulted his watch and realising it was nearly two thirty p.m. He'd decided it was pointless to wait any longer. Hamilton wasn't going to be in any fit state to talk for a while.

"Formby, stay in the hospital until he comes back from his operation. Let me know if he's conscious. If he is, I'll come over, otherwise I'll send someone over to watch him and you can get off."

"Do you seriously think they'll try to get at him?" questioned Aiden.

"No, not really, but I don't want to take any chances," replied Harris brusquely and, turning to Josie, he said, "Grimley, stay here with Miss Hamilton for now. I don't want her to go back to her cottage, although I don't think she wants to go back there anyway. She'll probably want to stay the night here. If so, well and good. We'll get someone over here to babysit her and you can go home as well. But I don't want her left on her own at any time. So, if she does insist on going home, you'll need to get at least two officers to stay over with her." Turning back to Aiden, he added, "Formby, you can arrange that for her."

Aiden and Josie exchanged glances. Oh well, another few hours to kill. It came with the job; exciting stuff, sitting in hospital corridors drinking undrinkable vended coffee, but an order was an order, and there was Anna to consider.

"I'd like to 'phone a couple of my friends," Anna said as they approached the reception area. "They're probably wondering where I am and they might have tried to contact me."

And I need to hear their voices, she thought, *to reassure myself that I'm still me, that it's just circumstances that are making me feel so unreal and detached, so distanced from life.*

"We don't want to alert anyone to the fact that Michael is here. We've asked all the staff not to give out that information. Is it possible that you could wait until tomorrow?" asked Aiden, taking charge.

Anna felt almost mutinous; they didn't trust her. But then she suddenly understood what he was saying: they believed her and they wanted to protect Michael. She looked at Josie and softened. This was, after all, the person who'd been kind enough to take care of Brian. She nodded her compliance, and then had a sudden thought about Brian.

"Brian," she said. "I'd completely forgotten about him! Will you be OK with him for another night"

Josie grimaced to herself. That wretched cat, shut up in her flat! Well, she'd left him a box filled with dirt and hoped against hope that he'd used it this time.

"Yes, he'll be fine with me," she said with more enthusiasm than she felt. "I left him plenty of food and he can't get out. I'll be back to check on him later myself anyway."

CHAPTER 20

Russia
Saturday 18th May, 1996
8.00 p.m.

Alistair Lyons was tired. The day had all but exhausted him. He really was getting past the age to be gallivanting around in the same way that he had when he was younger. Today he'd been up at the crack of dawn to drive to Bath, then back to London (well, Heathrow) to board a plane bound for Sheremetyevo Airport.

As he lay back in his seat (a British Airways flight, not Aeroflot, thank goodness) sipping his vodka, he had to admit to himself that, tired or not, he missed the excitement of those younger days. The spirit of adventure still burned deep within him.

He glanced at Jeremy Colton who was sitting next to him, gazing pensively out of the window. They had talked non-stop from their first meeting at the airport and into the first hour of the flight. Now both needed time to think. This Michael Hamilton, as he called himself, who now seemed to have landed so conveniently in Harris's lap, had undoubtedly killed Alexander, and the reasons for that lay somewhere in the past. Of that they were both in accord. But when it came to his real identity and his possible motives for killing Alexander, their opinions differed.

Following Alistair's call, Jeremy had immediately driven over to his offices and let himself into the old archives room with its ancient shelving. Dusty boxes encased those old secrets, and the faded and musty papers which, if leaked, would once have spelt out a KGB execution for many an apparently innocent tourist. But the boxes on these shelves contained history now. Time had moved on and political situations had changed – in name, at least. Perestroika and Glasnost had been born and the Soviet Union was no more. The men who owned these names should be safe now. Indeed, most of them now were the innocent tourists that they had once pretended to be. But yet the threat remained. The enemy might have changed his clothing and smiled a more Westernised smile, but he remained as deadly as ever.

Surprisingly, it hadn't taken him long to find the information he needed. Alexander had been a great help to his country in the early '60s. Firstly, as a student with a Russian girlfriend, he'd been able to travel freely over to Moscow with her and he'd got very friendly with her father. No doors had been closed to him. In his short time as a postgraduate at Moscow University, he had served his country well. The information, albeit only in terms of his academic discipline, had been of great use to the scientists in England. And when he'd left Russia and his relationship with the girl had ended, he had still remained on good terms with her parents, visiting them on many an occasion and never returning without some useful information. Alexander's name had figured strongly on those lists, up to the time when he and Claire had decided to start a family. Jeremy remembered it well; he himself having been called into the meeting to help his superiors to try to persuade Alexander to continue their work. But Alexander had been adamant. His new wife was pregnant and he was not prepared to allow the risks that his activities carried to come anywhere near his family. He had insisted that no contact should be made with him ever again, and reluctantly his superiors had agreed. Even they could not force a man to spy if he had no wish to do so.

And that, as far as Jeremy was concerned, had been that. Until Lyons's telephone call, he hadn't really given Alexander much thought. But as he'd looked through the papers – initially to find the name of the Russian girl for Alistair – he'd come across other information that he either hadn't known about at the time, or hadn't then thought significant. Perhaps it was simply that with the knowledge of Alexander's death at the hands of a son who had been dead for thirty years, he was looking for anomalies. Alexander had not worked alone in Russia – he'd been the handler for a young dissident Russian biologist by the name of Pyotr Karev. The information, which the young Russian had provided to MI6, had come via Alexander, and was deemed of great value by his superiors. What struck Jeremy as slightly strange was that all contact with Karev had abruptly ceased in 1965. It was as if he'd vanished without a trace and, more significantly, no one, least of all Alexander himself, appeared to have made any comment on his disappearance. There was of course nothing strange in the sudden disappearance of a Russian dissident at that time, but the lack of comment was most unusual. MI6 might happily expose its agents to the greatest of dangers, but some comment on their fate was usual. Admittedly, it didn't seem that Karev had ever been to England himself as all his information had come secondhand via Alexander.

Jeremy had pondered the significance of this as Lyons was negotiating the perils of the M4 on a busy Saturday afternoon. Deciding to delve further into the papers to find an answer, he'd instead been astonished to find Sutherland's name linked constantly with Alexander's. He'd known of their friendship, but had assumed it was based upon their shared days at university and more diverse interests and hobbies rather than their shared MI6 connection. What he hadn't realised was that Sutherland, who had little contact with the scientific world at that time, had also been heavily involved in Alexander's gathering of information from Karev, and had actually accompanied Alexander on several occasions to stay with Natalya's parents. Why then had he denied any knowledge of Natalya to Lyons?

Jeremy's mind worked in complicated circles and he was incapable of approaching any problem from a simplistic viewpoint. He wouldn't have survived for five minutes in his profession without this ability.

His theory, which he had carefully expounded to Alistair Lyons over his mobile 'phone as Lyons drove along the busy motorway, was to him the obvious solution: Sutherland was the father of this imposter, Michael Hamilton. Whilst Alexander had been getting involved with the Spanish girl, Sutherland had seized his chance and made a move on Natalya. She had accepted him on the rebound while undoubtedly still in love with Alexander.

"But I thought she'd become involved with some Russian chap?" objected Alistair, carefully avoiding the car that had unexpectedly swerved out in front of him.

"Yes, and who told you that?" asked Jeremy smugly and, without waiting for an answer, added, "Sutherland did, of course!"

"But why would he come to the UK and take on the identity of Alexander's dead son? Why on earth would Alexander let him do that, and bring him into his home six years ago if he was Sutherland's child? And why the hell should he kill Alexander?"

Jeremy smiled. This was what he liked best: the most complicated solution to a simple question.

"Because, my friend, maybe Alexander thought that he was his child. Let's not be naïve – Natalya could easily have been sleeping with both of them at the same time, or maybe she lied about the dates and told Alexander the child was his." His smile widened although Alistair couldn't see it. "You know, we both know that when we were young, Graham Sutherland hadn't quite got his sexual preferences in order, although from what you've said it seems like he's made up his mind now."

"Oh, come on, Jeremy, what difference does it make whether he was or is bi-sexual or not. Lots of people are. Your theories are too farfetched for words. If Sutherland thought our Michael Hamilton was his son, well, can you explain why he couldn't bring his son into this country in his own name? Why bother passing him off as Alexander and Donna's child? And if Alexander thought the child was his, why not bring him into the country openly as Natalya's child? Why go to all the trouble of passing him off as a dead baby?"

"Well, maybe Sutherland was too afraid to admit to whoever was his current lover that he might have fathered a child, but still wanted the boy to be near him. And Natalya perhaps agreed. It must be a better life in the UK than present-day Russia. He's probably selling to the Russians. You said yourself you thought there was some dodgy deal with Mayhims. So he persuaded Alexander to bring him to England. Alexander might have agreed, thinking that the boy was his. Maybe the real birth certificate shows Sutherland as the father, so Natalya and Sutherland probably made up some story to convince Alexander to use the dead child's birth certificate. Or maybe Natalya registered the boy without a father, making him purely Russian. Perhaps he couldn't get a passport – we all know how difficult that still is over there. And as for why he murdered Alexander, well, I would imagine that somehow Alexander found out what had really happened and threatened to expose or harm Natalya and Sutherland, and Michael – or whatever his name is – killed him first."

Alistair had smiled affectionately at the 'phone, before saying, "Jeremy, you are a classic. That is probably the most convoluted theory that I've ever heard!"

"Well, you know what they say: truth is stranger than fiction. Have you got a better idea?"

"Yes, I have, and a much simpler one: Michael is the son of Alexander and Natalya. Alexander brought him over to help him with his work, discovered that Michael was secretly working with Sutherland for the Russians and tried to kill him, but Michael being younger and much stronger retaliated and killed Alexander instead."

"And the false birth certificate?"

"Well, I'll borrow from your theory there. Natalya registered him as illegitimate and he couldn't get a passport easily so they took the easy option. After all, the chances of being found out were quite remote. I don't suppose any of them could have imagined what was going to happen."

"Well, there's only one person who can put us

straight. I think we're both in agreement that Natalya Miloslavskaya has the answer, and I say we go over there to confront her."

"And how exactly do you propose that we find her?" Alistair had asked mockingly. "Or do you imagine that she'll still be living at the same address, waiting for us to call? We are, you know, talking about events that happened some thirty years or so ago."

And so the call had ended. Alistair had continued along the M4, his mind busy with his thoughts, interrupted within the hour by another call from Jeremy.

"Alistair, don't come all the way into the centre of London. I'll meet you at Heathrow. I've collected your passport from Jenny and got a flight and a hotel booked for us."

"For God's sake, Jeremy, that's a bit extreme. Can't we talk about this first?" Alistair had been prepared for immediate action earlier, but this had taken him by surprise.

Jeremy had sounded almost childishly excited on the 'phone. "No. Listen, Alistair, I made a couple of assumptions."

"Oh, yes, and what assumptions might those have been?"

"Well, I started from the simplest perspective". He couldn't see Alistair's look of amused disbelief. "And I figured that Natalya would probably have retained her maiden name and wouldn't have moved far from her home. I also assumed that she'd have continued her career but with the limitations of bringing up a child on her own."

"Big assumptions, Jeremy."

Jeremy sounded hurt. "No need to be so sceptical. As it turned out I was right: Natalya Miloslavskaya is living within twenty miles of her childhood home and working in the microbiology department at Moscow State University. Most people would have predicted a greater future for her, had it not been for the fact that apparently she has remained unmarried and has brought up a son single-handedly. Not such an easy feat in Moscow in recent years."

"And that son – would he be our elusive Michael?" Alistair asked with a smile, just as a lorry overtook, causing the car to pull suddenly, making him grip the wheel and almost lose Jeremy's next words.

"Well, yes, I'm sure he is, but he's not called Michael: her son's name is Nikolai, and strangely enough, after an apparently blameless childhood and school record that would have left most people speechless with admiration, this paragon of virtue went on to study microbiology at Leningrad University, graduated six years ago with the highest honours and then almost immediately chose to drop out, take to a life of drugs on the streets and was heard of no more..." His voice faded to return more strongly. "Quite a coincidence, wouldn't you say?"

"He's called Nikolai, you say? Well, he's not named after either of them, then. Nothing to go on. Could be either," said Alistair.

Jeremy wouldn't give up. "Not necessarily. Maybe his middle name might hold a clue?"

"Well," Alistair smiled, "what is it? You're not going to tell me it's Graham are you? What is the Russian for Graham anyway?"

"I don't know."

"Well, what is his middle name then?"

"That's just it: I don't know what his middle name is." As Alistair burst into laughter, Jeremy continued defensively. "It was just a thought. I don't really think the name thing means anything. They could have called him any name they liked."

"Well, I guess there's only one way to find out."

And so the decision had been agreed to visit Natalya. Alistair's sense of adventure had been activated then to the point that when Harris contacted him minutes later with the news that they had Michael (or Nikolai, or whoever he might be), and that he might soon be available for questioning, he had no doubts that a visit to Natalya was still the best solution. After all, the son might lie but he felt sure that Natalya would tell the truth.

It was too late to call on Natalya by the time the taxi had deposited their weary selves at the Hotel Rosja. Jeremy looked with less than hopeful anticipation at its forbidding exterior, but perhaps this might be the one hotel in Moscow that would at least be warm. The night air, having only managed to reach a maximum of nine

Celsius during the day, was distinctly chilly, and he was familiar with Russian hotels: heating, unless you paid a premium, was never high on the agenda. He shivered slightly as he followed Alistair's cigarette smoke into the foyer. Despite the earlier storms, London had definitely been warm for May, whereas Moscow would appear to be compensating. The bleak interior did little to raise his spirits, or his temperature. He wished he'd packed warmer clothes, and looking at Alistair's back, he guessed he felt the same. His friend appeared to have shrunk as his muscles contracted in a vain attempt to conserve warmth.

They exchanged a brief gloomy look as the dour clerk checked their passports. If Moscow, on this brief encounter, was representative of what was happening in Russia as a whole, there wasn't much hope. The twin-bedded room into which they were directed had little but bare essentials, and no apparent form of heating apart from a large rusty radiator in the corner. Alistair rested one hand lightly on it, and as quickly pulled it back as it seemed to have been filled with ice cubes.

"Well," said Jeremy breaking the silence. "I hope you weren't expecting luxuries. This was all I could get at such short notice, and it is only for one night."

Alistair shrugged. No point in complaining. They were here now and it wasn't meant to be a holiday after all.

"I suggest we get ourselves a drink and something to eat before turning in. What do you say?"

The hotel boasted a small bar, open all night, with snacks available at a price. They ate what they could: black bread and some unidentifiable bean stew. Better not to even attempt to guess at its contents, but at least it was warm. There was little incentive to continue their discussions over the case. Their spirits were depressed by their bleak surroundings, and both felt a keen sense of anticlimax. Perhaps tomorrow would bring more enthusiasm.

CHAPTER 21

Russia
Sunday 19th May, 1996
7.30 a.m.

The following morning, Alistair and Jeremy made their way down to the hotel restaurant (if indeed the few scattered little tables and chairs and the unprepossessing food counter could be called a restaurant). They ordered a bowl of kasha each and some black bread rolls (at least there was butter this morning) and a pot of black coffee. The young waiter brought their meal over to them. At least this boy was friendlier than the desk clerk had been last night. As he poured their coffee, Jeremy decided to test his rather rusty Russian and asked if the waiter knew of Natalya Miloslavskaya. The waiter look rather confused at Jeremy's attempts and replied in very broken English.

"No, I know not it."

Jeremy continued, this time in English, in the very slow painful way that English people often adopt when addressing foreigners. "And... Nikolai Miloslavsky...

Do… you… know… of… him?"

The waiter shook his head and smiled, anxious to please, though obviously keen to get back to his duties. But Jeremy had one last question for him. Speaking more quickly now he said, "And Boris Miloslavsky. Do you know of him?"

Neither Alistair nor Jeremy were prepared for the look of fear that passed over the waiter's face. He stared at them for a long minute, as if trying to assess if they were the enemy, and then probably deciding that they were just two blundering Englishmen. He spoke so quietly and quickly that they had to strain to catch his words.

"No, no, Boris Miloslavsky, no, you not need. He oligarch, he powerful man, he hurt you, he… no, not good. You go home, not safe you stay, not ask." And pocketing the tip that Jeremy hastily thrust into his hand, he scurried off without a backward glance.

They stared at each other in surprise for a moment and then Jeremy nodded. "Ah, yes of course, makes sense." He took a sip of his bitter coffee and suppressed a grimace. "Ugh, what do they put into this stuff? Yes, Natalya's father always had connections in the right places. Of course he'd be part of the new corrupt regime and he'd have taken advantage of the new post-Soviet privatisation. These oligarchs, they're not popular with the Russian public but they're quite influential in modern-day Russian politics. Boris Miloslavsky is probably sitting at the right hand of Yeltsin. Bet you any money that our Michael Hamilton, aka Nikolai Miloslavsky, is working with his grandfather. Perhaps Natalya has no idea. Maybe she's not involved at all, and perhaps she genuinely believes her son actually is living on the streets. Looks like this Boris Miloslavsky might hold the key to our puzzle and this Nikolai is the go-between involved in the corruption with Sutherland and his grandfather." He finished in a downhearted tone. "The address we have for Natalya Miloslavskaya is in quite a poor neighbourhood from what I could see; not somewhere you'd expect to find the daughter of a wealthy, influential post-Soviet oligarch. Perhaps she is estranged from her father and her own son and won't be able to help us."

"Come on, finish your coffee and stop your speculations. Guesswork will get us nowhere. Let's go and confront the lady and ask her, shall we?" said Alistair briskly, standing up and stubbing out his cigarette in the overflowing ashtray.

After collecting their overnight bags, they asked the morose desk clerk to book a taxi for them and went out into the bitterly cold morning to wait for it.

The taxi driver stopped outside a blank concrete-faced apartment block. Alistair and Jeremy asked him to wait for them, and stood outside for a moment. Jeremy checked the address again: yes, this was correct, this was where Natalya Miloslavskaya lived. Up the concrete steps they trudged. Amazingly, her flat was right in front of them so no searching required.

As Alistair knocked heavily on the neatly painted door, a beacon of cleanliness compared to its shabby neighbours, it occurred to Jeremy that perhaps his conceptions hadn't been too far out. If Natalya lived in such an impoverished apartment block, she could well be estranged from her affluent and powerful father.

Alistair was preparing to knock again when the door was flung open to reveal a slight woman standing in the gloom of the hallway. She nodded at him, and then quickly stepped backwards as she noticed Jeremy standing behind Alistair. Suddenly, she moved forward and pushed past them to look down the concrete steps at their taxi, waiting in the morning mist. That seemed to satisfy her so she nodded again and indicated for them to follow as she turned and led the way back into her apartment.

Alistair looked puzzled, turning to Jeremy. "Is she expecting us?"

Equally perplexed, Jeremy shook his head and followed Alistair down the hallway.

They walked through the open door into a large sitting room, tastefully decorated but strangely barren of any personal possessions. Alistair's first thoughts were of pity. *How the Russians live,* he thought. *I knew it was bad, but to have nothing; none of the creature comforts that we take so much for granted.* And then, as his perceptions sharpened, he realised that this was a room deliberately made bare. Two large suitcases and some hand luggage stood on the floorboards. Nothing remained to make this room homely.

Natalya had moved straight across to the largest suitcase and now turned to face them expectantly, gripping its handle and lifting it with an ease that belied her stature.

If time could stand still for Alistair, it did in that moment that Natalya turned round to them and the pale morning sun broke through the mist and shone through the window directly onto her face. She smiled, clearly under the assumption that the taxi they had come in was the one she was expecting. Alistair recalled the faded black and white photograph; all that Jeremy had been able to produce of the Natalya who had so enchanted Alexander Hamilton. This Natalya, more than thirty years on, was the same person: her rich, abundant auburn hair, some silver streaks showing now, was still beautiful; her eyes, slanting slightly, were as dark as winter nights; her face, perfectly formed with high cheekbones, the skin without its youthful bloom now, was still stretched firmly across one side of her face, but the other side... he looked away, unable to meet her eyes. One side of her face was lined by deep scars that stretched in hideous parallel lines from her cheekbone to her jawbone, cutting deep down through the flesh, almost seeming to separate one side of her face from the other.

Jeremy was the first to recover his composure. With an ease that Alistair could only recognise later, he spoke slowly to Natalya in Russian, probably explaining that they were not about to drive her to wherever it was that she desired, and presumably to request her to speak in English, for she put the suitcase back down onto the floor and replied almost immediately in accented, but fluent English.

"I am so sorry. I mistook you for my taxi driver. I did wonder why it should take two of you." And then she smiled, a lovely crooked smile, natural enough although it had the effect of pulling her scars more tightly across her face. "You must excuse me. I am not in the habit of inviting strange men into my home. This is a mistake, you have come to the wrong address, and I must ask you to leave."

Jeremy spoke again, quickly, to forestall her as she briskly turned to lead them out of the room.

"Please, Miss Miloslavskaya, we would like to speak to you about your son, Nikolai."

She turned slowly to face them, no expression in her dark eyes.

"I don't know how you know my name, but I have nothing to say about my son. I don't know who you are, or why you are here, and I don't care, but my son left home years ago, and I do not know where he is. Now, would you please go? As you can see, I am about to travel."

Alistair found his tongue, his initial shock and embarrassment fading as he began to see Natalya rather than her scarred face.

"Where do you plan to go? Miss Miloslavskaya, I

must tell you, we have reason to believe we know where your son is, and we have some questions to ask you that may help us with our enquiries."

"You cannot know where my son is. He lives on the streets – drugs. He is no longer my son, I do not even speak of him. Now, I am asking you again, please leave." And she turned her back on them to stare out through the window, presumably to look for her own expected taxi.

Alistair glanced across at Jeremy, shrugged his shoulders, and said briskly, "Well, we have reason to believe that your son is living in England under the assumed name of Michael Hamilton—"

He got no further. Natalya whirled round, eyes wide with fear, her face white.

"No, this is not true, you cannot say this. You must not say this! Who are you? Why are you here?"

Alistair continued more softly. "We are your friends. We can help you and we know where your son is. He is in some trouble. Can you postpone your journey for a while so that we can talk to you? We might be able to help your son. We mean you no harm. We are police from England."

Natalya stood indecisively for a moment and then as Alistair produced his ID, her face crumpled and she dropped all her defences. "Trouble? What trouble? He is fine. On Wednesday, I speak to him on Wednesday morning on the 'phone. He is expecting me today. I cannot delay my journey, my flight to England is booked. He booked my flight for me. Travel is not so easy for us as for you Westerners. I cannot miss my flight, I have to go. He said he would meet me at the airport. He has booked for me a hotel. I must go. Please leave now, just go."

Jeremy and Alistair exchanged a look. So she was fully aware that this Michael Hamilton was her son, Nikolai.

Alistair continued. "Your son has had an accident—"

Natalya's hand flew to her mouth and she let out a cry, "No, it cannot be!"

Alistair held up his hand. "No, wait, please hear me out. He'll be fine, he's not badly hurt, but he's in hospital at the moment, the Royal United Hospital in Bath. We are travelling back to England today as well. We can meet you there later, I promise we will help you. But can you just tell us: why is he living in England assuming the name of Michael Hamilton, pretending to be the son of—"

Natalya interrupted him, putting her finger to her lips. "No, you mustn't speak these words, no one must know, it is too dangerous. You mustn't speak of it here." She looked around fearfully, as if the walls in her empty room might be listening. "I will talk to you in England. Do not speak of it here."

Alistair was about to reply when a heavy knocking reverberated around the barren rooms.

"My taxi, I have to go, but—" Natalya looked even more distracted, her voice rising, almost breathless in her anxiety. "In hospital, in Bath? Of course, his home is in Bath, he booked my hotel in Bath. I must go to him, but I have my luggage. What can I do? I must go to the hotel first, yes, I shall get a taxi from the airport to the hotel and then I shall go to the hospital, but I must see him, he's hurt. What happened to him? I must see him as soon as I can—"

More banging on the door, this time threatening to tear the whole apartment block apart.

As Natalya looked set to panic, Alistair picked up her two suitcases. "Natalya," he said firmly, and she looked startled as he used her first name. "Calm down, trust us, he will be fine. Do as you just said: go to your hotel, then go to the hospital. But take your time. We'll meet you at the hospital and you can see him. Then we can talk there. Everything will be all right."

Natalya hesitated, then took a deep breath and nodded slowly, obviously having decided to trust him. Jeremy picked up her hand luggage as she opened the door to the impatient taxi driver. They made their way down the concrete steps and the driver threw her luggage into the boot of the taxi as Natalya climbed into the back seat.

The taxi accelerated along the road, out of their sight. As Alistair stood watching the disappearing taillights, Jeremy broke into his thoughts.

"You might have misled her there, old friend. We don't actually know how badly hurt he is. You rather gave her the impression he'd be OK. I've no idea what's going on here, but it does seem that far from being estranged, she's obviously been in very recent contact with him, and something seems to be making her very frightened to talk about him here."

Alistair was as much annoyed with himself as he was with Jeremy's remark. Of course he knew he'd deliberately misled her, but she hadn't been able to wait so he hadn't had time to go into details. She hadn't given him that time. And anyway, they hadn't expected her to be packed and ready to go off like that.

He looked at his friend, anger evaporating and guilt surfacing. "I know, for God's sake, I know but, Jeremy, look, did you expect this? Of course you didn't, any more than I did. We naively thought we could interview her, get all the answers and go back and sort it all out. Well, it hasn't quite turned out like that. We'll have to get to the airport and get the next available flight out and meet her back in England. Ironic, isn't it?"

Jeremy nodded but made no reply as they walked across to their waiting taxi, his thoughts turning inwards. When he was young, he'd obediently complied with directions from above, he'd accepted orders unquestioningly, and as he'd got older, he'd given those orders himself and sent young recruits out into the field. This was the first time he'd acted so impulsively and taken himself out into the field with no word to anyone, and he was beginning to experience a self-doubt hitherto unknown. Like Alistair, Natalya's scarred face had taken him totally by surprise, but had moved him. Not that it should have made any difference, but she'd had a certain vulnerability about her. He was left desperately wishing that she hadn't left so soon and that they could have discovered more about her. He glanced across at Alistair. He shouldn't blame him for twisting the truth, after all, he'd done far worse in his time. He just hoped, for her sake, that her son, whatever he might have done, whatever he was mixed up in, wasn't too badly injured when she eventually got to see him.

And for the first time he welcomed his imminent retirement.

CHAPTER 22

Somerset
Sunday 19ᵗʰ May, 1996
5 p.m.

Aiden stood up from the chair outside Michael's room as Harris strode down the corridor towards him.

"How is he? Any change?" Harris asked.

Aiden shook his head. "He still hasn't come round yet, but the doctor thinks that the sedatives should wear off soon, although he's still on strong painkillers. As I told you earlier on the 'phone, the operation was a success although they had to dig quite deep as the wound had closed over. They were very worried about the infection so he spent the night in intensive care. But they pumped him full of antibiotics, kept him sedated and they think they've caught it in time and got the infection under control now."

"And the Hamilton girl?"

Aiden indicated inside the room where Anna was asleep, curled up in a foetal position in her reclining chair next to Michael's bed. Josie was sitting on a hard-backed chair by the window, reading a book, but keeping a watchful eye on them.

"She's OK. Refused to leave the hospital. She's asleep at the moment, must be exhausted poor thing. Apparently she was awake throughout the night and most of today whilst they were still quite worried about him. They've given us the bullet fragment. I've had it sent to the station so that they can send it off for analysis. Hopefully it won't be too difficult to check for a match with the gun that killed Professor Hamilton."

"Hmm," grunted Harris. "I've got no doubt it'll match, but won't prove a thing."

"Unless they can determine that it was fired first?" questioned Aiden. "If that was the case, Michael Hamilton could have been defending himself."

Aiden didn't quite know why he wanted to find excuses for Michael. It wasn't even as if he knew him, although for some reason he did feel a certain degree of sympathy for him. It was probably Anna's devotion to him that had moved him.

Harris looked at him sternly. "That, Formby, would depend entirely upon the circumstances; circumstances which, I must remind you, we are not much nearer to understanding, and until we do, this person calling himself Michael Hamilton is still just as guilty in my eyes."

Aiden wasn't going to be intimidated by Harris. "Any news on the man who was chasing him – did they find him?"

"No, and at the moment we're not looking, but as you know the accident occurred close to where Summers lives."

"Sir, can't we watch their houses? Deploy some extra manpower here. After all—"

Harris interrupted irritably. "No, Formby, we can't, not until we have something more definite to go on. Unless you want to pay for it out of your salary? All we have at the moment are a few coincidences and the word of a young woman who would appear to be devoted to our prime suspect. Until we can interview Hamilton, or whoever he is, we are not going to get anywhere, and you might as well accept that. I'll be off now. Just call me if he comes round." And he turned and strode off down the corridor.

Aiden shrugged his shoulders. Sometimes he wondered why he'd chosen this profession – it was so frustrating. It was obvious that Sutherland was involved up to his irritating neck in all of this. Harris must know that as well as he did. It was almost as if the man was held back by something, although in fairness he could see Harris's predicament. You couldn't really just drag in a man like Sutherland, question him and pit his words against Anna's without any real proof. But why couldn't they go out there and find some evidence? Watch Sutherland? He'd make a mistake soon, well, he already had: he'd lost both Anna and Michael, so he must be reaching panic point himself. *What was his name – that commander from Scotland Yard? Oh yes, Lyons, that was it.* Perhaps he was preventing Harris from making any progress?

Aiden opened the door, smiled at Josie and carried a hard-backed chair from the corridor into the room for himself, settling down next to her and taking her hand in his.

After about half an hour, they were joined by Dr Barnes who had come along to check on his patient. He adjusted the drip and then leant over Michael, who had started to move his head restlessly on the pillow. Anna still slept soundly. Dr Barnes moved away from Michael and started to make entries in the file at the foot of the bed.

Suddenly Michael's eyes opened. He turned his head and saw Anna lying motionless in the chair and muttered something that they couldn't quite catch. Henry Barnes turned and spoke firmly to Aiden.

"Don't expect too much from him yet. He's been through a bad time and although we think we've got the infection under control, he's still on a very large dose of strong painkillers, not to mention the effects of anaesthetic from the operation and the subsequent sedation. I wouldn't agree to his being questioned formally yet." Implicit in his tone was, *don't bring Harris back yet.*

Aiden moved slowly across to where Michael lay. *Strange,* he thought, *I've thought of nothing but trying to speak to this man for four days, and yet now I'm face-to-face with him, I feel inhibited.*

"Michael, how are you feeling?" he asked softly.

Michael shifted his head slightly and fixed his gaze upon Aiden. He licked his dry lips and said, "Where am I?"

"You're in hospital. You've had an accident, but you're safe."

"What have you done to Anna?"

Aiden hadn't noticed the slight foreign intonation before.

"She'll be fine, she's just tired. She's asleep," he said gently.

"Who are you?"

That was easy to explain – why hadn't he immediately introduced himself?

"I'm Detective Inspector Aiden Formby. I'm involved in the investigation into your father's... into Professor Hamilton's death, and we were hoping that you could help with our enquiries."

Michael continued to look steadily at him, almost as if he were trying to reach inside him, thought Aiden uncomfortably.

"What have you done to Anna?" he repeated with suspicion.

How to explain? Aiden looked involuntarily towards Anna who still lay curled up in the chair, completely relaxed, oblivious to this new drama. Dr Barnes looked across with something approaching sympathy, but still wary in case Aiden upset his patient. Aiden leant forward, trying not to react as Michael attempted to move his head away. *Mistake,* he thought, *this one is on the defensive still. He doesn't trust me. I should be careful.*

"Anna will be all right, I promise."

"Then why is she just lying there? What's wrong with her? How do I know who you are? How do I know you haven't harmed her? Why should I believe you? And where's Sutherland? I want to talk to him!"

As Dr Barnes moved forward in concern, Michael fell back onto the pillow from which he had raised himself, white-faced and gasping for breath. Aiden stepped back to allow Dr Barnes to get closer to his patient.

"Please, Michael, calm down, it's all right. Anna is fine, she's just asleep," Dr Barnes said gently. "Let me get you some water. Are you in pain? Do you need some painkillers?"

But Michael hadn't finished. Turning to Aiden, he said dully, "No, I don't want any more drugs. And my name isn't Michael. I'm not called Michael, tell him not to call me Michael. Don't call me anything. Just leave me alone."

He turned his head away wearily, muttering, "I thought she'd escaped. Where's Sutherland? I'll talk to him, I'll help him, tell him I'm sorry, the tape I gave them was the wrong one, the data was scrambled, I'll give him the correct one, just don't hurt Anna."

Dr Barnes managed to get Michael to drink some water and then looked at Aiden with a frown. "It's too soon – he's very distressed. He's not ready to talk to you."

"Just another moment. I'll be careful." He turned to Michael and addressed him as such. What else could he call him? "Please, Michael, listen to me: Sutherland isn't here. You're safe from him."

Michael pulled himself up again, suddenly noticing Josie in her uniform, his voice rising.

"I told you, I am not Michael Hamilton. If you really are the police, I will admit it: yes, I killed Alexander Hamilton. But if you have hurt Anna, you are no better than they are. Yes, I will talk to you, I'll tell you everything, but only when I know that my mother is here and she and Anna are both safe. If you've hurt her, or my mother, I shall say nothing."

And he lay back, drained by the effort, closed his eyes, shutting them out, and seemed to drift back into whatever restless state of sleep he'd been in before.

There was a stunned silence in the room. Josie remained quietly on her chair, keeping her eyes down, but watching from beneath her lashes. Aiden stood quite still, looking apprehensively at Dr Barnes who appeared to be speechless, staring first at Michael, and then at Aiden, his frown deepening, replacing his normally pleasant expression. Suddenly he broke the silence.

"Detective Inspector, you and I need to talk!" he said forcefully. "Now!"

"Yes, of course, let's go out into the corridor," suggested Aiden mildly. "Please excuse us for a moment, Jo," he added before they left the room.

Once outside, Barnes could contain his anger no longer. "What the hell is going on here, Detective Inspector? Just exactly who is this patient that I've been treating? I thought I was treating a person by the name of Michael Hamilton. I've seen some of his recent medical history. I've been sent the records from when he broke his leg a few years ago, but now he's just said that he isn't Michael Hamilton. No wait, let me finish," he said as Aiden tried to speak. "This is totally unethical! I knew, well, I guessed, that this wasn't simple – police involved, a bullet fragment in his shoulder. But killing someone? And who exactly is he? Who is his mother? Where is she and why hasn't she been informed that her son has been admitted to our hospital? In my care! You do realise he could have died, and now it seems I've been treating the wrong person. Why is he so frightened, what is he so afraid of? He's just admitted to killing someone with the same surname he's supposed to have, but now says it isn't. And who the hell is Sutherland?"

Dr Barnes ran out of breath. He sat down heavily on one of the chairs in the corridor and looked crossly at Aiden. "I need some answers from you."

Aiden ran his hand across his eyes. "Dr Barnes, I can only apologise," he said. "I understand how you must be feeling, but we don't actually have the answers ourselves yet."

"So, until now, you were also under the impression

that my patient was Michael Hamilton?"

"Well, no, er, yes. Well, in the beginning we…" Aiden was finding this difficult; he wasn't sure how much he should say. Then he took a deep breath, looked at the doctor and decided that he deserved to know at least some of the truth.

"OK, please bear with me. I'll try to fill you in as best I can, but I must repeat that we are nowhere near understanding the full story ourselves yet. You might have seen a news report last week that a professor – Professor Alexander Hamilton – was found dead in his research laboratory at Mayhims last Wednesday?"

Barnes shook his head. "No, I didn't, but now I'm thinking that must be the person who my patient has just admitted to killing?"

"Yes. We wanted to keep it quiet so we didn't release any details and kept a lid on what we've found since. Evidence started to mount up against your patient, who we at first believed to be Alexander Hamilton's son, Michael Hamilton. He became our prime suspect. They worked together at Mayhims and we had reason to believe he shot his father and ended up getting hurt himself in the process, hence the bullet fragment." Aiden paused for breath as Dr Barnes nodded, anger forgotten, leaning forward with interest.

"Michael Hamilton disappeared after the incident and during the course of our enquiries we discovered that he wasn't who he said he was. Alexander Hamilton and the managing director of Mayhims, Graham

Sutherland and even Anna Hamilton all seem to have believed that your patient was Michael Hamilton, Alexander Hamilton's illegitimate son by a Spanish woman. Yet we now know that Alexander Hamilton, at least, must have known that he wasn't the person named on that birth certificate. One of our officers was shot – killed." Aiden paused for a moment, trying not to let Paul's face appear before him. "He was killed whilst he was interviewing Anna Hamilton at her home on Friday evening. We know that this supposed Michael Hamilton also went to her home that evening and we at first believed (although now it seems more doubtful) that he was responsible for the death of our officer."

"I am so sorry to hear of your colleague's death. Please accept my sympathy," said Barnes with genuine concern. He hadn't missed the look that had flashed across Aiden's face when he mentioned it. "So, Anna Hamilton must also have witnessed this? No wonder she's so traumatised. But how can you be sure that he's *not* the child of the Spanish mother? He does have a slight accent, although I couldn't place it myself."

Aiden was quiet for a moment, wondering how much he should say, but suddenly decided that if he couldn't trust Barnes, then who could he trust? "Please, I must ask you to treat this information with the utmost confidentiality."

Barnes nodded. "Yes, of course. I appreciate your honesty and I won't mention any of this to anyone else. You have my word."

"OK, we'll get on to the question of the mother later. Anna Hamilton turned up at the station in a dreadful state yesterday morning, with an almost unbelievable story. Her clothes were blood-stained from the blood of our officer, and she maintained that yes, her brother had turned up on Friday evening, but then three strange men – no, four – had walked into her home, killed our officer and taken herself and Michael Hamilton, who was already in a weak state due to his untreated shoulder wound, to Graham Sutherland's house against their will."

"Aha," said Barnes. "So that's why my patient is afraid?"

"So it would seem, but as I said, Anna's story is quite hard to credit. She maintains that she managed to escape from Sutherland's house yesterday morning, and that her brother is completely innocent of any involvement in our officer's death. Subsequently, this Michael Hamilton also managed to escape and ended up literally falling in front of a car, supposedly whilst being chased by someone, thus ending up here, as your patient."

"And have you questioned this man, Sutherland?"

Aiden looked embarrassed. "No, not as yet. My superior officer wants to speak to Michael Hamilton – or whoever he is – first. There's also a commander from Scotland Yard who's got involved in the case but as yet I have no idea why. As I said, we, well certainly I, don't really have many answers yet."

"And the mother?" Barnes reminded him.

Aiden sighed. "To be honest, I'm even more in the dark about that than anything else. As I said, we believed at first that Anna Hamilton and Michael Hamilton were half-brother and sister. Anna was told that Michael's Spanish mother had an illegitimate child with Alexander Hamilton, and then allegedly died some six years ago, resulting in Michael Hamilton going to live with Anna and her parents, and working alongside her father. Anna's own mother also died a year or so after that, but there was never any question that she was this Michael's mother."

"Hmm, that doesn't make sense as he seemed to be talking about his mother as if she were still alive. He didn't seem to be hallucinating; he seemed genuinely concerned for her," said Barnes.

"Well, no, it shouldn't make sense, but then we got information – indisputable evidence – that the real Michael Hamilton died in a car crash with his Spanish mother when he was just a couple of months old. So whoever this person is, your patient, masquerading as the dead Michael Hamilton, may well have a mother somewhere. But I had no idea that she even existed up until just now."

"Then that would also mean that this Professor Alexander Hamilton had a child with yet another woman – my patient's mother," said Barnes in bemusement. "It is all a bit hard to believe."

"Yes, and if so, why not use that birth certificate? At least it would be genuine."

They sat for a minute, both lost in their own thoughts, trying to figure it all out, when they were interrupted by Josie poking her head round the door.

"Anna's awake. She'd like a cup of tea. Shall I go and get one for her? Michael is still asleep."

"Yes, of course," said Aiden, standing up. "Stretch your legs. I'll go in and take over."

Barnes also stood up. "I appreciate your frankness, Inspector, and I promise what we have discussed will go no further. Now, I need to check on a couple of other patients. Please sound the buzzer if you need me. I'll be back soon anyway." And off he went down the corridor, his back stooped as if he were looking for answers from his feet.

CHAPTER 23

Somerset
Sunday 19th May, 1996
5.30 p.m.

Aiden went back into the room where Anna was sitting up in her chair, gazing at Michael. She looked up as he entered.

"Is it really true that he woke up? Oh, how I wish I hadn't been asleep. He's very restless, seems to be talking in his sleep, but I can't understand anything he's saying. Josie couldn't tell me what he'd said when he woke up. She said I had to hear it from you, but she did say that he was worried about me. I really wish I hadn't been asleep! Why didn't you wake me?"

There it was: the accusatory tone that he'd been half expecting.

"Sorry, Anna. The truth of the matter is that when he suddenly awakened, he took us all by surprise. He wasn't awake for long. We told him that you were safe, and he saw you for himself, which seemed to reassure him. He's on very strong pain medication and he needs to sleep, but he's over the worst, and hopefully he'll be back with us again soon."

Anna smiled wistfully. "So, can you tell me what he said?"

"Well, mainly it corroborated what you'd told us: he seems very worried about Sutherland, he was concerned about your safety, and he mentioned a tape."

"Oh yes, he was supposed to be finding a tape for them that he'd hidden."

"And he mentioned his mother. He's worried about his mother."

"His mother? But I thought his mother died six years ago? Oh no, that's not true. Inspector Ravell said it wasn't true. His mother died when he was a baby—" Anna's face crumpled. "Oh no, that's not true either, is it? Oh, Michael, what lies have you told?"

Aiden stood by awkwardly, wanting to comfort her but afraid that if he did it might make matters worse. To his relief, at that moment, Josie pushed the door open holding a cardboard tray containing four polystyrene cups: tea for Anna, undrinkable coffee for herself and Aiden, and an extra one for Barnes who wasn't there to enjoy it. *Lucky sod,* thought Aiden as he burnt his lips on the tasteless, scalding liquid. His thoughts drifted back to Paul, who'd died for reasons that perhaps only Michael could explain; poor Paul whose whole life had been one of tragedy. And then he thought of Paul's mother, who had screamed at Aiden as he'd given her the news of Paul's death.

"I have no more sons to give, you've taken them all! What more do you want from me?" she'd said before collapsing into hysterical weeping. Aiden had stood by helplessly, not knowing how to comfort her. There was no comfort to be given – she was right.

His 'phone bleeped. He excused himself to Josie and Anna and went out into the corridor. Harris's voice crackled into his ear.

"I'm on my way over. Lyons and his friend from MI6 will be with you shortly."

"MI6?" questioned Aiden, slightly taken aback.

"Yes, look, I'll explain when I get over there. Sorry, I wasn't at liberty to tell you before, but there is a connection with Russia. They've just been over there on a flying visit and they're on their way back from Heathrow. Should be there soon. They want to meet at the hospital, not at the station. A Russian woman should also turn up – she's our Michael Hamilton's mother—"

Aiden tried to speak.

"No, don't interrupt – you can be present when they all turn up. I'll see you soon." Harris ended the call.

Aiden stared at the now silent 'phone, his thoughts in turmoil. He didn't know what to think, and was almost as shocked at Harris's apology as the news that whoever Michael Hamilton actually was, he really did have a mother, and a Russian one at that. But Harris hadn't seemed surprised so he must have already known and chosen not to share the information with him. Aiden felt a sudden surge of anger. No wonder Harris had felt the need to apologise! What other information had he kept from him? Well, he could stop feeling guilty that he hadn't told Harris that Michael had woken up, albeit for such a short time. Serves him right, and he hadn't given him the chance anyway.

He decided that he ought to update Barnes on this latest development. He would need to be there if the mother suddenly turned up in case it upset his patient. He put his head round the door to let Josie know where he was going, and that he'd update her when he got back. And off he went in search of Barnes.

Barnes was easy to find. He was already on his way back to the room, accompanied by a small, dark-haired woman who was gesticulating and apparently talking non-stop. Barnes stopped when he saw Aiden walking purposefully towards him. He raised his eyebrows and pulled his companion forward, effectively causing her to stop speaking for a moment.

"Ah, Inspector, may I introduce Natalya Miloslavskaya. The mother," he added in an undertone.

Aiden looked down at Dr Barnes's companion. His first impression was of large dark eyes regarding him solemnly, in a face… oh, God, a face at once so striking and yet so tragic, scars, running down half her face, but the other side still beautiful.

She smiled crookedly, holding out her hand and, if Anna had been there, she'd have seen the person she knew as Michael Hamilton in that smile.

"Delighted to meet you," she said quaintly, her voice

slightly accented. "You must be a friend of my son's?"

Taking her hand awkwardly, he replied, "I, er, well, er…"

He looked appealingly at Barnes. Hadn't the man explained the situation? Apparently not, as her next words proved.

"I have come to see my son. I understand he has had an accident. The police came to see me in Russia, but I was just leaving so I couldn't talk with them. They're going to meet me here. I am glad you're here with my son. This kind doctor is taking me to him." And she smiled sweetly at Barnes who appeared to be quite mesmerized by her.

She hadn't understood, or perhaps hadn't heard, Barnes refer to him as inspector, he thought with dismay. She took him for a friend of Michael's. Well, they were about the same age, he supposed. He nodded glumly, rapidly deciding that explanations could wait and turning quickly, he indicated for her to walk ahead of him down the corridor.

"So, we get to meet the mother. She's Russian. Harris has just 'phoned me. I was coming to tell you," he whispered to Barnes as they followed her small determined figure down the corridor.

Barnes gave an amused smile and whispered back, "She certainly is one hell of a lady."

They watched as she pushed open the door, pausing on the threshold, and then, before they could stop her, she threw herself across the room and onto the bed

311

where Michael still lay asleep, almost dislodging the drip that was attached to his hand.

Josie looked at them as they entered the room, her look of comical amazement at Natalya's precipitous arrival almost making Aiden laugh out loud.

"Kolya!" cried Natalya, hugging him to her. "Oh, Kolya, you're hurt! They told me that you were fine."

Anna had leapt to her feet as Michael, rudely awoken but still half asleep, attempted to free himself from Natalya's embrace. He pulled himself away, and then, recognising his mother, he lifted himself up off the pillows, holding out his good arm to embrace her, pulling her in to him tightly.

"Kolya?" she questioned, her voice rising, but he put his fingers to his lips and burst into a spate of Russian that left the others bewildered, but seemed to have the effect of reassuring Natalya.

Anna had quietly resumed her place in her chair once she'd realised who Natalya was, but she kept her hands on her lap. This was Natalya's time with her son.

The door burst open again and Harris entered, staring at each of them in turn then, focusing on Natalya, he spoke in his normal brusque tone. "Ah, you've arrived then, and your son is awake. Good, now we can question him and get some answers."

Natalya looked up, her hair falling back from her face, surprised at his tone, and then looked around the room, as if taking in for the first time the others who were there. She extricated herself from Michael's arms and stood upright to face Harris, hardly noticing as her son fell back heavily on the pillows, or as Anna's hand found his and gripped it tightly.

"What is this?" she demanded imperiously. "Who are you? Why are you here?" She looked at Aiden imploringly. "You are his friend, you tell me! What is going on? Who is this man?"

Harris suddenly noticed her scarred face and was lost for words for a moment. Aiden too couldn't find his voice; he was way out of his depth here. Barnes spoke into the silence, addressing the room at large, refusing to look directly at Harris.

"Chief Inspector, I would like to introduce Miss Natalya Miloslavskaya, Michael's mother." And he moved across to where Michael lay, to stand protectively behind Natalya.

Harris recovered, his tone more deferential now as he addressed Natalya. "Miss Milo... Misolaskeya."

"Miloslavskaya." She corrected him, unsmiling, seeming to share Barnes's dislike for Harris.

"Yes, sorry." Harris was getting flustered now. "Yes, Miss Miloslavskaya, please do sit down. I am Detective Chief Inspector Harris. I do apologise, we were expecting you, but you took me by surprise. Would you like a drink? A cup of tea or coffee perhaps?"

But she was not to be so easily mollified. She sat down in the chair on the other side of Michael's bed, but spoke with some hostility. "No, I do not want coffee. I want an explanation! Why are you here?" She looked around the room again, suddenly taking in Josie's uniform. "What is going on? Why are you police here?" And without waiting for an answer she sat down again, turned to Michael and repeated to him, more sternly now, "Nikolai, what is going on?"

Michael had pulled himself back up into a sitting position. Anna was rearranging the pillows behind him to support him. His voice, starting quietly, gained in strength.

"Mama, I will explain, but you must understand, these people need an explanation too. Things have happened here that you know nothing about – bad things – but I'm glad you've left Russia. At least you're safe, and Anna's safe too." His voice faltered but then he turned to Harris, saying, "I will talk to you now. I will tell you what you want to know."

Harris was back in control now. He stared at Michael. "Michael Hamilton, I have to tell you that you are still regarded as the major suspect in the murder of Alexander Hamilton."

Natalya opened her mouth to speak, but a look from her son stopped her. Harris continued.

"I certainly do want to hear what you have to say, and I have every expectation of placing you under arrest so I must warn you that everything you say will go on record and may be used as evidence against you. WPC Grimley, write this down."

Josie glanced at Aiden for reassurance but he was staring open- mouthed at the scene that was unfolding

314

in front of them. She smiled to herself and then reluctantly took out her notepad.

Harris's bulk seemed to fill the room as he looked squarely at Michael. "Did you kill Alexander Hamilton on the night of Wednesday fifteenth May?" he demanded.

"No, Nikolai, no, not Alexander!" came a cry from Natalya.

"Yes." A brief reply, a meaningful glance to Natalya to remain silent, and an imploring glance at Anna who had buried her face in her hands. What more damage could one word do?

"Could you explain to me why you killed him?"

There was a long pause. Michael looked down; he appeared to be having difficulty in formulating his next words. Finally he looked up. "This is not a simple story and there is no simple explanation. It involves my past, and my mother's past. I cannot explain without her permission."

Harris looked questioningly at Natalya; strange how her scars faded to the eye after a while, the undamaged side of her face becoming the more prominent. She nodded her assent wordlessly, a look of horrified disbelief still on her face. Michael continued.

"My name is not Michael Hamilton. I am not related in any way to Alexander Hamilton, nor to Anna."

Anna raised her head and looked at him, her expression impossible to read.

"My name is Nikolai Miloslavsky, and I am the son

of Pyotr Karev and Natalya Miloslavskaya. I was born in Moscow on fifteenth September, 1965. I never knew my father, he… He died before I was born." He stopped, unable to continue.

Harris spoke impatiently. "So, get on with it—"

Natalya interrupted, her face tense, the scars standing out lividly now on her white face. "I think it is for me to tell this part of history. If my son thinks it relevant, I will tell it."

Harris's 'phone bleeped and he held it to his ear, listening with a scowl. "Right, OK, sir, yes, she's here, yes, he's conscious and talking. OK, we'll wait for you. I'll come to meet you. See you in a moment, sir."

He turned to Natalya. "Miss Milo… Madam, another officer will be here very soon and it would be better if he could be present when you tell your story, rather than you having to repeat it." And he lumbered out of the room.

There was total silence in the room for a moment. Anna sat gazing blankly ahead at the wall; she seemed to have retreated into a world of her own. Natalya leant back in her chair, eyes closed, lost in her memories. Dr Barnes moved forward to lean over Nikolai who was lying back on his pillows, looking drained.

"Michael, sorry, Nikolai, have some water, please," and he managed to get him to sip some water.

Aiden leant towards Josie and whispered in her ear, "Hey, Jo, this is some story that we'll be able to tell our kids."

Josie smiled at his casual reference to 'our kids', a promise of their future as a family, although she knew – they both knew – that the drama that was unfolding in this hospital room could never be shared.

CHAPTER 24

Somerset
Sunday 19th May, 1996
6 p.m.

Minutes later, Harris was back, accompanied by two weary-looking but distinguished men in smart suits. Aiden recognised Commander Lyons; the other must be his friend from MI6.

"Right," said Harris briskly. "Please allow me to introduce Commander Lyons from Scotland Yard, and his associate, Mr Colton. They will both remain present during any further interviews in this room."

Lyons smiled and spoke to the room in general. "Apologies for intruding, but me and my friend Jeremy Colton here were at Oxford University with Alexander Hamilton, and that is the reason for our involvement in this matter." He took a small portable voice recorder out of his pocket. "We will be recording everything that is said in this room," he said, and then, looking across to Josie, he continued kindly, "No need to take notes, WPC. We'll give you access to the recording later."

Josie pocketed her notebook, breathing a secret sigh of relief.

Harris turned to Lyons. "Just to update you, sir," he indicated Natalya. "This is Miss Mil—" Luckily, he was saved by Lyons before he could stumble over her name again.

"Yes, we've already met Miss Miloslavskaya. Natalya, how are you? I hope your journey was good and you found your hotel without a problem." Alistair smiled warmly at Natalya, who was sitting up straight now, attempting an unconvincing smile in return.

Nikolai was also more alert now, sitting up and staring suspiciously at the newcomers, as Harris introduced the other occupants of the room, leaving him to the last.

"And this is the person who we believed was Michael Hamilton, the son of Alexander Hamilton. He has now admitted that was a lie, and has identified himself as Nikolai Miloslavsky."

"Aha," said Lyons, smiling at Nikolai. "Nikolai, at last we meet." He turned to Natalya. "I understand from DCI Harris that you were about to update us on the beginning of Nikolai's story."

Natalya took a deep breath, steeling herself to go on and, as Nikolai said nothing, she started to speak. "I met Alexander Hamilton at Oxford University in 1960. We were friends and in time we became lovers." She stopped, looking almost defiantly at her audience. They remained silent so she continued.

"Alexander was different from the boys I'd met in Moscow. England was different from any experiences I'd had before. You must understand, Russia was a communist country. Yes, I had an English mother, but she had embraced communist beliefs, and my father—" She faltered, unconsciously touching her scarred face. "My father was a true communist. He believed wholeheartedly in his ideology, but he was favoured, living the life of the elite, a communist aristocrat if you can believe that such a contradiction can exist. He could not begin to understand the injustices perpetuated on the proletariat. He took an active part in these injustices himself. This was his way of life." And here she stopped again and looked down at her hands. They sat patiently waiting. Even Harris could feel her pain, not understanding where she was heading, willing her to continue. She looked up after a few moments.

"Alexander used to visit with me at my parents in Moscow. He became very friendly with my father. At first, he did not agree with my father's politics and they would argue fiercely, but yet my father enjoyed that, he would see it as a challenge. He would talk more openly to Alexander than to anyone else, especially to me. I was often excluded from their discussions." She paused for breath, uncertain how to continue, unsure of herself.

Nikolai looked at her in silent support; no words were spoken.

"I continued my studies at Oxford, but then the political climate became more uncertain. I cannot even remember what it was that triggered off my parents' fears, but they recalled me to Moscow in 1963 as soon as I graduated. I was to continue my further studies at Moscow University, and somehow my father arranged for Alexander to come over to study there as well. It didn't work out well for us. Once in Russia, he became too much under my father's influence; he became almost as committed to the communist regime as my father. He idolised my father, he helped him, and I could not agree with that, so I could not stay with him." She stopped again for a moment. "You see, my time in the West, short though it had been, had taught me the value of democracy, of freedom for those who were less fortunate than myself. When my relationship with Alexander came to an end, he returned to England to continue his studies there. For a while I did not hear from him, although I know he kept in touch with my father and continued to help him." She stopped and looked around. "May I have a drink now, please? I have travelled a long way today."

Harris looked across at Josie who got up reluctantly. She didn't want to miss the rest of the story.

"WPC, coffee please. I think we could all do with some."

After taking their orders, Josie almost ran to the vending machine, clutching the makeshift cardboard tray Aiden had thrust at her. Inserting the coins, she cursed the machine for its slowness. As it slowly digested and accepted each combination in turn, she wondered what she was missing.

There was silence at first whilst they waited for Josie to return with the drinks and then Lyons started to speak, unconsciously rolling an unlighted cigarette between his fingers.

"I don't understand. I happen to know that Alexander was working for MI6 at that time, and yet you tell me he was working with your father. How can that be?"

"You will understand," said Nikolai grimly from his propped-up position in the bed. "Just hear her out."

"I do not know anything about that. As far as I knew, Alexander was helping my father and Russia. He was giving scientific information from England to my father who passed it on to the KGB, but you see, I was not so close by now. I was, as my father said, 'tainted by the evils of Western capitalism'."

Natalya paused as Josie returned with the drinks and silently handed them out. Then she laughed bitterly.

"He it was who lived the life of the wealthy corrupt capitalist, but he could not see it. But I continued my studies at Moscow University, and there I met Pyotr, my Pyotr." Her eyes softened and her voice became faraway. "He was everything I'd always dreamed of, so handsome, so passionate. I loved… do you understand? I loved him from the depths of my soul, and he loved me as much, but he also wanted to fight for freedom. He had not had the opportunities that I had been given; he had the intelligence but not the position. He was proletariat but yet he hated communism. He dreamt of a

Russia without communism and I think it is better that he never lived to see how our country is now." She paused to sip her coffee, trying not to pull a face at its watery bitterness.

"Please continue," said Lyons politely, trying not to show his excitement. The pieces of the jigsaw were beginning to fall into place, albeit some of them were upside down, but she must finish. He absentmindedly put the cigarette to his mouth, fumbling in his pocket for his lighter, and then quickly removed it after a frown from Barnes.

"Pyotr met a man called Graham Sutherland, a friend of Alexander's. Although they had opposing politics, still they were good friends. Graham Sutherland was involved with British Intelligence you see, whilst Alexander was helping my father and the KGB."

Lyons and Colton exchanged looks, and Nikolai scowled but kept his silence.

"Alexander didn't know this, but Graham Sutherland helped Pyotr to provide information to the British Secret Service – MI6, I suppose, as you mentioned earlier – and it was this Graham Sutherland who carried the information that Pyotr supplied over to England. Pyotr was proud of the chance to try to help his country free itself of the tyranny of communism, and I was proud to support him, but I had to keep it secret from my parents. And then—" She stopped, distress pulling down the contours of her face, her scars highlighting her emotions. "And then, he was betrayed. I did not know by whom, but at that time they took no prisoners. He disappeared. Word got to me that he had been executed. I was beside myself with grief. But then I found out that it was my father, my own father, who had given the order for his execution. He hadn't known that we were lovers when he sent my Pyotr to his death, but when I told him that he had killed the man I loved, the man I was to have married, he was beside himself with fury. I had betrayed him and his country. I was no longer his daughter, he said. My mother tried to protect me. She understood – she had never shared his fanatical patriotism, and her British socialism had long worn away. She stayed with him only because she had no other options; he was a powerful man. But I hated him then and I have hated him ever since."

She paused again for a moment, the grief and the bitter memories making her face harsh in the brightly lit room.

"Alexander was there when I found out. He was staying with them at the time. He tried to help me but my father was relentless. If I consorted with traitors, then I was one myself. But my father did not know then that I was pregnant with Pyotr's child; that he had ordered the execution of the father of his own grandchild."

She stopped and buried her face in her hands. Nikolai had fallen back on his pillows, his face grey, shocked by these unexpected revelations. Barnes fussed over him anxiously.

Lyons began to speak, the cigarette becoming mangled in his restless fingers. "I'm sorry if this is causing you too much distress."

"No, I have not quite finished yet. Kolya?" She looked towards Nikolai with concern as she continued. "I'm so sorry that I have had to say all of this. I never told you the whole story before, and I know it will be as painful to you as to me, but you need to know. Can you bear it?"

Nikolai nodded.

"Alexander tried to persuade me to leave Moscow to return to England with him. He promised to look after me, but I refused. He had a relationship with a girl, a Spanish girl, who was pregnant also, but he was prepared to leave her for me. I refused – how could he leave her? But even if I could condone that, I did not love him. I loved only Pyotr. My father, when he found out about the baby, was beside himself with fury. 'Go with Alexander,' he said, 'or lose your baby. You have shamed and betrayed your family name and your country. No one wants you here'. But I refused. For days I shut myself in my room while my mother brought me food when she dared – my father's anger was extreme. And then I recovered my strength. I loved Pyotr and I would have his child. I would survive, for Pyotr and for his child's sake. I went to my father and I told him I would leave. I would never see him again. I would have my child and bring it up alone, proud to be Pyotr's widow, even though we had not had the chance to marry." She stopped again, her hand going to her face, touching her scars.

"He lost his temper and he hit me. He hit me so hard that I fell against the window. It shattered and cut my face to pieces. My scars, the scars you try so carefully not to look at, were caused by my own father." She stopped, unable to continue now, the memories too painful.

There was complete silence for a long moment, but then Lyons spoke gently. "Miss Miloslavskaya, Natalya, I'm so sorry. This must be so painful for you to recount. But there is something that doesn't quite make sense. I'm not doubting your story, but are you sure that Alexander Hamilton was working with your father and giving information to the KGB? We have reason to believe that he was working for MI6 at the time you mention. Indeed, we know that it was he who was the handler for Pyotr Karev, not Graham Sutherland. We have the original documents. As you said, Pyotr never actually came to England himself, but all the information he supplied came via Alexander Hamilton."

Nikolai had raised himself up from the pillows, speaking with some effort. "No, you might have thought he was working for MI6, but he had been turned by my grandfather and he was a double agent, secretly working for the KGB, as was Sutherland. If you don't mind, I can take over from my mother now. It's all right, I'm fine," he said, addressing his last words to Dr Barnes.

"You've heard my mother's story, my story too, although there were some parts I wasn't aware of. I was brought up by my mother but we had no official contact with my grandparents, just regular secret visits from my English grandmother. But my grandfather's influence still ruled our lives – he was a powerful man. My mother told me that I was the son of a heroic man who had tried to influence a change in Russia, and that I should be proud of him. I grew up with that ideal to cherish. I understood from an early age that my grandfather had a different ideology and had hated my father and what he stood for. I accepted that, but until now I had no idea of the part he'd played in my father's death." A look of pain crossed his face. The recent revelations about his grandfather had obviously shaken him.

"Life wasn't easy for us. My mother was a single parent who worked hard and struggled to keep a roof over our heads. Occasionally, she would receive a visit from a man from England – that man was Alexander Hamilton – and I considered him to be our friend. At that time, I had no idea that he had even known my father; he never mentioned him and it was never discussed. And I had certainly never met, or even heard of Graham Sutherland then. I finished university. There had been many changes in Russia and my mother was afraid for my future. She wanted better for me, and I can't say that I looked forward to living the rest of my life in Moscow." He stopped for a moment, indecision showing on his face. "As I've said, my grandfather had influence and he prevented my getting an international passport. I couldn't travel, I couldn't escape. He hated me, but I didn't really understand why. He wouldn't see me, yet he couldn't let me go. Alexander Hamilton came to visit soon after my graduation. He had a plan, he said. If I would pretend to be his dead child, use that child's birth certificate, I could travel to England on a false passport and work with him. My mother thought it was a wonderful idea although I had my doubts. But it was better than the alternative, so I agreed, if my mother would accompany me. But she wouldn't leave for fear of the reprisals on my grandmother. I eventually agreed, and we devised a plan: I would pretend to disappear, drop out, apparently taking to a life on the streets of Moscow. And so I came to England, passing myself off as the dead son of Alexander Hamilton, as your brother, Anna, living a lie. I'm so sorry."

Anna shook her head blindly, but still kept her hand over his.

"I worked at Mayhims with Hamilton, and of course with Sutherland who was aware that I wasn't Hamilton's son. I didn't know then that they had been involved in the betrayal of my father. I didn't even know then that they'd known my father—" Natalya tried to interrupt but he shook his head slightly and continued. "I mostly enjoyed life and I enjoyed the work. But I hated the secrecy, the deceit, and I missed my mother although, as Michael Hamilton, I could freely travel to visit her. Each time I saw her, I tried to persuade her to come to England, so that we could end this charade, but she still worried about leaving my grandmother. My grandmother knew that I was safe and I managed to see her secretly when I visited my mother. So time went on. I became Michael Hamilton; I thought as him, I acted as him. But all the time I wanted to be myself again, and then my grandmother became very ill and she died." He stopped, the strain of speaking for so long beginning to show, but with an effort he continued. "It changed everything. My mother could now leave Russia and her past behind, and I could stop pretending to be Hamilton's son and Anna's brother."

He fell silent for a moment, as if unsure of his next words, and then he looked at Anna and said simply, "Anna, I'd fallen in love with you." As she tried to speak, he continued quickly. "No, don't say anything, you don't know it all yet. I had hoped you might come to feel the same for me once you knew that I wasn't your brother. I realise it's impossible now but I wanted you to know. I felt desperate at times. I came so close to telling you, but I couldn't."

The others had remained quiet whilst he was speaking, but as he paused yet again Natalya looked across at Anna as if seeing her for the first time.

"Anna? You are Anna, the daughter of Alexander? Of course you are, you have his looks."

Anna sat perfectly still, outwardly calm, her face unreadable. But her mind was in turmoil, swirling with emotions that made her feel dizzy, and her heart was beating too fast. For the first time since that dreadful evening, she felt a flutter of hope. And she hardly dared think that she might be able to give in to those feelings that she hadn't even been able to acknowledge to herself. She opened her mouth as if to speak, but no words came. Instead, she just nodded blindly at Natalya. *I can't take all this in,* she thought. *He loves me – Michael, no, not Michael, he's called Nikolai – but he loves me, and he's not my brother; he's no relation to me at all. There's nothing to stop us, it should be all my dreams come true, but it's not, it's just a continuing nightmare. My father, oh what has my father done?*

Harris cleared his throat. "Yes, er, perhaps you could continue, Mr, er…" *Damn it, what was his name? Stupid, unpronounceable foreign name.*

Josie suppressed a giggle; the buildup of tension in the room was beginning to affect her. She wanted to look at Aiden but she didn't dare. She knew if she did she'd either burst into fits of hysterical laughter or tears, or both.

"Miloslavsky," said Nikolai coldly, looking at Harris with some hostility before continuing. "I didn't go into work the day after my grandmother's funeral. I spent the day trying to help my mother make arrangements to come to England. It was difficult arranging things by 'phone. We had to be secretive – my grandfather mustn't find out or he might try to stop her out of spite, but luckily she had a passport from her student days and had always kept it renewed." He paused, indecision on

330

his face, and then took a deep breath.

"That evening, that Wednesday evening, I went to Mayhims to speak to Hamilton. I knew he would be working late in the laboratory. I told him about my grandmother's death, and of my mother's intention to travel to England. I was excited, for it meant I could discontinue the charade of being Michael Hamilton and I could finally become myself. He misunderstood, thinking I meant that I would no longer work with them, and he became very angry. He threatened me, telling me I had to finish the project before I could leave or he would report me to the Russian authorities." Nikolai paused again, closing his eyes as he made an effort to get his thoughts in order.

"I was confused. I'd had no intention of leaving and the project, as far as I was concerned, was making good progress. We thought we might have some hope of developing an AIDS vaccine, and my work into ways of making the virus dormant was going well. I couldn't understand why he was getting so agitated. I laughed, not really taking him seriously, and went over to the computer meaning to show him how advanced we were, but he pushed me to one side and shut it down, wiping the keyboard and mouse immediately. I was getting concerned now: he was behaving completely out of character and I started to worry that he might be having a breakdown. I managed to get the computer open again but he hadn't shut it down completely. In his haste he'd left some files open that I hadn't seen before. He tried to stop me looking at the data, but I could see he'd been using my investigations – not to make the gene dormant, but to accelerate its growth. I challenged him: why had he done this? Then he lost his temper with me. He told me that I was an idealistic fool, that I was the son of a worthless traitor and that he and Sutherland had taken great pleasure in betraying my father to the KGB."

Natalya cried out. "No, Nikolai, not Alexander! He was our friend."

Anna still remained silent but her face was white, and her hand holding his was shaking. Nikolai looked at his mother, his face drawn and grey.

"I'm so sorry, Mama. He loved you too much. You see, he was jealous of my father. He'd wanted you for himself, and when he discovered that you were expecting me, that you were pregnant by my father, his jealousy became too much to handle. His hatred for my father consumed him. Because he was working for both the Russians and the British, he was in a position to betray my father with Sutherland's help." His voice faltered but he carried on. "He and Sutherland never stopped living their double life. They eventually gave up any pretence of working for MI6 but they were still selling out to the Russians. They had all the contacts through my grandfather and his corrupt friends and they'd arranged a big commercial deal. Hamilton seemed to enjoy telling me all this. He was like another person, a person that I didn't recognise. He said I looked too much like my father. I think he'd hated my father so much for so long that his hate had spilled over on to me; I was the living proof of your love for my father."

Natalya gazed unseeingly at him as he paused to catch his breath. "I couldn't take it all in. I knew we weren't really close, but I had no idea of the extent of his hatred for me. I couldn't make any sense of what he and Sutherland had done to destroy my father all those years ago; these two men with whom I had been working closely for six years to have had such a terrible secret. And he must have sensed my confusion because he suddenly changed tack. He tried to persuade me to help. Imagine the power of being able to accelerate the AIDS virus to such an extent that you could quickly overpower another nation, and still keep the vaccine for yourself? This was what they were promising the Russians. It was important to them that they got it finished – they needed the money, Mayhims needed the money, and they'd lost their consciences long ago."

Nikolai paused again, accepting a glass of water from Barnes, gulping some down before returning the glass and continuing.

"I was so shocked. I said I would never help, it made me feel sick to the stomach. I thought I'd left corruption behind when I left Russia, and I'd believed in him and the work that we'd been doing, and all the time he'd been using me. He and Sutherland had been using my research work for their own corrupt end. I shut down the computer and said I was leaving. I started to walk towards the door but he went over to his desk and opened the drawer and took out a gun. I'd never seen it before. I had no idea that he would have such a thing. He said if I didn't agree to help, he'd kill me, and make it look as though I'd tried to kill him. I stopped and turned back. I was going to try to reason with him. I didn't think he'd seriously try to hurt me, despite what he'd said. But he just pointed the gun at me and fired. I thought the bullet had hit the pillar next to me but something still hit me in the shoulder – it hurt, but I didn't really register what had happened, it all happened so quickly. And then he started to move towards me, aiming the gun at me – he was going to shoot again. I just threw myself at him and as I struggled to get the gun from him, it went off again but he was the one who got shot. I couldn't help him, Anna. I'm so sorry." His voice tailed off and he lay back on the pillow, closing his eyes wearily. No one spoke for a moment; Nikolai's words had shocked them all.

"Did you not think to call a doctor?" asked Harris gruffly, breaking the silence. Nikolai didn't respond at first and Barnes moved forward in concern, but then Nikolai opened his eyes and pulled himself up with an effort.

Looking at Barnes, he shook his head. "I'm all right," and, as the doctor stepped back reluctantly, he continued. "Well, yes, of course I thought of calling for help, of course I would have done, but there was no point: he was dead. I could tell that. He had died instantly. I didn't know what to do, I hadn't meant to hurt him, I was just trying to get the gun off him. But I knew that no one would believe me – why should they? And then I remembered the data on the computer. I couldn't just leave it on there. Sutherland could get someone else to continue the work. I opened it up again, took a copy of the original data and then I scrambled the hard disk. I knew no one else at Mayhims had the knowledge to immediately unscramble it and it would take Sutherland a long time to find anyone else with the expertise. Then, as a precaution, I took a copy of the scrambled data as well. I had no clear idea what to do, so I 'phoned the police. I couldn't just leave his body there for someone to find the next day. Then I left the laboratory. I didn't even have my car there, I'd walked, you see, it was a lovely evening."

Yes, thought Anna, listening from faraway, as if in a dream, *it had been a lovely evening, the lull before the storm.*

Nikolai was still speaking, although his voice was getting fainter now.

"I walked and walked, not really knowing where I was going, but I knew I had to get to Anna, and then I thought, I can't go there. Sutherland would be looking for me, he'd be bound to think I would go to Anna. I couldn't go to the police as they wouldn't believe my word above Sutherland's. They would arrest me and I would have to admit to my true identity and then I would get sent back to Russia. My mother wouldn't be able to leave and my grandfather would exact his punishment.

I had nowhere to go. I couldn't go back to my flat – that was surely the first place he'd look – and I couldn't go to any of my friends and put them at risk. I 'phoned Anna. I needed her, but it was the wrong thing to do because I couldn't tell her what had happened; I couldn't talk to her until it was safe. So, I hid out in the fields near her cottage. At least there I felt close to her. And then I thought maybe if I just kept out of sight for a while, until my mother was safely in England, it might be all right. Well, it could never be all right: I'd killed a man, a man I thought was my friend but who had turned out to be my enemy. But once my mother was safely here, I would go to the police and take my chances. I'd already booked her flight to England for Sunday… oh, of course," he said, looking at Natalya. "You're here, it must be Sunday, I've lost track of time. My shoulder was hurting quite a lot by this time and I was tired so I found a hedge in the field and I just lay down in the shelter of it. I suppose I slept but I can't really recall much about the next day or so. I had no food, no water even, until it rained," he said with a twisted smile. "And then I had plenty to drink. I just remember being so cold even though the weather was warm, and starting to feel terribly ill. Eventually – I don't know why, I suppose I wasn't thinking straight, maybe it was the storm – but it all got too much and I changed my mind and decided I would go to Anna for help. I couldn't 'phone her again, the battery in my 'phone was long dead, so I just went to her cottage. But when I got there your officer was with her."

He stopped for breath. His head was starting to hurt as well now but they were all staring at him expectantly; he obviously wasn't allowed to stop yet. He looked at Anna apprehensively, but she just sat there, gazing at him, clutching his hand, her expression unreadable.

"Anna believed what the officer must have told her: that I'd murdered her father. Well, it was right in a way, although I hadn't meant to hurt him. But I knew I had to get away again. I couldn't afford to be arrested then, not until I knew my mother would be safe. I still had the gun. I tried to keep him away but he just kept coming closer..."

"You were going to shoot Inspector Ravell?" interrupted Aiden, unable to contain himself, all the sympathy he'd been feeling starting to evaporate.

"No, I just wanted to get away," Nikolai replied, shaking his head and immediately regretting it. "I can't really remember much about what happened next but I wasn't going to shoot him, I wouldn't have done that. I just wanted him to back off so that I could get away again, out of Anna's cottage. But then I can't remember anything else until I was sitting on the sofa and Richard Summers and his men were there. He knew what had happened and he said I had to help them. I didn't think," he said, lowering his head, "I didn't think that they'd do what they did. I thought they just wanted me. I said I'd help if they'd leave Anna and your officer behind, but they killed your officer. They just shot him. I knew it was my fault, I'd led them to Anna's cottage. Sutherland told me later that killing your officer was part of their plan to frame me. If I refused to help him, he threatened to kill me and Anna, and to set it up to look like I'd had a breakdown, killed Hamilton, your officer and Anna, and then killed myself." He closed his eyes, reliving those awful moments.

Like Aiden, Lyons was feeling a strong sense of sympathy for Nikolai, but he wanted to hear the whole story.

"Nikolai, you're doing well, you've had a bad time. It does seem that you've had little choice in what has happened, but finish your story, please. It is very important that we hear everything. We need to understand."

Nikolai opened his eyes. "But it was still my fault. I'm so sorry. I brought danger to Anna's home. They shot your officer, Anna was sitting next to him, he fell on her, oh, God, so much blood, and I couldn't do anything to help. Then Carl hit me, and I don't really know what happened next. Everything is so patchy. I don't remember any more until I woke up in Sutherland's house. They'd cleaned up my shoulder and they gave me painkillers, which made me feel a bit better. My shoulder didn't hurt so much but I still felt strange and lightheaded. They had Anna there so I had no choice but to agree to help them. I took them to where I'd hidden the tapes, but then I overheard Summers on the 'phone. He was talking to Sutherland and from what he said, I worked out that Anna had managed to escape. So, I pretended that there was only one tape, and I gave them the scrambled copy. The other is still hidden safely. They won't know any different until they try to reinstall the data, which they'll find difficult anyway without my help. Summers took me back to his house and locked me in his upstairs office. He had a gun, which might have been the one that I'd had earlier at Anna's. I don't know what happened to it. My shoulder had started to hurt quite badly again. I suppose the painkillers had worn off."

He paused for a moment to take a deep breath. He was getting very tired now.

"I heard Sutherland come in. They had an argument – the walls were very thin, I could hear every word they said, and I knew for sure then that Anna had escaped and they hadn't found her. Sutherland didn't want me to be in Summers's house as he was afraid that the police would come round, so I heard them make a plan to move me to another house where his men were waiting. I knew I wouldn't stand a chance of escaping from all of them, so when Sutherland left, saying he'd be back soon with the others to take me, I knew I had to act quickly. I knocked the office chair over, hoping that the noise would bring Summers up to check on me. It worked, and I hid behind the door as he came in. I hit him with his brass paperweight and I managed to get out of the house."

He stopped again, looking confused.

"Well, I can't really remember what happened after that. I had got out of the house but he was right behind me and he had his gun. I couldn't have got very far, my shoulder was hurting so much by then, so I don't know why he didn't take me back. I don't really know how I got here."

"You had an accident. You fell into the road in front of a car," said Aiden gently. "And when that happened, there would have been witnesses. He wouldn't have stayed around."

Nikolai nodded. Whatever; he was too tired now, he didn't really care anymore. He looked at Harris. "You can arrest me now if you like, take me away if you want, I don't care, but you should also go and get Sutherland and Summers. It was Carl Webb, he's one of their men, who killed your officer. Two others, John Wilson and Mark Robbins, were there as well, they were a part of it. They're all contractors who sometimes work for Mayhims; Summers manages them. I don't know much about them but I do know one of their addresses: John Wilson's. I had to give him a lift home once when his car wouldn't start. He doesn't live far from my flat in Bath. But before you do what you have to do, I would like to have some time to speak to Anna privately, and also to my mother, please."

There was complete silence in the room as he finished. Josie looked at Aiden who smiled reassuringly at her. Anna's hand tightened over Nikolai's. Lyons opened his mouth to speak, but before he could, Harris stood up and went to stand over Nikolai.

"Young man, you've made some serious accusations, but there's no solid proof in anything that you've said so far. We will need that tape before we can even think about bringing Mr Sutherland in."

Lyons frowned at Harris, but before he could speak, Nikolai pulled himself up in the bed, pushing off Anna's restraining hands.

"Yes, disbelieve me if you like, but everything I've said is completely true. You've heard what my mother has said and Anna will be able to confirm what happened to your officer, and how we ended up at Sutherland's house. And yes, I can tell you where the tape with the data is. I told you, I didn't give them the right one, it's still hidden." He fell back on the pillow and closed his eyes.

Barnes spoke up, looking directly at Harris but addressing them all.

"Enough," he said firmly. "He's exhausted, he's had enough, and I should think that you've heard more than enough. I should remind you that this is my patient and he's just had a major operation. You do realise he could have died of septicaemia if we hadn't treated him when we did. In fact, he probably would have done. As it is, he spent last night in intensive care and he is under my medical supervision. He needs to rest, and you need to leave."

Lyons stood up stiffly, his voice gruff. "Sorry, doctor." He turned to Harris and said reprovingly, "That was harsh and unnecessary. I believe him. I'm sure he's telling the truth. It'll be easy enough to prove anyway. We've already got forensic evidence that backs up some of his story. As soon as he's ready we'll get the other names and that address that he promised and leave him be. We need to bring in Sutherland and Summers and put this to rest."

He looked at Natalya who was sitting staring at her son with a frightened look on her face.

"Natalya, are you all right?"

She looked up at him and he could see the tears in her eyes.

"This is all my fault. I had no idea that Alexander could be like that. I sent my son to England in his care, to be safer there than in Russia. I trusted him. And how could he have found it in himself to betray Pyotr? Yes, I knew that Alexander had betrayed his country but I thought I understood that kind of betrayal as after all, was that not what my idealistic Pyotr did also to his country? But to betray Pyotr. How could Alexander do that? I thought they were friends. Pyotr thought they were friends. Yes, I knew Alexander loved me still, he tried so often to make me leave and marry him, but I didn't think he was capable of such cruelty. Oh, I'm so sorry. He was your father," she said as she turned to face Anna.

Anna shook her head, her eyes as full of tears as Natalya's.

"It's all right. Yes, he was my father, and I loved him,

but I don't think I can really ever have known him. I'm finding it so hard to understand how he could have done those dreadful things. I'm almost glad that he's dead. If he was still alive, I could never forgive him, and I'm just so relieved that my mother never had to hear this." Then she had a sudden thought. "Did my mother know that Nikolai wasn't Michael Hamilton?"

"No, Anna, your father didn't want your mother to know. As far as she was concerned, Nikolai was Michael, his illegitimate son by Donna," replied Natalya.

Anna sighed. She and Natalya had something in common: their fathers had both betrayed them, but whatever her father might have done, he hadn't scarred her physically as this woman's father had.

"I'm so relieved that she didn't know. My father wasn't easy to love. I don't think he had much love really for me or my mother, but he treated my mother well. She wasn't unhappy, and I didn't know any different. Until I met Micha... Nikolai. It was only then that I learned what it was to love. But, Natalya, you shouldn't blame yourself, just because he loved you so much. We were all taken in by him. He must have had a side to his character that we never saw. But tell me one more thing: did he try to persuade you to leave with him after he married my mother?"

Natalya shook her dark head, and then pulled her hair back off her face to reveal her scarred face more clearly. "I thought that when he came back after my father had done this to me that I would never see him again, but he still wanted me, even though I was pregnant and he had a pregnant Spanish girlfriend himself. I wouldn't listen to him. I said I could love only Pyotr, even though I had lost Pyotr, although of course I didn't know then that it was he who had betrayed him." She stopped for a moment, the pain showing in her eyes. "But then he stopped seeing his girlfriend and came to visit me again, asking if he could be with me, act as the father to my unborn child. I refused him. I said we could be only friends; we could never be lovers again. He wouldn't give up. It went on for one, maybe two years, and then one time he came over and said he had met your mother and that he would marry her if I still said no. I was so relieved. I told him to be happy with her and we agreed to still be friends. So, yes, he still came to visit me and Nikolai after that, but it was just as a friend, and I knew he called to visit my parents too, but I didn't discuss that with him. I had no idea that he was still working with my father, and nor did my mother."

Nikolai stirred and opened his eyes. He frowned when he saw Harris but pulled himself up to a sitting position. Harris went over to Nikolai's bedside and Dr Barnes glared at him warningly, but he shook his head and addressed Nikolai uncomfortably.

"Mr Miloslavsky, I apologise. I wasn't trying to imply that you were lying. I realise that you've been through a lot recently. We'll go and bring in Sutherland, Summers and the others now. But if you feel you're up to it, then I'd be grateful for the location of the tape, and then we'll leave you in peace."

"Is he under arrest?" Anna asked, before Nikolai could reply.

Harris opened his mouth to speak, but Lyons got there first this time, smiling at Anna.

"Well, we'd prefer him to stay where he is for now, but I don't think there's much danger of him moving too far for the moment anyway. But no, I think that we'll be able to exonerate Nikolai from any blame of intentionally causing your father's death. In fact, it seems that he acted in self-defence and your father's death was no more than a tragic accident. You will obviously both be required to give a statement regarding the murder of our officer, though."

Nikolai looked at Anna, his eyes dark with emotion. "Anna, I'm so sorry. I've caused you so much pain. Although I didn't mean to do it, I'm still responsible for the death of your father, and I understand if you don't want to see me again, but I shall—"

Anna interrupted him, saying firmly, "No, Michael." Then she smiled. "Oops, sorry, Nikolai. Don't apologise, it should be me apologising. It was my father who tried to kill you. But neither of us is responsible for what he did or what he caused to happen. We couldn't have prevented it nor can we undo it. And we will find a way to put it behind us." And then she leant over, putting both her arms around him and resting her face against his, whispering in his ear so only he could hear.

"And no, you won't get rid of me that easily. I shan't let you out of my sight from now onwards, although I can't promise that I'll always get your name right." She rubbed her cheek against his. "By the way, I quite like this designer stubble, but I'm not too keen on a full beard, far too tickly, so we'd better get you better and out of here as soon as we can." She felt him relax as she smiled again and slowly released him, moving to one side so that Josie could come over and sit down next to him with her notebook.

As Josie scribbled down the information that Nikolai gave her, Lyons turned to Harris.

"Until we've brought them all in, it would be wise to leave Formby here with Nikolai for protection and WPC Grimley for Anna and Natalya, if she plans to stay. Contact the station and get some armed backup and then go and bring in Sutherland and his nasty little friends. If I know him, once he's cornered he won't give you too many problems, but we must remember that they do seem to have a fair few guns between them. I'll meet up with you back at the station."

Harris nodded and pulled out his 'phone, speaking briskly as he left the room.

Lyons turned to Colton. "Jeremy, old pal, I think we'll need to take another look through those old documents. Seems like our old friend Alexander Hamilton was a double agent all along, responsible for the betrayal and disappearance of Pyotr Karev, and Sutherland was up to his neck in it with him. And now we know that Alexander didn't break off contact with the Russians even after he married Claire, we should be able to build quite a case. We'll keep the lid on it though, keep it out of the press. Nickolai's name needn't be made public. It's already been reported that Alexander died in a tragic accident in the lab. We'll talk to the other employees, make sure they keep silent about any other details they might know, and Michael Hamilton can quietly disappear. Nothing more needs to be said. We can help Nikolai and Anna make up a convincing story." Here he turned to smile at them. "Seems like you two are going to have to do a bit of explaining to your friends."

And then he turned back to Jeremy. "And most certainly, no one needs to know that Natalya is here in England. We'll also have to make sure that Sutherland and Summers don't get to talk to their Russian buddies. Might need some help with that, a bit of misinformation from your MI6 colleagues, maybe some help from MI5 as well..." He stopped suddenly and looked more closely at Jeremy. "What? Oh no! I know that look of yours, Jeremy! What devious plot are you hatching now?"

Jeremy grinned, suddenly looking about twenty years younger. "Well, I've already thought up a story to give out," he said and his grin became mischievous. "Sorry Donna, RIP and all that, but you'll become the villainess of this piece. No one but Harris and those present here, and Sutherland of course, knows the whole truth of Michael Hamilton, and we'll find a way of silencing him. So, here's the story that I propose: Supposing that when Donna went to Spain, her baby, Michael Hamilton, died when he was just a few months old, a cot death maybe. She doesn't tell Alexander but instead goes to Russia and tracks down Natalya. We know that she knew about her and was jealous of her. She manages to steal Natalya's baby, thinking that Alexander fathered that baby as well. She brings the baby to England as her own child, the dead Michael Hamilton. Somehow, she's managed to keep his birth certificate, and as his death would have been registered in Spain, no one would spot the anomaly. Everyone, including Alexander and even Nikolai himself, could then have been fooled by this, and Nikolai's fictional past as Michael Hamilton becomes reality. Who is going to check? Why would anyone think to? The truth can often be stranger than fiction and, in this case, it actually is. And it makes sense that no one would connect a baby dying in Spain of natural causes and a baby kidnapped in Russia, with an illegitimate child being brought up in England by his Spanish mother and supported by his English father. It's highly unlikely that the news of a kidnapped baby in Russia would even have been reported in England back then. Years later, Natalya finally tracks down Nikolai, and since DNA testing has now developed she can prove that he is her long-lost son. Anna and Nikolai thus discover that they're not in any way related after all and can be together as a couple, and Nikolai is free to use his real name. His hospital stay can be explained away as the result of his accident with the car in Bath."

His audience gazed at him speechlessly as he sat back and looked around the room, smiling smugly. Only Alistair had witnessed Jeremy's fruitful imagination at work before, but even he was taken back by the speed with which Jeremy had thought up his convoluted story. But Jeremy hadn't quite finished yet.

"Of course, that story might only work for friends. Nikolai might need to assume his true identity if he wants to use any qualifications gained from his Moscow days. Somehow, I don't think that Mayhims will be in existence for much longer." He paused for a moment, thinking, and then smiled again. "No, that's OK, Nikolai, I can arrange to get you matching qualifications from the university in England where you were supposed to have studied as Michael Hamilton. Yes, that would work better. But I think you should lose any connection to Boris Miloslavsky. Better to leave that name behind you now. You could take on your father's name, Karev. In fact, Natalya should do the same. We can get that arranged for you." He looked across at Natalya. "Did you manage to get to England without your father's knowledge?"

Nikolai sat up straighter, turning to Jeremy, and spoke for Natalya, who seemed to be lost in thought. "Mr Colton—"

"No, it's Jeremy, please," interrupted Jeremy with a

smile.

Nikolai smiled back. "Jeremy, I just don't know how to begin to thank you. I'm lost for words. I can never repay you for finding a way to give me my life back, safety for my mother, and for giving Anna and I the chance of a future together. But yes, I booked and paid for my mother's flight as Michael Hamilton, and my grandfather has no knowledge of my life here. As far as he's concerned, I'm still lost on the streets of Moscow, or even dead. He wouldn't think to make any connections with her disappearance. He might make a few enquiries and he might even find that she did come over to England, but powerful as he might be in Moscow, he won't have any influence in England, especially without contact with Hamilton, Sutherland or Summers, so he probably won't make much effort now. It will be safer, and such a pleasure to take my father's name, better for my mother too." Turning to Natalya he said questioningly, "Mama, what do you think?"

Natalya suddenly came to life, brushing her hair back from her eyes, and looking from Alistair to Jeremy. "Oh yes, thank you so much. There is still so much I need to understand, but one thing I do understand: you are putting a lot of effort into helping us and I must also add my deepest thanks for that."

Alistair smiled at her. "Our pleasure, my dear." Then he glanced at his watch, which had the effect of reminding him of how long ago it was that he'd last had a cigarette. He got up quickly, addressing the room at large. "Good gracious, is that the time! I must get on and head back to the station. Formby, you're in charge here now." Turning back to Natalya, he added, "Natalya, my dear, do you want to stay here for now with Nikolai or shall Jeremy give you a lift to your hotel?"

Natalya looked across at Nikolai who was now leaning back against his propped-up pillows, looking exhausted but relaxed, with Anna sitting protectively next to him, and she smiled.

"Yes, I will leave now, I am tired. I have had a long day, with too much emotion. And I think he is in good hands."

Nikolai gave her a sleepy smile as she leant over and kissed him on the cheek, and then she gave Anna a warm hug before turning to Dr Barnes, smiling her crooked smile.

"Dr Barnes, please make sure you look after them both well. I shall be back here tomorrow."

Henry Barnes surprised himself by leaning forward, taking her hand and kissing it. "And I, dear lady, shall look forward to seeing you tomorrow," he said, meaning it.